ISLAND OF SHADOW AND LIGHT

A NOVEL

PAUL KONWISER

Paperback ISBN 978-1-63226-162-5
eBook ISBN 978-1-63226-163-2

This is a work of fiction. Names, characters, places, and incidents are either the product of the author's imagination or are used fictitiously, and any resemblance to actual persons, living or dead, business establishments, events, or locales is entirely coincidental.

Published by All Night Books
An imprint of Easton Studio Press
PO Box 3131
Westport, CT 06880
www.allnightbooks.com

Book and cover design by Alexia Garaventa

AUTHOR'S NOTE

Hawaiian locals speak a dialect known as Pidgin. The book contains much dialog in Pidgin, but varied somewhat so as to be understandable to non-Pidgin speakers. I think of it as Pidgin lite.

Island of Shadow and Light was written several years ago. This was before the fire consumed much of the town of Lahaina. My heart goes out to the victims.

Thanks to my granddaughter Dominique for her contribution to the cover.

My deepest thanks to Celeste Mapuana Volivar Fry, who convinced me to take the manuscript out of the drawer where it resided for far too long.

Mahalo to my beloved Sandy.

1

No one knows about the murder yet. They soon will.

On Maui's remote northwest shore, far from the golden beaches and glittering luxury hotels, sheer black sea cliffs rise out of the Pacific. Cool aquamarine waves from the Aleutian Islands end their 6,000-mile journey here, crashing in white salt spray and deep-throated thunder against the lava precipice. The body lies on a rock slab 300 feet above the sea. It is the site of an ancient *heiau*, a stone temple, rumored to have been used for human sacrifice. Leading to the site, a lonely road clings precariously to the steep rock wall.

As the setting sun touches the horizon a lumbering tour bus laden with sunburned vacationers heads toward the heiau. The bus takes up nearly the whole width of the road, as it travels inches away from a steep fall onto the rocks below. It's the "Spooky Hawai'i" tour, and most of the passengers are by now wishing they had taken the sunset cruise instead. The slick and colorful brochure for the tour had made it sound like an easy fifteen-mile jaunt out of Lahaina. There was not a word about traveling on the most dangerous road on Maui, just as darkness descends on the island.

The tourists are being entertained over the bus's PA system by a "native" guide, a local who is actually Filipino and Chinese and Caucasian, but who looks Hawaiian to them. The dark and handsome young man has told his charges to call him "Kimo." His real name is Jeffrey. At this point in the tour, his job is to scare them, but not too much. When they arrive at the *heiau*, which he has told them is pronounced "hey ee ow," they file off the bus. Kimo slips behind the vehicle and quickly changes from his aloha shirt and white slacks. When he emerges from behind the bus to face the assembled group he is bare-chested and wears a *malo*. Now, in contrast to his formerly cheerful manner, he speaks in hushed and somber tones about human sacrifice, about people with their brains battered in by the high priests. It's a canned spiel, not necessarily historically accurate—that's not the point. Giving folks a thrill is the point. Then, chanting in Hawaiian and beating solemnly on a small gourd drum, he leads them up a stone staircase to the temple.

When they get to the top of the steps, there is still a little light left in the sky. In front of them is a clearing on a cliff overlooking the ocean, the *whump* of the waves crashing into the rocks far below. Kimo stops chanting abruptly and turns to face them. His expression is stern; he looks to the tourists like a Hawaiian of ancient times. "Behold, the rock of sacrifice!" he says, raising his arm and pointing to a small stone platform on the ocean side of the clearing.

There, silhouetted against the horizon, stands a slight, white-haired man, a stone hammer in his hand, his shirt covered with blood. And on the rock, the figure of another man lying with his crushed head on the stone, chunks of skull and brain scattered about.

A middle-aged woman puts her hands up to her cheeks and gasps, a look of horror on her face. Her husband says to her, "For pity's sake, Phyllis, it's just a dummy. It's part of the show."

Kimo looks in the direction he's been pointing and drops his arm in shock. "Holy shit!" he says. He takes off running across the clearing toward the old man, shouting at him. "Uncle! Uncle!"

One of the tourists runs after him, capturing everything on his video camera. A great show. The rest of the group watches in confusion.

"It's his uncle," a woman says.

"Nah, they call everybody uncle here," someone else corrects her.

Kimo gets to the old man, the tourist close on his heels. The place is covered in gore, and the old man is dripping blood. He stands over the body, the stone hammer tightly gripped in his hand. The tourist eagerly starts shooting video of the body, the gore, and the old man, the final streaks of sunset adding what he thinks is real artistry to the scene.

"Uncle, what you did?" Kimo asks.

The old man looks up at him, a stunned expression on his leathery, dark-skinned face. "I'm so sorry. I didn't mean for him to get hurt. I warned him. It's all my fault. All my fault." Kimo gently takes the hammer from him and lays it on the ground. He puts his arm around the old man's shoulder and leads him slowly away. Some of the tourists drift closer.

"Please, folks, get back on the bus," Kimo pleads with them.

The camera-toting tourist has his smiling face pressed to the viewfinder as he zooms in on the body on the rocks: "Wow, is that realistic!" Kimo pulls a cell phone from under his *malo* and punches in a number. The tourist teases him, "Hey, you're really spoiling the ancient Hawaiian atmosphere with that phone."

"This is not part of your tour, man. That guy is dead," Kimo tells him.

The tourist lowers his camera, his face reflecting uncertainty as to whether or not Kimo is just kidding him. Then he looks at the pieces of glistening brain tissue lying on the rock. In fact, he is standing on a hunk of it in his brand-new open-toed sandals. *Not kidding*, he decides, and immediately throws up.

Kimo gets an answer on his phone. “Danny, it’s Jeff. I’m at the *heiau*. Lissen brah, you gotta call da cops. Get one dead guy ovah heah . . . Yeah, dead guy . . . No, he *mahkeh*, brah . . . Head all bus’ up.”

Kimo glances over at the tourist who is now on his knees barfing his guts out. “No, easy, brah, it’s not one of the tour people, no . . . Hey, and listen, it was uncle wen do ’em . . . No, Uncle Sunny, dat *kupuna* from da kine . . . How I know? He tole me, brah . . . He say he wen do ’em.”

2

John Rossi was having the dream again, gliding like a long-winged bird thousands of feet over a thick and unbroken layer of cottony white clouds. Above him the sky was a crystalline blue. He could hear the sound of wind, and he thought perhaps it was the wind on his wings. And another sound, very faint—a simple flute, poignant and haunting music from some exotic land. Somehow it made him feel very sad. His arms extended, he was getting tired and wanted to set down somewhere. He had been soaring above these endless clouds for as long as he could remember, and there had been no sign of land. Then, off in the distance, he saw it: a dark triangular shape poked out of the white blanket. A mountain top. He aimed for it, but suddenly the music changed and got louder, and he recognized a Beatles tune. The sound of the music affected him, and instead of wings he was just a human high up in the sky, but now plummeting earthwards. He became aware that he was naked and began trembling with cold as his body picked up speed, headed for the certain death that awaited him.

He awakened suddenly in the dark room, with the blankets in a heap on the floor next to the bed. He was sweating, and the wetness chilled him in the cold room. The alarm radio was playing music from a classic rock station. He lay there for a few moments, shivering as he came to full wakefulness. This was different from the other times. This time the dream felt much more real.

He got quickly out of bed. There was no time to think about dreams. He was showered, dressed, and on his way out the door within fifteen minutes. His rubber-soled boots crunched on the frozen crust of snow and ice as he crossed the parking lot to his car. He sat down shuddering on the cold seat and started the engine. Then it was back outside to scrape the ice off the windows with a plastic scraper. It took a good ten minutes of hard rasping before he had cleared enough of his windshield and was able to drive off to work. An ice storm was blanketing Northern New Jersey. On this bitter January day the normally easy drive from his apartment in West Orange to his office in the warehouse section of Newark was going to be a slippery and perilous adventure.

Nearly an hour later, he pulled up to the old brick building housing Rossi & Son Electrical Contractors and hit the remote control for the garage door opener. The big industrial door rolled up with a frigid metallic clatter, and he drove on in. He could see that most of the utility trucks were still in the garage. That meant that the crews were having trouble getting in through the storm, and Rossi & Son was going to be backlogged, probably for the rest of the week. After parking his car inside, he walked up the worn wooden steps to the offices above the garage as the metal door rattled closed behind him. Dependable old Louise had made it in to work, no surprise there. She smiled up at him as he walked in. She was just hanging up the phone.

"I just talked to Brian at Intercontinental," she said.

"Yeah?"

"According to Brian, the whole office is 'like wired backwards,' " she said, using her fingers to denote the quotation.

"What do you mean wired backwards?"

"Got me. I'm just telling you what he said."

"Who was our man on that?" he asked her, pretty sure of what the answer would be.

Louise didn't answer, but she gave him a certain familiar look.

John grunted. "Okay, call him back, and tell them I'll get over there as soon as I can."

He walked into his small office and sat down at his desk, rubbing his eyes in exasperation. He was going to have to bail Tony out once again. The phone immediately started ringing, but Louise didn't pick it up. After ten or so rings, he grabbed it himself. "Rossi Electric."

It was Angela. "How come you're answering the phone yourself? You should let Louise get it. That's what you're paying her for."

"She must have stepped away, sweetheart," he said. "You're up early."

"I know. I woke up thinking about Henrietta, and I couldn't get back to sleep."

John had to stifle a groan. The wedding guests. Again. Angela said, "You know, if we don't invite her, I don't see how we can invite Nick and Carmen."

"We can't not invite Nick. He's been a friend since grammar school."

"Then we can't leave Henrietta out."

"Fine, then don't."

"But if we invite her, then what about Alice?"

John was about to say, "What about Alice?" in a tone that would have been the opening salvo in yet another annoying squabble with his fiancée. At that moment the lights in the office dimmed momentarily and the phone line went dead. *Saved by the storm*, thought John. He got up and grabbed his parka, and headed for the door. Maybe he could get out of the shop before

Angela would think to call him on his cell. Louise was back at her desk, as he passed in a hurry.

"The phone just died," he said.

"Must be the ice."

"I'm going over to Intercontinental."

"Okay."

"I'm going to take a truck," he yelled back over his shoulder as he thunked down the stairs in his work boots.

It was always cold in the garage, even during the summer. The place could hold a dozen or so of the green-and-yellow utility trucks owned by Rossi & Son. Normally they would be out on various jobs by this time of the morning. He had ordered snow tires put on the trucks a few days ago. He hadn't gotten around to doing this on his own car yet, so the truck was going to do better in the icy conditions out there. He could leave his cell phone in the car and fend off an argument with Angela for a while.

Besides, he had to admit to himself, he liked driving the truck. He had started out in his father's business as a teenager working in the shop, restocking electrical parts coming back from jobs at the end of the day. He had worked out a system for keeping track of parts and tools. Within a few weeks he had figured out a way to cut inventory carrying costs in half. His father seemed unimpressed, and his brother Tony just laughed and said it was all bullshit. After all, his dad had run the shop for years without ever needing any "goddam system." But they had let John have his way. Soon, not only were the cost savings obvious, but other systems he put in place to find items more easily made the whole business run smoother. So they promoted him to be a helper. He worked with Mike, a master electrician, and he quickly learned the trade. Mike not only knew his stuff, but he was glad to pass on the knowledge, especially to an eager and intelligent helper. It wasn't long before John was better at the job than anybody except Mike himself.

Climbing into the truck, he remembered with pride the first time he got sent out on a call by himself. It was on a pleasant summer morning, before the daily heat and humidity had built up. He had grabbed his web tool belt, entered the garage with manly strides, and hauled himself up into one of the big utility trucks. He'd fired up the powerful V8 engine and driven out. It was just a minor residential deal, fixing a bad outlet. But he was doing it on his own. He remembered driving up to the house, parking the truck in the driveway and walking up the steps, a studly *chang chang* resonating from the tools on his belt. A pretty young woman answered his knock. He smiled at her with a confidence he had never felt before with a good-looking girl. "Electrician," he said to her. Fifteen years ago, and he recalled it like it was yesterday. He had just turned seventeen.

The ice was changing to snow as he drove out to Intercontinental Wholesalers, an absurd name for a tiny local firm that didn't do any business outside of Essex County, let alone the country. Intercontinental was owned by Angelo Mancini, a "reputed" mob guy. John knew for a fact that the man was connected. John's father had gone to school with Angelo, from kindergarten through high school, and they had always been pals. John didn't know if Intercontinental was some kind of a front or maybe an entirely legitimate enterprise. From a business standpoint, they seemed like regular guys to John, and he had always tried not to be judgmental. After all, he was engaged to Angelo Mancini's daughter.

He rolled the truck to a stop in front of Intercontinental, a run-down brick building in an industrial section of Newark. In an ugly city, this was a particularly hideous building in a downright scary neighborhood. Add in the fact that it was January in the middle of a winter storm, and it was truly an appalling place to be. As he carried his tool bag up to the front door, it opened, and a couple of goonish-looking guys sauntered out. One of them stopped and looked at John, who was standing there in swirling snow dressed in his fur-lined parka.

"Hey, look who's here. The Hawaiian snowman."

John grinned at Vincent Mancini, his future brother-in-law.

"How you doing, Vinnie?"

"Not so good. They're sittin' in the dark up there. You gonna be able to fix it?"

The guy with Vinnie said, "I hear he can fix anything."

"I'll have a look at it," John told them.

Vinnie smiled and clapped him on the shoulder, and he and the other guy walked off down the sidewalk; John went through the door and up a flight of stairs. He thought about Vinnie's crack. Hawaiian snowman. They'd never fail to comment on his racial background. At least this remark was friendly. Yes, he was adopted. Yes, his skin was dark. But marriage to one of them was going to make life easier, he was certain of it. There was a lot to love about Angela Mancini. He knew they could make a good marriage if they both worked hard enough at it.

At the top of the stairs, he was greeted by a cute young blonde receptionist. About half the lights were on. She told him there were also dead outlets in the coffee room. Another fuck-up by his brother. He headed for the circuit breaker box. In about twenty minutes he had everything working again, and the receptionist was brewing coffee.

"Does this mean that Tony won't be coming back again?" she asked him.

John knew in that moment that Tony was screwing her. The guy couldn't keep his dick in his pants to save his life. Tony's wife must know about his philandering—couldn't possibly not.

"I don't think he'll be needed. I'll tell him you asked, though." The girl reddened and quickly left the room. *I don't know why I said that*, John thought. *I'm just so tired of covering for Tony.* No matter how hard he tried to please his adoptive parents, it was never enough. He excelled at school, Tony dropped out. He made all-state in wrestling; Tony was a third-stringer. He got a full scholarship to Yale; Tony dropped out of Fairleigh Dickenson, or Fairly Ridiculous as he had called it. Still, they just loved Tony. If it hadn't been for his sister, he would have run away from home years ago. It was only Lizzie who made him feel at all a part of the family. He stopped himself. He was starting to think like a kid again, like the way he had felt growing up with this family of strangers.

He was on his way out the door when the receptionist stopped him. "Phone call for you. Angela Mancini," she said. He walked over to an empty desk. One line on the phone was blinking and he punched the button. Angela sounded exasperated. "Why don't you answer your cell? I've been trying to reach you for an hour."

"I took a truck. I forgot my cell phone in the car."

There was a big sigh from her end. "Okay, listen, I just wanted to say I'm sorry to be bothering you with all this stuff while you're working."

"No, really, it's okay."

"I thought you hung up on me there."

"The lines went dead."

"Yeah, I know. Louise told me. They're working again." Her voice turned sweet. It was the Angela he loved. "You would never just hang up on me, would you, Johnny? Even if I aggravate you?"

"No, sweetheart, never."

"Okay, just wanted to be sure. We're still going to have dinner?"

"Yeah, sure. I think the storm is letting up. I'll come by around six."

"Okay, Johnny, see you then. I'll try not to call again. Love you."

"Love you too, sweetheart. Bye." He hung up the phone. The wedding planning was creating some stress in their relationship. He had to admit to himself that he had some worry about these tensions between them before they were even married. But hell, what marriage was perfect, anyway? Not any that he had ever known about. And the really important thing was how marriage to Angela would finally turn his life around and make him a member of the family. Everything else was small stuff.

Outside, it had almost stopped snowing, just a few flurries now, but it seemed to be windier and a lot colder. He shuddered as a couple of snowflakes stole their way past the hood of his coat and down the back of his neck. He zipped his parka a little higher as he walked toward the truck. Vinnie and his companion were coming up the sidewalk, carrying steaming cardboard cups of coffee from the shabby little luncheonette down the street.

"You get these guys squared away?" Vinnie wanted to know.

"Everything's fixed," John told him.

The other guy said. "Told you. This guy can fix anything."

John looked at the man curiously, and Vinnie introduced them. "John, this here is Bruno Ricci, my cousin from Chicago." John shook hands with Bruno.

Bruno said, "And you're marrying Angela. Lucky man."

Vinnie said, "Hey, she get ahold a you? I got a call from my dad. He said she seemed agitated."

Great, John thought. *She thought I hung up on her, and she called her father.* His face evidently reflected his concern.

Vinnie said, "No, she was worried about you, that's all."

John said, "A misunderstanding. We got disconnected. The storm."

"Disconnected," Vinnie echoed, looking at Bruno.

"Sure, the storm. It's logical," Bruno said.

"Logical, sure. Just a misunderstanding," Vinnie said, nodding his head. They stood there and looked at each other for a long moment.

Finally Bruno spoke. "Vinnie, let's fuckin' go inside. My coffee's gettin' cold here," he said, shivering and stamping the sidewalk with his fashionable but thin-soled Italian loafers.

"Okay, see you later, Johnny. Good man," Vinnie said, giving John a firm but friendly punch on the shoulder.

They went into the building, and John climbed into the truck and started it up. He drove back toward the shop, shuddering on the cold vinyl seat, waiting for the heater to start working. He thought about Angela. He had first met her years ago, when she came to work for Rossi Electric. She had just graduated from secretarial school, and his father had agreed to hire her as a favor to his old friend Angelo Mancini. She was pretty and bright, and a fast learner. John had been sixteen then, and had had a serious crush on her. Sometimes he got the impression she was flirting with him. Of course, she was untouchable, an Italian virgin daughter of a mob guy. John knew that as a dark-skinned adoptee, even if he happened to have an Italian last name, he stood no chance with her. That, naturally, made her all the more desirable, and for a time it seemed his every waking thought was filled with fantasies about Angela.

Two years later, she was gone, married to a proper Italian young man, who had some sort of a role in the Mancini family business. About twelve years after her marriage, her husband mysteriously disappeared. Some said he had been killed after betraying family interests. John's father had hinted that he had been turned by the feds and was in a witness protection program. Whatever the truth of the matter, Angela was treated as a widow, but a widow with a huge black mark against her. To make matters worse, she was unable to have children. She was no longer a desirable marriage partner, at least for a regular family member. She was closing in on forty years old, and she was damaged goods.

John's father and Angelo Mancini had gotten the bright idea to get John and Angela together. Two undesirables. Their engagement had brought great joy to both families, and John felt a level of acceptance and approval by his adoptive family that he had never known before. It was good. It was going to work.

3

Back at the shop, operations were returning to normal, although they were well behind schedule. Most of the crews had come in and had been dispatched to various job sites. He went upstairs to his desk to handle the pile of message slips there. Lots of calls probably related to the storm. He flipped through the pink squares of paper. Message triage. Big customers got top priority. Small guys would get a call from the office, maybe get a crew dispatched later in the afternoon.

One of the message slips was from Miriam Putnam. The "Please Call" box was checked, no message. Jimmie's mom. Ever since his blowup with Jimmie a couple of years before, he had been out of touch. In all the years he had known Jimmie, he couldn't recall ever getting a call from his mother.

He made some of his important business calls first, but the call from Mrs. Putnam was weighing on his mind. Why would she be calling him? What was going on with her son? James Edward Putnam. Crazy WASP name for a guy with half Navajo Indian blood and a face like an Apache warrior. And John, with his Waikiki beachboy looks and the Italian surname. It was natural that they would become friends. Not just friends. Soulmates. Compadres.

Blood brothers. Maybe her call was some kind of attempt at reconciliation of the two kids who had grown up together. Not that that would be possible, not unless Jimmie had changed.

Finally, despite the press of pending work, his curiosity got the best of him, and he dialed her number. She must have been sitting right next to the phone, for she answered it instantly.

"Hi, Mrs. Putnam. It's John. John Rossi."

"Oh, Johnny," she said, and the next thing he heard were sobs.

"Mrs. Putnam? Are you okay?"

"Johnny, it's so good to hear your voice."

"What is it? What's happened?" This brought on a fresh spate of sobbing, before she could barely compose herself.

"He's dead. Jimmie's dead."

John was too stunned to speak. He had never imagined this. He'd never lost a friend his own age, never expected to. And certainly not Jimmie. They may have been angry at each other, but it would get straightened out someday. Jimmie couldn't be dead. Jimmie was eternal.

"Are you sure?" he asked. A crazy question, but this couldn't be so, couldn't be happening. She seemed to understand this.

"Yes. He's been identified. He's dead."

A million questions popped into John's head at once. Where, why, when? And above all, how could this be happening? Couldn't it all be some terrible mistake?

"Johnny, there's something important I need to ask of you. Can you come over?"

"Yes, of course. I'll be there as quick as I can. Same house?"

"Yes."

"I'm on my way."

"Thank you, Johnny," she said and the line clicked dead.

He hung up the phone. He thought of calling Angela to tell her. But he had become engaged to her after he and Jimmie had had their big falling-out, and she didn't know Jimmie. He would have called his parents, but they had never liked Jimmie, never lost their prejudices against an "injun." Even his sister didn't like Jimmie that much. She thought that John was only hurting himself socially by hanging around with the only other dark-skinned kid in the school. John's best friend should have been white. He realized that he was on his way to console his friend's family, but he had no one to console him. He grabbed his parka and headed for the door.

"Sorry, Louise. I have to go out." She might have protested. They were still behind schedule and the phones were ringing continuously. But she saw the look on his face.

"Is something wrong?"

"Yeah. A good friend has—" he was about to say "died," but his lips couldn't form the words. *Passed away?* Then, again, he had the crazy thoughts. *This can't be true. He's alive. It was a tragic case of mistaken identity, had to be. Jimmie's car had crashed and a fire broke out, burning the trapped man inside. But it wasn't Jimmie. He had lent his car to a friend. He would come to work tomorrow in a cab, angry as hell at his pal for not returning the car, not knowing anything about the accident. But he would be alive. Or a small plane went down somewhere, and they just presumed there were no survivors. But one guy had made it and crawled away from the wreckage. He would be found. John would find him . . .*

"Yeah, something's wrong. I'll call you as soon as I can."

He drove his car to Jimmie's house. Up Bloomfield Avenue, then onto Watsessing Street, past the park where they had played as children. A narrow strip of grass now, but in his child-memory, a vast plain. The steppes of central Asia. The Pampas of Argentina. The veldts of Africa. A park stretching as far as their young eyes could see, full of daily adventures—climbing trees, sneaking up on picnicking girls to scare them, blowing up tent caterpillars with firecrackers, building a lean-to out of fallen branches.

He drove past the Smith house, where he and Jimmie had first met. Nine years old, they had been. The Putnams had just moved to the neighborhood, and he had never laid eyes on Jimmie before. It was a birthday party for the Smith kid—John couldn't remember his first name—on a warm day in May. John had rung the bell. He had gotten there late, he didn't recall why. He could hear the other kids playing inside the house. The door was opened by Mrs. Smith, a tall, pale woman. She gazed down at him standing there on the front steps with his dark little hands clutching the present for her son. She reached down and took the gift from him. Then, instead of inviting him in, she motioned to him to follow her back down the front steps. She led him to the side of the house, opened the gate to the back yard, and waved him through.

Back in the yard there was a small wooden picnic table, and a little dark-skinned kid sitting there wearing a party hat, sullenly eating cookies from a plate. Jimmie. He barely looked up at John when he sat down across from him.

"I'll bring you boys some cake." Mrs. Smith smiled at them, scuttled up the steps and went in the back door of the house. John watched her go. He was confused. Jimmie didn't say a word, just kept on eating his cookies and drinking from a glass of milk.

"How come we're out here if the party is inside?" John finally asked him.

"Oh, grow up!" Jimmie practically snarled at him.

"Huh?"

"They don't want *us* in *there*," he said, motioning his head toward the house. They could clearly hear the sounds of the other kids inside, singing "Happy Birthday."

"Why?" John asked him.

Jimmie extended his skinny brown arm and placed it next to John's. They were a virtual match in skin tone. "Duh," Jimmie said, mockingly. John quickly pulled his arm away. This couldn't be right. Mrs. Smith returned with two paper plates with a piece of cake on each.

"Here you are, boys." She set the plates down on the table and hurried back inside. John stared at the plate of cake in front of him. It was just the kind he loved, white buttercream frosting, lemon filling, a blue flower on top. Jimmie dove right into his piece.

As a little brown boy growing up in a white neighborhood, John had certainly felt the sting of prejudice, especially from certain kids in school. But this! Not being allowed to be in the house because he looked different. This was a stunning shock he had never before experienced. He couldn't help himself. The tears started to flow. He felt ashamed, crying in front of this boy he didn't even know. The kid looked tough, like he would never cry himself. John didn't want to be a crybaby, but he couldn't stop. He gave himself away with a snuffle, and Jimmie looked at him, as if about ready to yell, "Crybaby!" Before Jimmie could say anything, John said, "I'm not eating that."

"You don't want yours?" Jimmie asked him, reaching for the plate.

"I'm not eating the fucking thing," John responded. He had surprised himself with the obscenity, but Jimmie seemed delighted. He stopped eating and put down his plastic fork. "You're right. We can't eat this stuff. Fuck!"

Even with a face full of tears, John laughed despite himself. He had always been a good boy, an altar boy, with perfect grades in deportment at Sacred Heart School. He had never known how good it could feel to be bad. The impulse that moved him next surprised him even more. He suddenly stood up, picked up the plate and walked toward the back steps of the house. He stood at the bottom of the steps, put a leg back, and with all his strength, hurled the cake at the back door. It splattered against the screen with a satisfying squish and thump.

"Wow!" said Jimmie. He got up and took the rest of his cake over to the steps and threw his own plate at the door. For a moment they stood there, side by side, admiring their handiwork. Then they could hear someone coming from inside the house, and Jimmie said, "Holy shit, we gotta get out of here!"

They ran, laughing, to the back of the yard where they vaulted a low chain link fence into the back yard of a house on the next street over. They kept on running and laughing, gleefully guilty, until they reached the park. They sprinted across the field into the bushes surrounding the park and climbed up into a maple tree, boosting and pulling each other up into the branches, concealing themselves in the leafy foliage. They were still laughing, but John, the heretofore perfect kid, the one the nuns pointed out to others as a model of good behavior, couldn't imagine what the consequences of his actions might be. On the other hand, he had never felt so liberated, so much like his own person.

"Man, I can't believe you chucked that cake!" Jimmie said.

"You chucked yours too."

"I never thought of doing that. I always ate their cake and took their shit. Not anymore."

"This happened to you before?" John asked.

"All the time. In Mississippi, where we lived. If you're an injun, you hang out with other injuns, not whites."

"I never really thought about it before."

"Your parents are white, I'll bet."

"Yeah. I'm adopted," John told him.

And so they got to know each other, the Indian and the Hawaiian. They stayed in that tree and talked until dark, until they knew that if they stayed any longer they were going to get into even more trouble at home. Before they left they made a pact. They were going to show them all. They would be the best students, the best athletes in their school. Not take any shit off anybody. Jimmie took out a penknife, and with a cut to their fingers they declared themselves blood brothers. It was from that time forward that John focused on becoming strong in mind and body. And he never cried again.

John pulled to the curb in front of Jimmie's house, a house he knew as well as his own, maybe better. He and Jimmie had set up a gym in the back yard, moving it to the garage in the winter. They had kept adding equipment over the years, earning money mowing lawns as kids, doing part-time jobs later, building strength so that no one would dare push them around. They went out for sports too. Not team sports, but the individual, fighting sports, boxing and wrestling. When they weren't working out, they were studying, drilling each other on math and later algebra, then trigonometry, critiquing each other's essays in history and English—tough critics, both of them. They were inseparable friends who would have gotten teased about being queer for each other if anyone had dared. No one did.

John sat in his car for a moment, and a sudden emotion got hold of his gut. He would never see Jimmie again. But this was too much to bear, and he went back to his mantra: *He's alive, he crawled from the wreckage, it was someone else, he's out there somewhere, I'll find him . . .*

He got out of the car, walked up the front steps onto the porch and rang the bell. After a moment Miriam Putnam opened the door. He hadn't seen her in maybe three years. As soon as the door was closed behind him, her arms went around him and she hugged him, sobbing. For him she had always been a tower of strength, and this all felt so very strange. As for himself, he couldn't cry now. He hugged her right back. He was going to be strong for her. And he was somehow going to straighten this all out, correct the mistake. Finally, her sobs subsided, and they walked to the sofa together and sat down.

"Tell me what happened," John said gently.

Tears started flowing again. "He was murdered."

It was the last thing he expected to hear. "Murdered? How? Where?"

"In Hawai'i. They said he was bludgeoned to death." John sat there, stunned. Hawai'i. How could that be? What was Jimmie doing there? Now the mantra changed: *Revenge. Find the killers and avenge Jimmie.* Finally she calmed, and took the wind out of his sails.

"They caught the guy who did it."

"But why? Why would somebody kill him?"

"They said it had something to do with his work. Somebody got mad at him."

"But what was he doing in Hawai'i?"

"He took that job. The one he wanted you to take. They sent him instead."

"Oh, my God!"

This was a different kind of pain, and it was almost too much to bear. Years of Catholic upbringing brought forth a surge of guilty feelings. He wasn't going to be able to find Jimmie, or even comfort his mother. *I'm responsible for this.*

Sensing his feelings, she said, "Johnny, I know what you're thinking. But it's not your fault. I know you two had an argument about this. But it was his decision to go in your place. Jimmie's decision." She reached out and put a hand on either side of his face, made him look directly into her eyes. Her voice was firm, commanding. "Don't you dare go feeling guilty about this. Don't you dare."

John got hold of himself, but he was still a bundle of conflicting emotions. "How is Mr. Putnam?"

"You didn't know, forgive me. He's in the hospital. He had a stroke."

"Oh, God. This is terrible. When did all this happen?"

"They called early this morning. Billy just collapsed. I was with him in Saint Barnabas until now."

"I can't believe all this is happening."

"I wish it were yesterday," she said, wiping tears from her eyes.

They sat for a moment. She said, "Johnny, I need to ask you to help with something."

John responded eagerly, "Anything. Anything I can do."

"I need you to go to Hawai'i to bring Jimmie home."

4

Hawai'i. This just couldn't be. Not this way. For all the thoughts he had had over the years about the land of his birth, he had never imagined that the first time he was going to see it would be like this. Of course it wasn't really the first time, although he had no real memories of Hawai'i. He had come to the mainland, adopted, at age four, a child born out of wedlock. His birth mother had been a teenager. She had died giving birth to yet another illegitimate kid at a Catholic hospital. The local bishop had a good friend from the seminary who had a parish in New Jersey, and he had asked him to find a family to take the boy. John knew all this because the Rossis had told him. They were not like some adoptive parents who wouldn't even tell their kids they were adopted. Of course, there was no hiding the fact that John had a different racial background from the Rossis.

It was hard to find people to take in a non-infant child. But the Rossis, good Catholics with a strong sense of responsibility and an inability to have children of their own, had agreed to bear this burden. To say that they had been surprised to see that this little kid was brown as a coffee bean would be an understatement. Apparently, they had not realized that little Hawaiian kids could have such dark skin. But the commitment had been made, and they would honor it, good people that they were. They would raise this little brown child as they had promised—would do their duty, despite the stares of others, the looks from family and friends.

And so they did. The little boy got a new name, John Edward Rossi. Naturally, as soon as he had been legally adopted and there was no giving him back, Teresa Rossi had gotten pregnant and a few months later gave birth to respectable white Italian-American children—twins, a boy and a girl. As much as she wanted to do right by Johnny, how could she help it if she loved her own true children just a little bit more? And so he grew up—part of this family and not a part—in this Roman Catholic, almost entirely Italian enclave in Northern New Jersey.

Then he met Jimmie, and everything changed for him. He rebelled, but not in a way that his parents or teachers could complain about. He didn't misbehave. He rebelled by excelling at everything he did—school, sports, work. He and Jimmie became the most popular kids in school, but as much as the other kids wanted to get close to them, the boys remained aloof in many ways, their own special unit. No one else was granted entry to the exclusive Jimmie and Johnny club.

When John was thirteen, they went to a new school, the junior high. There was a new set of teachers, and one of them, Mrs. Struble, took a special interest in him. Mrs. Struble was a kind-hearted and compassionate woman, close to retirement. She had often regretted a career teaching class after class of the same white middle-class teenagers, year after year. When John showed up in her classroom on that first day of school, she asked him to stay after the others had been dismissed. She asked him about his background, where was he from.

"Bloomfield," he answered, surprised at the question. She realized her mistake at the same time that it occurred to John that he was being singled out because of his color. He would have been resentful, had it not been for the special attention of this kind and gentle woman. He realized she had a genuine interest in who he was, an interest that had never manifested from within himself. One day after class, she told him she had something he might like. She reached under her desk and pulled out a small musical instrument case and handed it to him. It was shaped, he thought, like a miniature guitar, but when he opened it he found that it contained an ukulele.

"My brother brought this back from Honolulu when he was there during the war. He passed away years ago. It's been gathering dust in the attic for a long time. I thought you might like to have it."

It was a beautiful instrument, and he stood there running his fingers over the wonderfully shaped and polished wood. Mrs. Struble walked over to the map in the front of the room and gazed longingly at the Hawaiian Islands, her eyes glistening.

"My brother said that Hawai'i is the most beautiful place in the world. My husband and I always wanted to go. We thought there would be time." Her voice broke, and it took her a moment to recover herself and continue. "After he died, I didn't want to go to such a romantic place on my own." She turned and saw him examining the ukulele. "It's made of koa wood," she told him.

"What is koa?" he asked her. It was the first of many questions he would ask over the next couple of years, and the start of a remarkable friendship that would lead him, finally, to begin to discover his roots in Hawai'i.

That evening, sitting with his parents in the living room after dinner, he had shown them the ukulele, and announced his intention to learn to play it, "Just like they do back home." He was unprepared for their reaction, his mother's sudden tear-filled exit from the living room. He sat there on the sofa, dumbfounded, realizing he should be feeling guilty about something. His father looked at him sternly. "You've hurt your mother very badly, John. And you've made me angry."

"Why? What did I do?"

His father rose up out of his easy chair and walked over to John. "*This* is your home," he said, jabbing a finger at the living room floor. "Not some island somewhere. *This* is your home."

So John went to his room put the ukulele away, stashing it far under his bed, and taking it out to play in his room only when no one else was around. And Mrs. Struble continued to guide him toward books about Hawai'i and Polynesia. He read everything he could get his hands on. His rebellious nature was taking hold, plus the natural defiance of a teenage kid. He was going to learn about his roots.

Thinking back on it now, he thought of it as his Hawaiian Phase. He had gone from aggressive denial of being any different from the other kids to a determined effort to find out anything and everything he could about the place of his birth. He began to accumulate books: picture books, history books, books about island culture. These he kept at Jimmie's house, so the Rossis wouldn't know. A cardboard box in Jimmie's basement contained the books, the magazine clippings, a paper flower lei, all his Hawaiian stuff.

Jimmie had reacted with complete bemusement to all this. He seemed to have no interest in his own background. He just wanted to be like the other kids, like the best of the other kids. He wanted to be so admired for his accomplishments that no one noticed that he looked a little different. Meanwhile, John was saving his money for a plane ticket. He studied airline timetables, and he had his routing all figured out. American Airlines flight 321, a 727 leaving Newark at 1:00 a.m. to Chicago. It was cheaper to fly at that hour. Then AA 465, another 727 leaving Chicago at 6:20 a.m. with stops in Omaha and Albuquerque, arriving in Los Angeles at 10:21 a.m. Finally, a United 747, flight 8, leaving Los

Angeles at noon, arriving in Honolulu at 2:10 p.m. A one-way ticket was all he needed. He wanted to go to Hawai'i and find his mother's grave, find out if his father was still alive, and maybe locate a brother or sister. His real family. They would welcome him with open arms and flower leis, and sweet Hawaiian music. At times the longing was so great he could almost taste the island air of his homeland, and he longed to be with a family who looked just like him, to get away from the Rossis and go home. His real home. But all that was kid stuff, and it was a long time ago.

He never made it back to work that day. He spent the rest of the afternoon with Mrs. Putnam. He took her to the hospital to look in on Jimmie's dad. He was "stabilized" they said, but no one knew how he was going to come out of it, how functional he would be. They called the airlines and found out there was a direct flight on Continental Airlines from Newark to Maui, where Jimmie was. A place called Kahului. During his Hawaiian Phase, the name would have sounded exotic and enticing. Now it just seemed odd and foreign, and much too far from home. He made a reservation for the flight the next morning. Now all he had to do was tell his parents. And Angela.

5

He picked her up at her house at six that evening. She looked terrific, dressed for dining out in a slinky black dress and a fur coat, her long dark hair down halfway to her slender waist. John thought of his desire for her when he had been sixteen. Now she belonged to him.

He was quiet as they drove to their favorite restaurant. In contrast to his strained mood, she was full of bubbly chatter. She had had a wonderful day, talking on the phone with her friends about wedding plans, making key decisions on such things as what color of bunting should go on the tables at the reception. The wedding was months away, and he marveled at how much time one could put into planning the thing. He hated to dampen her mood by telling her of Jimmie's death, and he didn't know how to break the news that he was going to be leaving for a couple of days. He knew this wasn't going to go over well. He decided to wait to tell her about Jimmie until they were at the restaurant.

They were seated and had ordered when he finally asked her, "Do you remember me telling you about my friend Jimmie?"

"Of course, the kid you grew up with. You guys had a fight, though. Right?"

"Yes, we did. I haven't seen him or talked to him in two years."

Suddenly her mood changed. "So let me guess: You finally called him, and you guys are now buddy-buddy again, and now you want him to be best man at the wedding instead of my brother."

The all-consuming wedding. Everything in their lives was seen in relation to their upcoming wedding. The thought of Jimmie being best man at his wedding touched a point deep inside him. As they had gone through their twenties, they would sometimes joke about being each other's best man someday. Neither of them had ever married, and now that couldn't happen. He felt a surge of sadness, and he had to fight it back. She was startled to see his reaction, and she softened.

"Oh my God, Johnny. If it means that much to you—"

He interrupted her with a wave of his hand. "It's not that." He took a sip of water while he regained his composure. "Jimmie is dead. I just found out today."

"Oh, Johnny. I'm so sorry." She reached across the table to take his two hands in hers. "Forgive me. I should have realized there was something wrong as soon as I saw you tonight."

"You had no way to know. I would have called you, but you didn't know Jimmie, and I didn't want to tell you over the phone."

"Of course. What happened to him? I mean, how did he die? He was your age, right?"

My age, John thought. Thirty-two. You're not supposed to die at thirty-two. Dying is for old people.

"He was murdered, Angela. Somebody killed him." She just squeezed his hands harder. As the daughter of a mafia capo, she had some familiarity with sudden death by murder, and it was not the kind of shock it would have been for most people. Her mind went directly to the practical aspects of dying.

"When is the funeral going to be?"

"I don't know yet. He didn't die here. And they need to bring the body back."

"From where?"

"Hawai'i."

"Hawai'i? What was he doing there?"

"Working. He went there for his job."

"That's weird, huh. I mean he ends up in Hawai'i and you're here."

"Yes." John couldn't seem to get himself to tell the story of just how weird it was. Weird and ironic and totally horrible.

"His mom asked me to go there and bring him home."

Her tone changed instantly from supportive to suspicious. "Why you? You weren't friends anymore. Why doesn't she go?"

"Jimmie's dad had a stroke when he heard. She needs to care for him."

"Can't they just ship the body home? Won't a funeral home do it?"

John had discussed this with Miriam Putnam. There was more to it than bringing Jimmie home. She was Jimmie's mother and she needed to know what had happened to her only son, needed to hear it from a friend, hear it first-hand. She wanted John to talk to the police. Make sure they got the right guy. Get closure. A stupid word, and John hated himself for even thinking it, but he couldn't come up with a better one. He explained to Angela, and she seemed to understand, but clearly something was on her mind.

"What's troubling you?" he asked her.

"I don't know. It's silly."

"What, tell me."

"I guess I'm afraid that you'll like it there and never come back."

John looked into her eyes and held her hands firmly. "Listen to me, sweetheart. I am going to stay exactly one day. I already have my reservation, there and back. I leave tomorrow morning and I'll be back on Thursday. I have no connection to Hawai'i.

It's just an island in the middle of the ocean. It might as well be Madagascar, to me. I'm not staying. I'm coming right home."

"You better," she said, smiling hesitantly.

He drove her home after dinner. The skies had cleared, but it was bitter cold out. He told her about the box in the back seat of his car. It was the box of Hawaiian stuff from Jimmie's basement. Mrs. Putnam had kept it all this time, and he remembered how throughout junior high school, Jimmie had chuckled over John's obsession with Hawai'i. Then they'd entered high school. Without Mrs. Struble's daily influence, and with the onset of the usual hormones, the Hawaiian Phase was replaced by the Girl Phase. John discovered, as did Jimmie, that there were certain women in their all-white school who were attracted to men of color. Jimmie reveled in this discovery, bedding as many of them as he could. John also enjoyed his share, losing his virginity at age sixteen to a creamy-skinned blonde named Brenda Petersen, who proceeded to inform all of her friends that she had screwed one of the most popular kids in the class, and that it was true, dark men had big dicks and incredible sexual stamina. John didn't know if this was factual or not, but they kept coming on to him, and he kept enjoying himself.

Eventually, of course, it occurred to him that being sought out simply because he was dark-skinned was discrimination, no matter how you looked at it. How could you know if they really liked you or if they wanted to try "it" with a dark-skinned guy? John and Jimmie talked about this a lot. John was disappointed that Jimmie was not troubled in the least by it. "Keep 'em coming" was his motto. Thinking back on this in later years, John could see that it was a sign of an important difference in their personalities, one that would eventually split up their long friendship. Along with the girls, Jimmie's grades took a nosedive, and John couldn't see how Jimmie was going to get into the Ivy League college they had often talked about attending together.

Back at his apartment after dropping Angela off, he pulled his carry-on suitcase from the closet. It was plenty big enough for a short trip. He automatically started to throw in what he would need for a mid-winter trip, then stopped himself and took out the sweaters and replaced them with summer clothes from the back of the closet, stuff he hadn't expected to wear for months. The phone rang. It was Angela's brother Vincent.

"Hey John. Angela told me what happened. Anything I can do to help?"

"No, thanks. I'm okay."

"Well, anything you think of, now or while you're out there, just give us a call, you hear? You're practically a member of the family." There was a pause at the end of the line. "So you're coming right back in a coupl'a days, right?"

John realized the purpose of the call. The offer to help was genuine. So was the implication of what could happen if he didn't come back to Jersey immediately.

"You bet. I'm just there for a day."

"Okay, Johnny. You take care."

He hung up the phone. It was a damn good thing he was telling the truth. He had no intention of staying in Hawai'i, wished in fact that he didn't have to go.

The phone rang again—his mother, concern in her voice. "Angela says you're going to Hawai'i. Is that really necessary?"

"Mrs. Putnam asked me to go. I can't say no."

"You don't think it could be handled from here?"

"No, Mom, I don't."

"What about the business? Have you made the arrangements?"

"Nothing to worry about. I'll only be gone a couple of days. Tony and Louise can handle things while I'm gone."

"Okay, if it's just a couple of days."

"Out tomorrow, back on Thursday."

There was a moment of hesitation. "You've done a good job with the business. We depend on you, you know. Is there anything we can do?"

"Maybe call Mrs. Putnam in the morning? See how she's doing?"

"Yes, I'll do that. Come home safe, John."

"Thanks, Mom."

He hung up the phone. Rare words of praise from his mother. He and his parents had agreed on little, ever since John, then in his senior year of high school, said that he would be applying to college. Albert Rossi had assumed John would go directly into the family business. His father thought college was a waste of time, especially when you had learned a trade, as John had, and he announced over dinner one evening that John could do whatever he wanted, but he would be on his own financially.

John and Jimmie applied to all the Ivy League schools. John got early admission to Yale, with a partial scholarship and work program that would enable him to pay his own way. Jimmie's grades had slipped considerably in the last two years of high school. John tried to get him to apply to some backup schools, but Jimmie didn't seem worried. John was floored when Jimmie, like John, got into Yale. He pointed out to John that he had checked the box identifying himself as "Native American," and he figured that had done the trick. John had not done this, not wanting any special treatment.

They had looked forward all summer to starting school together in the fall. Toward the end of the summer that John expected to be his last working for his father, a new sign went up at Rossi Electrical Contractors. It read, "Rossi & Son Electrical Contractors." It was clear to John which son this was. Tony would be taking over the business eventually. While John had never had any intention of following in his father's footsteps, the rebuke still stung. Most of the fleet of trucks was scheduled for replacement that summer. As each new truck arrived, they had the new signage—"& Son"—added to the doors. Each one was an additional wedge driving apart the relationship between himself and his father. Each one was, to John, an affirmation that Tony was the true son and John was not.

At summer's end, four days before he was to drive off to New Haven with Jimmie, his father had had his first heart attack. Tony was fourteen years old. His mother pleaded with John to postpone the start of school and help run the business, just for a few weeks. So Jimmie went off to Yale by himself, and John ran Rossi & Son. "Don't get trapped," Jimmie kept telling him. "You can feel obligated if you want, but you don't owe the Rossis the rest of your life."

John assured Jimmie that it was only temporary, until his father got back on his feet again. He would join Jimmie in New Haven for the spring semester. But toward the end of the year there was a second heart attack. This one left his father weak and hardly able to breathe, and John was still needed. A year went by, and then another. John was genuinely sorry to miss the opportunity to attend Yale. The business courses he took at night at the local community college were hardly a substitute. But for the first time in his life, he felt accepted and needed by his family. He was barely in his twenties, and he was responsible for twenty-six employees and a multi-million dollar enterprise. He found that he enjoyed running the business, even though Tony would officially become his boss on Tony's twenty-first birthday.

Jimmie applied himself in school, and graduated with a degree in economics. He immediately got a job selling securities for Merrill Lynch. He was good at it, and made a bundle. He seemed to feel a responsibility to get his old buddy John out of Rossi & Son, and into a "real" job. About every other week, it seemed, Jimmie would call offering John a job with Merrill Lynch or one of the half-dozen other brokerage firms he worked for over the years, each one for a bigger salary and commissions. John would have liked the money, of course, but was not interested in the positions. He liked being his own boss.

Then, through a brokerage connection, Jimmie got a job working for Zodiac International Casinos. More than that, he was working directly for "Mr. Zodiac" himself, Charles N. Brewster. Brewster was supposedly going to be the guy to legitimize the gambling industry, take it mainstream. He was fabulously successful financially, and became a business media darling. A couple of marriages to glamorous trophy wives got him in the magazines and newspapers, and soon almost everyone in America knew who he was. He was building and running casinos for Indian tribes, at first in New England and later in the West. Jimmie was his point man in dealing directly with the tribes. It never seemed to occur to Jimmie that maybe he had been hired for no other reason than because he looked like an Indian. This really bothered John, and he often hinted at what he thought to Jimmie, but Jimmie didn't get it, or more likely, didn't care. This kind of discrimination had never bothered him in the least. If somebody wanted to offer him a big salary just because of the way he looked, well that was fine with him. It was a situation John would never have tolerated, and as Jimmie moved up in the organization John grew more troubled about what was happening to his friend.

About two years ago, he had gotten a call from Jimmie. He wanted to meet in an expensive restaurant in Manhattan. "This one's on me, Johnny. Or on Zodiac. I want to talk business."

"Not another job offer."

"Definitely not. You be there, buddy."

So on a rainy Friday evening, John drove into the city after work and took the elevator up to an elite restaurant on the top floor of a skyscraper on Fifth Avenue. Jimmie hadn't arrived yet. John checked his overcoat and was shown into a quiet booth in the cocktail lounge. He ordered a ginger ale. He had always been too disciplined to drink liquor. Jimmie showed up about twenty minutes later and slid into the booth opposite him.

"Hey!" Jimmie's standard greeting.

He was in his charming but high-pressure salesman mode, and John knew his pal was up to something. A pretty cocktail waitress immediately appeared to take Jimmie's drink order. "Vodka gimlet," he told her cheerfully. John could see him looking for her reaction, but she just smiled briefly and walked away to fill his order. Jimmie watched her go.

"That's the drink Cary Grant always ordered. Thought I'd try it out on her."

"A rare woman immune to the Jimmie Putnam charm machine."

"The evening is young," Jimmie said. "So how you been? It's been ages."

"It's been four days. And I've been fine."

"Nice place, huh?" Jimmie said, with a grand sweep of his arm out toward the spectacular view of the city across the room.

"Sure is."

"How'd you like to be eating and drinking in places like this from now on?"

"I thought you said this wasn't another job offer."

"Hey, this is not *just* another job offer. This is *the* job. The turning point in your life."

"Jimmie—"

"Just hear me out, okay?" Jimmie glanced around the room as if checking for the presence of enemy agents, and then leaned forward over the table conspiratorially. "Here's the deal. Zodiac International is planning to set up casinos in, guess where."

"Antarctica," John said with a sincere lack of interest that clearly vexed Jimmie.

"Hawai'i," Jimmie said, as if making an earth-shattering announcement. "Hawai'i! Can you believe it? They need a local type guy they can really trust to go over there and do the groundwork, get it set up. I told Charles I know the perfect guy for this. The perfect guy!"

"Yeah? Who?" John said, casually sipping his soda.

"Come on, Johnny, you cannot pass this one up. A deal like this comes along once in a lifetime. You'd be in on the ground floor of the operation. We're talking palm trees. Hula girls. It's perfect for you."

The waitress brought Jimmie's drink and said, "We'll have your table ready for you in just a few minutes." As soon as she left them, Jimmie picked right up again.

"Johnny, Hawai'i. You always wanted to go there, I remember that."

"That was years ago, Jimmie. It was kid stuff."

"But think about this. You get to return to the land of your birth. Name your own salary, and it damn well better be at least three times what you're making now, and I'm serious about that."

John didn't want to be thinking about it, but Jimmie was getting to him. He looked out across the restaurant to the towering windows. The exterior of the building was lit by floodlights, and in the glare of the illumination he could see that the rain was turning to sleet. His thoughts turned to balmy nights and palm trees, and maybe some little piece of Hawai'i of his own. It had been so many years since he'd considered these things, and he was surprised at how readily it all came flooding back. Jimmie was grinning at him, knowing that the hook was set.

Jimmie had apparently decided he'd better strike while the iron was hot. He'd set up a meeting with some high-level Zodiac people for the following morning in their New York City office. "It's not a job interview," Jimmie said. "It's a no-brainer—the job is yours based on my recommendation. They just want to have a look at you. If you can keep from pissing them off for about two hours, you're in," he joked.

As it turned out, John had been unable to avoid pissing them off. By the next morning, going into the city on a commuter train, dressed in a suit, tie, and overcoat, in the press of thousands of other commuters, he knew he would be making a big mistake to take this job. They just wanted a token Hawaiian to fill a slot in an org chart. Jimmie was happy to be the token Indian. John was not going to let that happen to him, and Jimmie should have known it. He was feeling increasingly angry at Jimmie for putting him up to this, and angry at himself for falling for it. By the time the elevator in the Zodiac office building got to the fiftieth floor his mind was made up. As the door opened he remained in the car and slammed his palm irritably on the down button.

Before the door began to close Jimmie and another man passed by and noticed him standing there in the elevator car. Instead of being able to flee, he found himself in the firm grasp of Jimmie, who was enthusiastically introducing John to his colleague.

"Dick, this is the guy I wanted you to meet. John, meet Dick Bennett."

John reluctantly shook hands with Bennett, a trim, late-thirtyish man in some sort of Italian suit and the slicked-back, self-assured air of a master of the universe. John felt an instinctual dislike for him. Bennett's handshake was nearly painful, his potent grip identifying him as one of those guys with toxic levels of testosterone who likes other men to know he works out.

"Jim has told me a lot about you. Thanks for coming in," Bennett said, leading John by the elbow toward a glass-walled conference room just off the lobby. Jimmie started to follow, but Bennett said to him, "Jim, how about getting us some cappuccinos from the Starbucks downstairs. You know how I like mine. John?"

"Not for me, thanks," John said, as Jimmie scurried obediently off. After all the bragging about his big salary and high level in the company, John could see Jimmie for what he really was: the injun they send out for coffee. As sour as his mood had been, he now felt even angrier. He went into the conference room with Bennett, and they sat down in expensive leather chairs at a large, highly polished wood table. John pictured himself in a room like this one, the only person of color there. And everybody looking at him, knowing that he had his job because of his appearance. And if coffee was needed, he'd be the one sent out to get it. It was about the worst job scenario he could imagine, a real nightmare, and he couldn't wait to get away from this place and back to his grubby, comfortable old office at Rossi Electric.

"So Jim tells me you're ready for the big time."

"Yeah, I can hardly wait to be able to get the coffee for you guys."

Bennett grinned at him, not sure if John was being a wise guy or was just trying to make a joke. John took a small pad and pencil from his suit pocket and got ready to write. "How *do* you like your coffee, Dick? Or is it *Mister* Bennett?"

Bennett's smile was fading quickly. "Jim didn't mention that you're a smart ass."

"No?" John said. "How thoughtless of him."

"This could turn out to be the shortest job interview on record," Bennett said, clearly irritated.

John looked at his watch and said enthusiastically, "I'm game. What *is* the existing record?"

Bennett stood up and glared at John, before stalking angrily out of the door.

"We about done then?" John called out after him.

Bennett did not turn around, but disappeared through a doorway. John gathered up his coat and went out to the elevator, mentally kicking himself for having acquiesced to come there in the first place. When he left the elevator in the building lobby, he nearly bumped into Jimmie, who was carrying two Starbucks coffee containers in his hands.

"Ah," he said to Jimmie. "Here's the boy with the coffee."

"What the hell happened?" Jimmie asked.

"I don't think he liked me very much."

"I don't get it. It was all set."

"Well, I just hope I didn't embarrass you too much."

Jimmie looked alarmed. "Why? What did you do?"

John was still feeling angry. "Don't worry, you're still their little injun."

Jimmie looked at him. "So what are you saying? You think I only have my job because I look Indian?"

"You said it, not me."

"You've always held that against me."

"No, I haven't."

"Yes, you have. You've always resented my success."

"You call this success?" John said, motioning toward the coffee in Jimmie's hands.

Jimmie just stood there, uncharacteristically silent. John knew that he had deeply wounded his old friend. Jimmie didn't say a word, just walked slowly into the elevator. The door closed behind him.

John should have gone after him, but he didn't. He should have called Jimmie that evening, but he didn't. Nor the next day nor the next week. Then his father had a third heart attack and was no longer able to be involved in the business. Tony was now officially in charge of Rossi & Son. One week with Tony running the business, and it was a shambles. Without openly admitting that her son was messing up, his mother had pleaded with John to help Tony out before Rossi & Son went down the tubes. John had worried that Tony would resent his help. Quite the contrary—he was immensely relieved. He could pretend to be the boss without having to do any real work. And John found that without his father there looking over his shoulder, he had a free hand to run things the way they should have been run. Before long they had hired three new crews and added extra trucks to the fleet. A year went by and then a second one, without a word from Jimmie.

Between running the business and dating Angela, he seemed to be finally earning his parents' love and respect. And when they had to order a new truck, his father made sure the lettering on the door read, "Rossi & Sons."

John's life provided a contentment and stability he had never expected to have. The one thing he had never thought he would do seemed right and natural. Hawai'i was a distant childhood fantasy.

6

John drove himself to Newark airport the next morning. The temperature was just above freezing and the gloomy winter skies looked menacing, with light snow flurries falling. The forecast was for heavy snow, but it was not supposed to hit until later in the day. He hoped the weather would hold up until he got away. He wanted to get this over with. The short-term lot where he parked would cost a few bucks extra, but it was convenient, and it was only the one night. This was not going to be a vacation. He had planned out the trip as he would a quick business trip to Detroit. Get off the plane and into a rental car, drive to the Zodiac International office. They were handling all the arrangements for Jimmie. He didn't have much respect for gambling operations, but he had to admit, these guys looked after their own. They had tried to dissuade him from coming at all, at first. But they seemed to understand, when he told them about Jimmie's mother, that he had to come. They set up a meeting for him with an assistant district attorney for Maui County. They had made all the arrangements to ship Jimmie home, and they were paying for John's hotel room. They had offered to meet him with a car and driver, but John preferred the freedom of his own car. Get in, take care of business, and get out.

He went through Newark airport security quickly and found himself with nearly two hours to kill. He bought a newspaper and went into an airport coffee shop for breakfast. As he ate his sausages and eggs he could see through the restaurant windows that the snow was falling heavily now. After breakfast, the gate area was crowded with tourists escaping dreary Newark in the middle of January. Their festive mood did not suit him under the circumstances. He went as far away from the crowd as possible but where he could still hear any boarding announcements, and sat down to read his paper. As seats in the immediate gate area filled up, the crowd spread out, and a young couple waiting for his flight sat down across from him. They sat and snuggled and giggled, and he guessed that they were newlyweds, maybe still a little tipsy from a wedding bash the night before. After a few moments he became aware of some of their conversation.

"Shhhh!" the young man was saying.

"Well, ask him," she whispered loud enough for John to hear.

"I'm not going to ask him. You ask him."

"I'm not going to ask him. You do it."

The man cleared his throat and spoke to John. "Hi. I hope you don't mind my asking, but are you Hawaiian?"

The girl looked on with interest to hear his reply. It occurred to John that, in all his life, he had never been asked this question. Most Easterners were unfamiliar with Polynesian faces. They always seemed to assume he was Puerto Rican, although he didn't really look remotely Latino. And now, the question having been asked, John found that he didn't know quite how to answer it. If he said yes, they would probably be babbling with questions about Hawai'i. But "no" wasn't exactly the correct answer either.

"I was born there, but I haven't been there since I was a kid," John told them.

"Wow, so you're a tourist too," the girl said to him.

John smiled at them. "I guess I am at that."

The young man said, "You sure don't sound Hawaiian. I mean, you talk like us."

John said, "I've spent my whole life in New Jersey."

"That's amazing. This is going to be really something for you then," the girl said.

"Shelly, let the man alone," her companion told her.

"No, I'm just saying," she said to him.

They were interrupted by an announcement on the PA system from the gate. "Passengers on Continental Airlines flight 8 to Maui, may I have your attention please. Due to the snow, we're going to be delayed in taking off this morning. We are told that we'll be boarding in approximately one hour."

There was a collective groan from the passengers. The announcement continued. "We'll let you know as soon as it's time to board. We regret the delay, and we thank you for your patience." There was an audible hubbub of passengers in the area.

"Let's go get something to eat. I'm hungry," the young man said to the girl and they got up to leave.

"Nice talking to you," the girl said to John as they walked off.

John smiled at her and looked out at the runways, where he could see snowplows in operation. He went back to the paper, working the crossword puzzle to help pass the time.

They finally boarded about an hour and a half late. John had a window seat on the left side of the plane. There had been few seats available at the last minute. The aisle seat was occupied by a bored-looking college student who sat down, covered himself with a blanket, and went to sleep. It looked like the middle seat would be empty, but at the last moment before they closed the door, a dark, heavyset woman, maybe fifty or so years old, came bustling down the aisle and stood in front of his row. She had all kinds of small packages to stow in the overhead before she finally took her seat. She did a double take when she saw John. She addressed him with a warm smile that seemed to embrace him.

"Aloha!" she said.

John couldn't help smiling at her. "Aloha."

"So what you doin' here in cold mainland in winter? Bet it feel good fo' go home, yeah?"

Again, John found himself stuck for a response. He knew that as soon as he opened his mouth she would know he wasn't a real Hawaiian.

"Actually, I grew up here. I've never been to Hawai'i before. Well, I was born there, but I haven't been back since I was a kid."

"Fo' real? Dass so sad. But good you finally going home, yeah?"

Her smile and her evident warmth made it easy to open up to this woman. "Well, I'm only going for a day. My best friend died there, and I'm going to bring him home."

She patted him on the hand. "Eh, you one good frien' fo' do someting li' dat."

Not exactly, John thought. Not exactly.

"So who's your *'ohana* ovah there, you know, your family? Maybe I know them. You look kind of familiar. You from Maui?"

"Yes, but my Hawaiian mom is dead. I was adopted."

"Oh, dass so sad. So maybe you find some family there."

"I wouldn't know where to look. Besides, I have to come right back tomorrow night."

"Too bad, too bad."

This seemed to stop her for a while and she sat in contemplation while the plane taxied for takeoff. They got to the end of the runway and the jet engines started spooling up to takeoff power. Suddenly she grabbed John's hand tightly. "You mind? Dis part really scare me," she said.

John smiled at her. "No, that's okay," and he squeezed her hand

She looked over at him. "You a *pono* boy, a good Hawaiian boy. Tings get better fo' you from now on, you have auntie's word on dat." She said the words with such conviction, he almost believed her.

She took a deep breath as the plane roared down the runway and lifted off. She kept gripping John's hand with one of hers and the armrest with the other, until they reached altitude and the engine noise leveled off.

"You like sleep now, jus' tell auntie and I no boddah you no moah."

"No, that's okay. I enjoy talking to you. What were you doing in Newark?"

"Not Newark. Went to Connecticut fo' visit my daughter. She living there now, married to one *haole* guy. You know what is *haole*, a foreigner, yeah? If I like see my grandchildren, I got to go there. Nice place, Connecticut, but it's not Hawai'i. So what happen to your friend? He wen go Hawai'i fo' vacation?"

"No, he was working there. For Zodiac Casinos."

"Casino? We don't have any casinos in Hawai'i. Only state that have no gambling allowed, you know."

"I didn't know that. I guess Zodiac is trying to be the first to have one."

"Oh, I hope not. Gambling bad for us. Already bad now. Make it legal, and auwe! We going be in big trouble ovah there."

"Well, I hope it doesn't happen then."

"Wait a minute, Zodiac. Who's the boss of that company?"

"A man named Brewster. Charles N. Brewster."

"Oh, I know about him. He stay married to Wainani Smith. She was Miss Hawai'i, you know."

She chattered away for the next hour and all through the meal, talking about Wainani Smith, among other things. In addition to having been Miss Hawai'i about five years before, she was also a genuine Hawaiian princess, an heir to the throne of the nation of Hawai'i. Not that there was one any more, a nation or a throne. But if there were a throne someday it would most likely be Wainani who would occupy it. Eventually auntie seemed to get bored with this topic and wanted to know more about John.

When was he born, when did he come to the mainland, who his family might be. John answered with as much information as he knew. He didn't mind the chatter. It was helping to take his mind off the purpose of the trip and what lay ahead, and talking to the first real Hawaiian he'd ever met served as kind of a cultural indoctrination.

Suddenly she rubbed her eyes and said, "I go sleep now." She closed her eyes and within fifteen seconds she was snoring softly. John thought that she could be around the age his mother would have been. He wondered if he might have some relatives still there. *'Ohana.* The Hawaiian word for family. He found that he couldn't sleep. He just kept gazing out the window at nothing, hour after hour, mostly seeing cloud cover and later, after they passed the coast, occasional glimpses of the ocean nearly eight miles below. He marveled that pilots had no trouble finding an island 3,000 miles out in the Pacific, the most remote occupied archipelago in the world.

At some point he must have dozed off, because he found himself opening his eyes and seeing something sticking up above the solid blanket of clouds far in the distance, a dark, pointed shape. He figured it must be an unusually shaped cloud, because they were still nearly an hour from landing. Yet there was something familiar about it that he couldn't quite fathom. He felt a poke on his arm. Auntie was awake and she was looking out the window too.

"Big Island," she said.

"That's Hawai'i?"

"Mauna Loa."

He stared out at the mountain peak poking out of the clouds. With a jolt, he recalled his dream, the same dream he had had so many times. Could he have a recollection of this? He tried to imagine himself as a scared little child, leaving Hawai'i. Had he been looking out the window then at this same sight, the island of Hawai'i growing smaller and smaller as it receded in the distance? Something in his gut told him he had, although try as he might, he could not invoke an actual recollection of it. Yet there was something here, something he knew. Maybe it was a memory he had suppressed all these years.

"Wonderful sight. Ho, feel good fo' come home, yeah?" she said.

"It does, and I'm trying to figure out why. I mean, I was so small when I left. I don't really remember anything about Hawai'i."

She put a chubby finger lightly on her forehead. "You don't remember it here." She moved her finger to her chest and touched over her heart. "You remember it here. Same ting for all us Hawaiians. These little islands are in your heart fo'evah, doesn't matter where you go."

She closed her eyes and sat back in her seat with a contented sigh, a smile on her face. At that moment he felt the gradual reduction of power in the jet engines as they began their descent. He watched as they flew past the Big Island. It seemed to continually change shape. First he had seen Mauna Loa, and as they went by, the second big volcano, Mauna Kea, came into view, then a third mountain, the Kohala Peninsula. He knew all the names. He had studied these islands in depth during his Hawaiian Phase, spent hours gazing at a map, longing to be here. He still could not see Maui.

Then suddenly there it was, Haleakalā volcano, and they were low enough to be flying below its peak. He had a clear view of the slopes of the mountain, radiant green in the sunshine. They flew almost to the other side of the island, then banked to the right to continue the descent to the airport. Now he could see the coast. He marveled at the colors of the water, intense greens and aquamarine near the shoreline, changing to a cobalt blue as the water deepened. He felt a tingling in his extremities, a sense of intense excitement. Something was happening to him, some feeling he had never experienced before. They were very low now, descending over sugar cane fields, emerald and waving in the wind. Off the wingtip he could see a town, and beyond that the shadowy mountains of West Maui, with deep valleys dark under rain clouds. He knew he had seen this sight before, his fingers and toes told him, and, as auntie had said, his heart. The plane thumped down on the runway, then turned and taxied back toward the terminal. On the side of the field opposite the terminals, he could see several large corporate jets parked on the tarmac. Finally they stopped at the gate, and he waited for the aisle to clear so they could exit.

"So, you're here," auntie said.

"I'm here."

She laid a brown hand on his arm. "Remember what auntie say. Your life going be different from now on." She got up from her seat and stepped into the aisle to let him pass.

"Aren't you getting off?"

"No, I going stay on da plane, go Honolulu."

The passengers in front of him had exited, and John stood up.

"Go now," she said, touching his arm. "Live your life."

"Thank you." He pulled his suitcase down from the overhead, and walked toward the door.

"Aloha!" she called after him.

He turned back to face her. "Aloha."

He filed off the plane with the other passengers, most of them chattering happily as they began their vacations. As he exited onto the jetway, he caught sight of the exterior skin of the plane. It seemed incredible that this same aluminum tube had just hours before been in the snow of Newark, and now was in this amazing and exotic tropical place. He followed the crowd through a doorway and down a flight of stairs, and suddenly he realized that there were no outside walls here, and he was outdoors. He could smell the scent of the balmy air, flowered and heady, and he took deep breaths of it, pulling it deeply into his lungs as if he were taking the first breaths of his life. It felt so wonderful and so familiar. He walked out into the open and now he could see the West Maui mountains in the distance. Suddenly overwhelmed with sensation, he felt himself go weak in the knees, and he sat down heavily on a smooth stone seat just outside the terminal. What was happening to him? What was this intense feeling he was having in his heart, his limbs, and his head? And then it hit him. It wasn't the hours without sleep or the jet lag. It wasn't even Jimmie's death. Tears filled his eyes and streamed down his face for the first time since the day he had met Jimmie. And he realized what it was: It was home. At long last, he was home.

7

He didn't know how long he had been sitting on the bench outside the terminal. He had lost all track of time, and there wasn't much of that left. He had to be on his way back to Newark by tomorrow. It hurt his heart to think about leaving this place, but he had responsibilities. He checked the time. His watch was reading 11:30. That would be at night in New Jersey, so it would be around 5:30 here. He tried to pull himself together and organize his thoughts. He was supposed to meet with a man who worked with Jimmie at the Zodiac office in Wailuku at 3:30, so he was a couple of hours late for that. He pulled out his cell phone and tried calling Zodiac's number, but just got a voice mail telling him the office was closed for the day. In truth, he was glad he could put it off for a while. His mind was in too much of a fog to concentrate. He left a message that he was tired from the trip and would be going directly to the hotel; he would go to the district attorney's office the next day. Picking up his bag, he walked down to the rental car shuttles.

Half an hour later he was on Highway 30 in a red Chevrolet Malibu, headed for his hotel in Kapalua. Crossing the central isthmus of the island, surrounded by cane fields, there was no longer any doubt in his mind that he had memories of this place. There was no specific recollection, just the complete certainty that he had seen all these things before. He drove with all the windows rolled down, even though it was windy. He had only a day to absorb this, and he wanted to take it all in as completely as he could. The road began to wind as it drew close to the coastline on the leeward side of the island. He was in a long line of traffic now. Most of the vehicles looked like rental cars, current models, in just a few colors, red, silver, blue, brown. Looking out over the water he could see another island, which he assumed would be Lāna'i. The road continued next to the steep cliffs of West Maui, through a short tunnel, and down onto a flat area close to the sea. Now he could see that there were two more islands ahead, and he realized that the first island he had seen must have been Kaho'olawe, with Lāna'i next and finally Moloka'i. It felt good to be getting the lay of the land, and he was surprised at how much he remembered from his readings about Hawai'i so many years before.

Soon he was in heavy traffic passing through Lahaina, most of the town to the left of the highway. He remembered that it was the police in Lahaina who were doing the investigation. He would have liked to talk to them about it, but he didn't know where the police station was. He figured he'd better get to the hotel and get some sleep, although he didn't feel in the least jet lagged, just a little tired. Then, just past the town of Lahaina, he saw a sign on the right-hand side of the road reading, "Police Department." There was a small white building on a grassy bluff. He turned in and drove up the hill toward the structure. As he pulled into the parking lot, he could see that the building was ringed by picketers. A dozen large Hawaiian men were carrying signs. He assumed it was some sort of labor dispute, but one hand-drawn sign contained a depiction of a noose. He wondered what was going on, and if he'd have any trouble getting into the police station.

As he walked toward the front door a couple of the pickets eyed him curiously, but made no effort to stop him. Two blue-uniformed cops were standing in front of the entrance. They looked him over, then stood aside to let him pass. He opened the glass door and walked into an open area with several plastic bench seats, and offices opening into the room. A weathered old Hawaiian man sat in one of the seats, his head held low, staring at the ground, his wrists handcuffed in front of him. He was dressed in worn clothing, a blue checked plaid shirt, brown shorts and rubber slippers. John was surprised about the handcuffs. The guy looked too old and beat to be a threat to anyone. Drunk and disorderly, maybe.

A policeman sitting at a desk at the far side of the room gave John a careful looking over. "Howzit bruddah? Help you?" the cop asked John.

John said, "I wanted to see if I could find out about—"

The phone rang at the policeman's desk and he picked it up, motioning to John to take a seat. He sat down opposite the old man, who ignored him and just sat bent over staring morosely at the floor. The cop at the desk continued to talk on the phone, and John pulled his cell phone out of his pocket to see if he had gotten any response to his voice mail to Zodiac. A couple of quarters came spilling out as he pulled the phone out, and they landed on the floor between himself and the old man. The man immediately reached for them with his calloused brown hands, manacled together. John thought, *Fine, let the old guy have them.* He was surprised when the man picked the coins up and politely handed them over, placing them carefully in John's hand, looking up at him for the first time. Then, as he touched John's hand and looked at his face, the old man's expression completely changed from overwhelming sadness to a beaming smile. He reached out with both hands and grabbed John's wrists, nearly pulling him out of his chair.

"Eh, you came! I knew fo' sure you was going come! I knew it!"

The policeman at the desk looked up in alarm and quickly ended his phone conversation. "Hey, you're not allowed to touch the prisoner!" he yelled at John.

John looked over at the cop helplessly. The old man just sat there beaming at him, holding tightly to his arms. The policeman got up from his desk and walked quickly over toward them.

"Uncle, you behave yourself. Let 'em go," the cop told the old man.

"You no understand. Dis Keoni. Years ago I wen save his life. Now he stay come back fo' save mine. I knew it! I knew it!"

The cop spoke to John. "You know this man?"

"I've never seen him before in my life."

"No, Johnny Boy, you jus' no remembah. You was too little den."

John felt a sense of shock. How did this guy know his name? The policeman said, "Okay now, uncle, let 'em go. He say he don't know you."

"Oh, he know me. He going get me outta here, fo' sure."

There was a commotion at the door, and the most beautiful woman in the world walked into the building. At least that's what she seemed to John. She had long black hair, a stunning island face, and a figure that might be a tad too heavy for a svelte New Yorker, but to John seemed just perfect. She wore a business suit and an angry expression on her face, as she strode over to John and the old man.

"What the hell is going on here?" she said to John. Her tone may have been angry, but all John could hear was the sweet island lilt of her voice. He just looked at her dumbfounded, but the old man grinned at her.

"Dis Keoni. He going help us."

"Who are you?" she asked John.

"It's some sort of mistake, I'm only here for my friend," he spluttered.

She bent down and spoke gently to the old man. "Uncle, the marshals are here. We have to go now."

"Where?"

"To Wailuku. It's better for you over there."

"Keoni can come too?"

"He'll be along later, okay?"

"Okay," he said and reluctantly let go of John's arms. More uniformed men had come into the building and one of them took the arm of the old man, who could not seem to take his eyes off John. The woman looked at John now more with curiosity than hostility. As they walked toward the door, John heard the old man tell her, "I no stay worry no mo'. Everyting going be okay, now dat Johnny Boy here."

Then they were gone, swallowed up in a swirl of uniforms—a half dozen marshals in brown uniforms and the blue-suited cops. They pushed their way through the riled-up and shouting pickets, and the old man and the woman got into a big white Ford van. They pulled away quickly, escorted front and rear by a couple of police cars. The picketers yelled angrily after them, waving their signs in the air. As soon as the van was out of sight, the men began to disperse.

The policeman from the desk spoke to John. "What da hell was that about?"

"You tell me," John said. "I don't even know who that guy is."

"That old man is just the most notorious criminal on Maui."

"You've got to be joking. What did he do?" John asked.

The cop seemed surprised at the question. "Murdered the guy from the casino. Where you been, brah?"

John felt as if he'd been punched in the stomach. He had just been touching Jimmie's murderer! He had had plenty of time to think about what he would do if he ever got his hands on whoever had killed Jimmie, and now he had literally had his hands on the man and hadn't even known it was him. But this old man murdered Jimmie? Why? Something in John couldn't quite believe that this was the guy. Illogical as it undoubtedly was, he felt that he would have known Jimmie's killer.

John said to the cop, "I just got here from the East Coast. The man who was killed was my best friend. James Putnam. That's who we're talking about, right?"

"Yeah, that's him."

"I came here to bring his body back home."

"Oh, hey, sorry you had to go through all this, brah. Sorry 'bout your friend."

"Thanks." John tried to make his next question sound casual. "Who was that woman?"

The policeman smiled at him. "Lani Miller. She's his lawyer. Some *ono*, yeah?"

Lani. What a beautiful name, John thought. The cop was still grinning at him.

"Listen, the other reason I'm here is to ask about the investigation," John said, but other thoughts were distracting him. He looked out the door in the direction the van had gone. "Are you sure he's the murderer?"

"Oh, yeah, dass da guy."

"Is there someone I can talk to about the case?"

"About what?"

"It's for Jim's mom. She wants to be sure that justice is being done."

"Yeah, okay. You gotta talk to the chief investigator. He's not here right now. Maybe you can come back sometime tomorrow."

"I'm going back home tomorrow. With the body."

The cop thought this over for a moment. "Try wait a little while, let me see what I can do." He went over to his desk and made a call, then motioned to John to come to the phone. The voice on the end of the line said, "This is Sergeant Peters."

"Sergeant Peters, this is John Rossi. I just came from the mainland to take Jim Putnam home."

"Yeah, so I understand. Sorry for your loss."

"Thanks. I sure would appreciate an opportunity to meet with you, get some of the details of the case."

"Well, you know, it's still under investigation, so I can't really help you out there. Maybe in a couple of weeks."

"I'm leaving tomorrow."

"Wish I could help you out, but I can't."

"His mom wants to know that justice is being done, that they got the right guy. Do you think they did?"

Peters hesitated a moment, before he asked, "Where are you staying?"

"I'm going to be at the Kapalua Bay Hotel."

"Okay, listen, I'm in Kahana right now, not far from the hotel. You go over there and check in, and I'll come by as soon as I can."

"Thanks, I'm grateful for your time. If you're going off duty, I'll buy you a drink."

"Sounds good to me. See you there. Maybe an hour or so."

John hung up the phone, thanked the cop, and went out to his car. He had driven less than a block to an intersection when he thought he heard the sound of a train whistle. And there, coming around a curve, was a small steam locomotive pulling a line of passenger cars. What was this thing doing on Maui? He sat in the car waiting for the train to pass, while looking out at the ocean and the island of Lāna'i. This was turning into the most bizarre day of his life. The old man, Jimmie's murderer, who seemed to know him. The beautiful woman who had left him smitten. His strong feelings of familiarity for a place he could not remember. And now a steam locomotive. Finally, the train passed and he drove back to the highway. A glorious sunset was taking place over the water, but deep in thought, he hardly noticed it on the twenty-minute drive to the hotel. He pulled under the portico and a bellman came out to greet him. He popped the trunk lid and the bellman reached in and grabbed his bag.

"Checking in, sir?"

"Yeah," John said, pointing to his bag. "I can manage that." As he got out of the car, the bellman politely handed the suitcase to him.

"Would you like me to park your car for you, sir?"

"Okay," John said handing him the keys.

The bellman gave him a valet ticket, and John walked into the hotel. The lobby was spectacular, with a ceiling a good sixty feet high and terraced floors at different levels overlooking a waterfall right inside the building. But what really struck him was that the lobby was completely open to the outdoors on the seaward side, where the last of the sunset was finally dissipating. Growing up in New Jersey, John could hardly have imagined a building where you simply didn't need outside walls.

He checked in at the small reception desk, where they told him that his bill and all expenses for meals would be covered by Zodiac International. He got his key and went up to his room. It was nearly dark now, but he could see the last of the sun's afterglow and he knew that there would be an impressive daytime view. He went out on the balcony, sat down in a chaise lounge chair and gazed out over the ocean. He could see the dark shapes of Lāna'i and Moloka'i, and on Moloka'i the headlights of a car blinked on and off, passing trees as it traveled along the shoreline. It was a warm, pleasant evening, and he was filled with nostalgia, he knew not for what. He began to wish he had left himself an extra couple of days here. But obviously that wasn't possible under the circumstances. He still had his meeting with Sergeant Peters, and he tried not to think about what time it was back in New Jersey. The warm evening air surrounded him like a down comforter on a cold night, and he found himself drifting off. Soon he was deep in slumber. He dreamed about his mother, his Hawaiian mother. Somehow he had found her, she wasn't dead. She was living in a little grass shack under a palm tree, by the sea. He went into the shack and it was auntie from the airplane, she was his mother. She stood up when he came in, hung a flower lei around his neck, and embraced him. He wanted to hug her back, but her phone started ringing, and for some reason he wanted her to be sure to answer it.

He startled awake. The phone in the room was ringing, and he leaped up to get it. "Hello?"

"Mr. Rossi, this is Sergeant Peters. I'm in the lobby."

"I'll be right down."

John went over to the bed and grabbed his winter coat, which he had carried into the room and slung over a chair. He started to put it on, then smiled at himself and tossed it back on the chair. *Tough to ignore a lifetime of habits.* He walked down the hall to the elevator and pressed the button. When it didn't arrive immediately, he took the stairs. He was grateful to Peters for coming to see him in his off hours, and didn't want to keep him waiting. He went out into the lobby. There were various terraced levels, and it suddenly hit him that he didn't have any idea what Peters looked like.

On one of the terraces a man was playing the guitar, and he found himself drawn in that direction. The music was soft and sweet, and somehow very Hawaiian. For the umpteenth time that day he was hit by a wave of nostalgia that he could not explain. He knew this music, had heard it before. As he got closer he noticed that there was a bar in the corner. A couple and a single man were sitting on easy chairs listening to the music. He figured the single guy had to be Sergeant Peters, and he was about to walk over to him when he felt a tap on his shoulders. He turned. A florid, heavyset man in his mid-forties was standing there with his hand extended.

"Sam Peters." John shook hands with him and they sat down on a sofa. John asked him, "How did you know who I was?"

"Hey, I'm a detective," Sam laughed. "No, seriously, it's not hard to spot somebody who just got in."

"What gave me away?"

Peters pointed at John's feet. "Socks."

"Yeah, well I started to walk out of the room with my overcoat."

They chuckled together about that and the bartender came over to take their order. John ordered a Coke and Peters a beer. The bartender said, "We also have a *pupu* platter if you like." Peters saw the puzzled expression on John's face. "Like little appetizers," he told John.

John suddenly realized how hungry he was. "Yes, that would be great."

Sam looked at him curiously. "So what's your story? John Rossi. You look Hawaiian, but you sound like New York."

John decided to give him the short version. "I was born here, but I've lived my whole life in New Jersey."

"Never been here since you left?"

"First time."

"Interesting. You're what they call a 'coconut.' "

"What does that mean?"

"Brown on the outside, white on the inside," Sam said.

John looked startled.

"Guess I shouldn't have said that," Sam said. "Said the wrong way at the wrong time to the wrong person, it could be taken as an insult. I certainly didn't intend it that way."

John smiled at him. "That's okay. It's pretty funny, actually. And accurate, as concerns me."

"Well, since you're here for only a day, I have just one evening to give you as much local lore as I can."

John chuckled. "I appreciate that."

"I understand you created quite a stir at the station."

"It was the weirdest thing. It was like the guy recognized me. He called me 'Johnny Boy.' "

"That's pretty typical for a kid named John."

"He also called me by another name. 'Koni' or something."

"Keoni," Sam said.

"That's it."

Sam smiled at him. "Hawaiian name for 'John.' "

John shook his head, not knowing what to think of all this.

"Is it possible that he knows you?" Sam asked.

"I don't see how. I was four years old when I left. I don't know. He's an old man."

"There's a little more to it than that. This is not some crazy old coot. Uncle Sunny is known as a *kahuna*. More than that, he's a healer. They have special powers."

John gave him an incredulous look. Sam lowered his voice and glanced around the room, suddenly self-conscious. "Listen, I'm from Chicago originally. I was a cop there so I have a healthy sense of skepticism. But after living here for ten years, I've seen a lot of stuff."

"What kind of stuff?"

"Crazy stuff. Look, all I'm saying is, you can't just disregard this *kahuna* business."

The bartender brought them their drinks and set them down on the table in front of them. "*Pupu's* coming right up, gentlemen."

Sam took a deep draught of his beer. "Okay, not much time, so down to business. You wanted to know the facts of the case. You have to know that I can't give you all the details, because it's an ongoing investigation. Plus, you have this possibly ambiguous relationship with the defendant."

"I told you, I've never met the man before, and I—"

Peters held up a hand to stop him. "All I know is that for the last forty-eight hours, since he was taken into custody, he hasn't said word one to anyone, not even his lawyer. Then you show up and all of a sudden he's Mr. Yakity Yak."

"I can't explain that," John said.

"Okay, I'll take your word for it." Peters took another long swig of beer. "Anyway, here's the facts: Sunny was found at the scene of the crime. He was standing over your friend. He was covered in blood. He was holding the murder weapon in his hands. When he was discovered by some tourists, he confessed to the crime. He did it on video tape."

"But why would he kill Jimmie Putnam?"

"Motive, yeah. This is where it gets kind of interesting. Your pal Jimmie was working for Zodiac International. They've been on the ground here for maybe a couple of years, trying to get the laws changed to allow casino gambling. They've been spreading around so much cash they're probably going to be successful. Zodiac wants to build in the Kalonahoa Valley, on the north side of the island. But Sunny is there farming taro. His family has owned land in the valley for generations, doing the same thing. Sunny won't leave, no matter how much money they offer him. James Putnam is sent in there to make friends with Sunny, but he doesn't tell Sunny or anyone else that he works for the casino. Somehow Sunny finds out Putnam is working for the opposition, is some kind of spy for the casino. Bang, there's your motive."

The bartender showed up again, with another beer for Sam and a plate full of appetizers. He winked at John as he set it down. "Got you a little someting special from da kitchen, bruddah. Fresh. Enjoy." John didn't know what he was talking about, but he dug right into the food, dipping two fingers into a small bowl of a purplish, pudding-like substance and licking it off delightedly. Sam was studying him with a curious look, and John finally noticed.

"What?"

Sam smiled at him. "Somewhere some synapses are firing."

"What do you mean?" John asked, hungrily dipping his fingers and sucking the purplish stuff off.

"That's *poi* you're eating."

"Is it?"

"With your fingers."

John looked embarrassed, as he realized how impolite he had been. He wiped his fingers off with a cocktail napkin. "Sorry, I was hungry." He looked around for the bartender. "We can ask for another bowl. It's delicious."

"No, no, that's okay, I can't stand the stuff. They say it's an acquired taste, but even after ten years here, I won't eat it. I'm beginning to think that it's a taste you acquire at birth, or not at all."

John was still feeling embarrassed at his lapse in manners, and wanted to change the subject. "So there's no question in your mind, Sunny did it."

Sam didn't answer the question directly. He said, "It's classic: motive, opportunity, and overwhelming circumstantial evidence. Plus a videotaped confession."

John sensed that something was being held back. He hadn't known Sam for more than half an hour, but he liked him, and his gut feeling told him this was a decent, honest guy.

He looked straight at Sam. "So you think he did it."

Sam, looked away, and sat in quiet thought for a moment, sipping his beer. "You know, after twenty years as a cop, you develop certain instincts about people, especially about crime suspects."

"And what are your instincts telling you?"

Whatever Sam was going to say, he evidently had changed his mind. He finished off his beer with a couple of long gulps and stood up, extending his hand to John. "It's getting late. I have to go. Thank you for the beer, and have a safe trip home."

John stood and shook Sam's hand, but he didn't release it when Sam tried to turn to leave. "Please tell me what you really think. I have to go home tomorrow, and I need to tell Jimmie's mom what happened."

Sam hesitated a couple of moments before speaking. "Okay, maybe I can say this to you, because it doesn't really mean anything in light of the overwhelming facts in the case. It's just one man's gut feel, you have to understand. And sometimes I do get it wrong."

"I understand that," John said

Sam looked John square in the eye and spoke emphatically. "There's no way Uncle murdered your friend. No fucking way." He turned and quickly walked across the lobby.

8

When John got back to his room, the message light on the phone was flashing. *Must be the Zodiac guys calling about the meeting*, he thought. He didn't feel like talking to them. He went out on the balcony and sat down. He didn't allow himself to calculate whatever unimaginably late hour it would be in New Jersey. All he knew was that suddenly he was wide awake. *What the hell am I supposed to do now?* There was the meeting with the Maui County district attorney in the morning. And for Jimmie's mom, he knew he would have to personally view the body before it was shipped back home. Not that there was any question about the identity. People from Zodiac who had known Jimmie for years had identified him. But what was he going to tell Jimmie's mom about the murderer? Sam Peters thought that Sunny didn't do it. And having accidentally met the man, John wasn't so sure either.

And then there was the other thing. Sunny seemed to know him, even knew his name. It could be some kind of crazy coincidence, probably was. Still, if there was some way to find out if Sunny knew his family, it could turn his painful trip into something positive. Oh yeah, there was one more item—talk about crazy. There was that woman, Sunny's lawyer. He didn't know anything about her, except her name. Lani Miller. He tried to shake off this feeling he had for a total stranger. Married, undoubtedly. Probably had two kids at home. No, three. And he himself was engaged to be married. It was nuts. But as he stripped off his winter clothing and slipped into bed, all he could think about was Lani. And that he was going to need an extra day here.

He awakened to bright morning sunlight streaming into the room, and squinted over at the alarm clock on the night table. It was 6:15. He had been so tired he had forgotten to set the alarm. After yesterday's eventful and tiring day it would have been better to get another hour's sleep, he thought. Then he realized that he had gone to bed at around 8:00 p.m. local time, so he had been asleep for over ten hours. After showering and shaving, he was feeling ravenously hungry. The message light on the phone was still flashing, and he remembered that it had been flashing last night. He'd gone to bed without checking. He picked up the phone and pressed the button for the hotel voicemail. As he expected, it was a woman from Zodiac, checking to see if he had arrived okay, reminding him of his 9:00 a.m. meeting with the D.A.

There was a second message. This one made his heart leap when he heard her voice. It was Lani Miller, wanting to talk to him urgently. She left a number, told him to call at any hour. He couldn't imagine how she had managed to locate him. Then he figured she must have talked to the cops. And there was a third message. Angela. Where was he? Why hadn't he called her? Was everything going okay? He rang off the voicemail and dialed her home number, getting her answering machine. It was around noon there, so she would be at work. He left a brief message, saying that he might have to stay an extra day to clear up some problems, he'd call her later. Then he dialed her office number, and left the same message on her voicemail there. He was glad he hadn't reached her. He didn't want to break the news personally about the extra day. Next, he called Zodiac. Yet another voicemail, it was not even 7:00 a.m., so they wouldn't be in the office yet. He hung up the phone and realized that he had subconsciously saved the best for last. He dialed the number for Lani Miller. She had said to call at any time. She had seemed pissed off at him the first time they met, and he was hoping that at least he wouldn't awaken her. To his surprise, she answered on the first ring, sounding wide awake. And still angry with him.

"Didn't you get my message from last night?" she asked.

"No, I'm sorry, I forgot to check before I went to bed," he said lamely. Even with an edge of anger, he loved the sound of her voice.

"I really need to talk to you."

"Okay, but I have to be at a nine o'clock meeting with the D.A."

"Can we meet before then?"

"Sure. Where?"

"In Wailuku, at my office. It's just a few blocks from the courthouse, where the D.A.'s office is."

"Okay. I'm just going to grab something to eat and I'll be on my way."

"I know a good place for breakfast if you're hungry."

"That sounds great," he said

"In fact, let's just meet there. You need about forty-five minutes to make the drive. When will you be leaving the hotel?"

"Ten minutes."

"The place is called Kimo's, corner of Main and Central in Wailuku. Do you have a map?"

"There's one in the rental car."

"Okay, I'll see you there in about an hour."

She hung up abruptly, and it suddenly occurred to him that she had not said why she wanted to meet him. And that he didn't ask her because he didn't care why. All he knew was that breakfast with Lani sounded like a perfect way to start the day.

Outside the hotel, he waited for the valet to retrieve his car. It was a glorious morning, warm even at this early hour. There were wonderful fragrances in the air, from some type of tropical flower, he guessed, and there was the fresh scent of the ocean. He wished he had gotten a convertible instead of a four-door sedan. The Malibu rolled to a stop in front of him, and he tipped the parking guy and drove off. He had a map, and from the bellman he had also gotten directions to Kimo's. It was a place well known to the locals, he was told. Most of the trip was backtracking the way he had come yesterday, through Lahaina and along the coast where the highway skirted the cliff and went through the tunnel. Going this way he had a great view of the slopes of Haleakalā, clear almost to the top. The peak was covered in clouds, the sun outlining its bulk. To his right were the West Maui mountains, its valleys in deep misty morning shadow. It was January. Newark was sitting under a blanket of snow. He was here. He felt alive for the first time in years. And he felt at home.

He drove across the isthmus between West Maui and Haleakalā and into Wailuku, county seat of Maui County. It was overcast in town, and rain threatened. He passed though the tree-shaded entrance to town on Highway 30, turned right at the traffic light onto Main Street, then turned left on Central Street three blocks from the courthouse. He had no trouble finding Kimo's, a clean-looking place in a modest strip mall in a half residential and half retail store neighborhood. He parked in the lot in front next to a couple of other cars and went in.

She was sitting at a booth on the far side, having coffee. When she saw him coming in, she smiled, and his whole world lit up. If she was beautiful when she was angry, she was stunning when she smiled. She stood as he approached the table and extended a hand to him, which he took, savoring the contact.

"This is self-service. Just go to the counter and get whatever you want. I'm just having coffee for now."

He couldn't think of a thing to say to her. He reluctantly let go of her hand and went to the counter. There were some odd breakfast items posted on a board over the counter, like miso soup, Portuguese sausage, whatever that was, and rice—for breakfast! He ordered scrambled eggs, bacon, and toast. He asked for poi, and the counterman laughed, apparently thought he was joking around. *Must not be a breakfast food*, John figured. He carried his tray to the table and sat down opposite Lani. He had been so hungry earlier, but all he could do was look at her. He sensed her embarrassment at his gaze, and he dug into his food. *She's a beautiful woman and must be used to this*, he thought.

"You eat and I'll talk," she said. "First, I want to apologize."

"For what?"

"Well, we seemed to have gotten off on the wrong foot. When I saw you at the police station, I didn't know who you were, and I thought you were trying to pull something with my client, to get him to talk."

"Yesterday was the first day I ever met him."

"Not according to Sunny."

"Yeah, I know. But I haven't been in Hawai'i since I was four years old, and I don't know him."

"He knows you."

"That's what he says."

"He knew your name."

"I know. I can't explain that."

She sighed in frustration. "Okay, I don't know what's going on here. All I know is that after he got arrested, Sunny was clammed up tight until he met you. He wouldn't give a statement to the police and wouldn't talk to me, either. He wouldn't have a bite to eat or drink until you came along. He got back to jail yesterday after he met you and ate three dinners in a row. So I called the cops and found out who you were and that you're leaving today. I told Sunny about it, and now he's not talking again. I'm trying to put together a defense here, and my client won't talk to me unless you're there. You see my problem?"

"Yes, I do."

"Please don't think I don't see your perspective. I'm very sorry about your friend, truly. You came to bring him home, and now I'm trying to get you to help the man accused of murdering him. I'd understand completely if you just got up and walked out of here. But you have to understand that, if Sunny talks, it may be to confess to the crime, so it could go either way. I'm willing to take the risk to find the truth."

"Do you think he did it?"

She smiled at him. "Never ask a defense attorney that question."

"I'm asking."

She put her hands on her cheeks, as she contemplated the question. He noticed that she was not wearing a wedding ring, and his heart leapt. She looked at him, seemed to make a decision about how much she was willing to trust him.

"Most of my clients are guilty. Most of them claim they're innocent. The cops have a videotape on which Sunny says he's guilty—according to them. I haven't seen it yet. I'm supposed to get a copy this morning." She paused a moment before going on. "But it's an odd situation for me. My client says he did it, and I don't believe him."

"Neither do I," John said firmly.

He wasn't sure if he said this because he truly believed it or because Sunny was his ticket to spending more time with this woman. Then he rationalized, *If I don't work with her I might never know the truth about what happened to Jimmie. And that's why I came.*

"Then you'll stay?"

"At least through today."

"I'm grateful to you for that."

She glanced at her watch. "You need to get over to the courthouse for your meeting. Do you know how long you'll be?"

"I think it's going to be brief. I got some information from Sergeant Peters last night."

She hesitated a moment before she said, "Maybe I shouldn't say this, but the D.A. is an elected position here."

"And?"

"The D.A. is a politician. He has a constituency to support. And that constituency is the establishment, meaning builders, the hospitality industry—"

"And casinos."

She smiled at him. "You're pretty sharp for a coconut," she said. Then she suddenly blushed. "Sorry, I shouldn't be calling you that. A coconut is—"

John smiled back at her. "I know what a coconut is."

"My point is, with Sunny, they figure they have an open-and-shut case. Not only that, they've got the perfect perpetrator, and the perfect situation. If Sunny is convicted, he won't be able to defend his land. If he stops growing taro up there, he loses his water rights. The casino needs that water to get building permits. Gambling is still illegal here, but that could change quickly, if public and political sentiment goes in favor of it. In Sunny you have a guy who represents traditional Hawaiian ways. If people think those ways include violence and murder, they might be swayed to allow casinos. Charles Brewster, the politicians he's been financing all these years, the labor unions, and the D.A. will take full advantage of this situation. For them, this couldn't have happened at a better time, and Sunny is the ideal defendant."

"Too perfect, maybe," John said.

"You're right."

"And this does bring up another interesting question."

"Yes," she said, as if reading his mind again. "With all this evidence against him, if Sunny didn't do it, who did?"

While he finished his breakfast, she told him where to find the courthouse and Wailuku police headquarters, where Sunny was being held. They agreed to meet there at ten, and they parted in front of the restaurant. She walked to her office, which was just around the corner. He watched her wistfully, her swaying hips, her glossy, waving dark hair. He kept watching until she was out of sight. Finally he got in his car, drove over to the courthouse building, and parked in the basement lot. The elevator took him up to the seventh floor of the eleven-story structure, the tallest building in Wailuku. He found the D.A.'s office and walked in. There was a receptionist at a desk.

"I'm John Rossi. I'm supposed to meet someone from Zodiac International here. I don't know who we're meeting from this office."

"Yes, sir you're expected. They're in Ted Wong's office, down the corridor, second door on the left."

John thanked her and found the office. The door was open, and a thirtyish Asian man behind the desk was laughing and chatting with a *haole* guy, a slender man of about forty with dark, slicked-back hair. He was wearing a perfectly fitted Italian-style suit, and looked like he'd be more at home on Wall Street than in this little government office in Wailuku. He was taking pretend swings with a golf club. It was clear that the two men were pals. John stuck his head in the door. The Asian guy said, "Help you?" in a friendly voice.

"I'm John Rossi."

The Asian man got up quickly from his desk, and came around to offer his hand. "Oh, hey, sorry, I wasn't expecting—"

John helped him out. "A coconut?"

The man laughed and shook hands warmly with him. "Something like that. I'm Ted Wong, assistant D.A." He motioned toward the *haole* guy. "Do you know Dick?"

"No, I don't," John said, shaking hands with Dick Bennett.

Bennett shook hands with an iron grip, and in that moment John remembered his ill-fated interview with the man two years before. He thought there was a brief flash of recognition in Bennett's face, but he couldn't be sure. Maybe Bennett was not the type who could distinguish one brown-skinned guy from another. Bennett's tone was cordial, but still business-like. "I'm sorry we didn't connect yesterday. I understand your flight was delayed," he said.

"Yes. A snowstorm."

"Hotel okay?" Dick asked.

"It's a wonderful place, very nice. Thanks for putting me up."

"Least we can do under the circumstances. Jim was with us a long time, and we owe him a lot. Horrible thing that happened to him. Horrible."

They mulled this over for a moment, then Ted spoke to John. "Well, hey, have a seat." John took one of the two guest chairs on one side of the small office and Dick sat in the other one near the desk.

Ted said, "I know you're on a tight schedule, so just let me know how I can help you and I'll do my best."

"Well," John said, looking at Ted Wong. "I already know some of the facts of the case from talking to Sam Peters."

"You've already spoken with the police?" Bennett seemed a little surprised, but he recovered quickly. "Well, then you know it's a clear cut case of murder, clear as could be."

John continued to talk to Ted Wong, but Dick Bennett was the one responding. "Are there other possible suspects?"

Bennett sounded suddenly exasperated. "Other suspects? This man Sunny lures your friend to a *heiau*. You know what that is?" He didn't wait for a response. "An old Hawaiian stone temple. And not just any temple, this one was once used for ritual human sacrifice. He gets Jim up there, picks up a rock, and bashes the guy's head in. And he's caught in the act, practically."

"But no one actually saw him do it," John said.

"Saw him, shit!" Bennett said to Ted Wong, "Show him the pictures, for crissakes!"

When Ted didn't immediately respond, Bennett grabbed a folder off Ted's desk and thrust it at John.

Ted said, "Dick, I don't know that we should—"

"No, let him see what this so-called *kahuna* did to his friend."

John looked at the grisly pictures of the murder scene. They were having the intended effect. Sunny had been photographed from many angles by the tourists, blood all over him, murder weapon in hand. Fortunately, there were no clear views of the body in these photos, and John was glad not to have to look at them.

"Plus," Bennett added, "we've got the guy on videotape, clearly confessing, 'I did it. I murdered him.'"

Ted said, "Well, actually what he says is—"

"Or words to that effect," Bennett interrupted Ted with an angry wave of his hands, annoyance in his voice. Then he seemed to calm down a little. "Sorry if I seem upset. Jim Putnam was a friend of mine, a good friend. No, we've got our man, John, we've got him. And we're going to crucify him in court. Too bad there's no capital punishment in Hawai'i."

The phone rang, and John half expected Dick to answer it. But Ted picked it up. "Yes? Oh yes? . . . I see . . . Thanks for letting me know . . . Okay, bye now."

He hung up. Dick glanced at his watch and said to John, "Well, I understand you want to view the body. That's fine, we've set that up for you. And then I guess you've got a plane to catch."

"I'm going to stay over another day. Is that a problem?" John asked.

Dick seemed quite surprised. "Really? You know a lot of arrangements have already been made."

"Is there something else on your mind?" Ted asked him.

"I don't know. My real reason for coming here was to let Jim's mom know that justice was being done. I just want to be sure."

Dick Bennett, an astonished expression on his face, was getting ready to say something, but Ted silenced him with a wave of his hand. He smiled at John, and said, "I understand you had breakfast with my ex."

For a split second, John didn't know what he was talking about. Then it hit him. "Your ex? Lani is your wife?"

"Was."

"How did you know I was with her?"

Ted grinned at him. "It's a small island, John."

Bennett was getting riled up again. "Who the hell's side are you on, anyway? What are you doing talking to her?"

"I'm not on anyone's side," John said. "Wait, that's not true. I am on Jim's side. I want to do the right thing by him, for his family. If there's some doubt in my mind, I can't just go home."

"Why would there be any doubt in your mind?" Ted asked him calmly.

"Because no one who knows Uncle Sunny thinks he would be capable of doing such a thing. Including me."

Dick Bennett blustered, "*Uncle* Sunny? What the hell is this?"

"John," Ted said reasonably, "I understand completely. You want to be sure. You need to be sure. We can keep the body on ice for another day, not a problem."

John turned to Dick Bennett. "If you don't want to pay for my hotel room, I understand your position."

Dick seemed to have calmed himself. "No, that's okay. I agree with Ted, you need to feel right about this. If there's anything else we can do for you, you have my number. Let me know when you're ready, and we'll take care of the arrangements."

John stood and shook hands with both men. Ted said, "And if there's anything this office can do, don't hesitate to call on us." As

John started to leave the office, Ted said, "Oh, and my ex-wife? Bear in mind that she thinks all her clients are innocent."

John acknowledged with a nod, and walked down the hall. *Maybe you don't know her as well as you think*, he thought to himself.

Following Lani's directions, he drove through town to Wailuku police headquarters, a couple of miles away. It was in a building that appeared to be brand-new. He found a parking space in a visitors area in front of the building and walked into the lobby. It was relatively unadorned; in fact, it looked as if it had just been completed. There was no reception area, and all the doors leading off the lobby were closed. Then he noticed the phone on a wall, with a directory next to it. There was a number for "CELL BLOCK" and he punched in the digits. A man answered. "Benson."

"My name is John Rossi. I'm supposed to meet Lani Miller here."

"Hold on a sec." He heard a muffled conversation in the background, then the man came back on. "She'll be right up."

"Thanks." He hung up and waited for her. Out the glass lobby doors, he could see Haleakalā. It was clear on top now, and the slopes were a luminous green in the intensifying sun. He marveled that people could live and work here, shop for groceries, commute to an office, do ordinary things, in the face of these glorious surroundings. He thought it would be a terrible distraction. Maybe you got used to it after a while. He thought about Lani. Her last name was Miller now, maybe her maiden name. Then he had an awful thought: maybe she was married for a second time. And he stopped himself. He was going to be on an airplane out of there the next day. What the hell difference did it make? He heard a metal door open behind him, and she came out into the lobby, a smile on her face. *God, she was beautiful.* John walked over to her. "Aloha," he said.

"Aloha," she answered. "Or as we say around here, 'Howzit?'"

"Howzit," John said, trying out the new word.

She led him though the doorway, and they went down two flights of noisy steel stairs to a sub-basement. "How'd it go with the sharks?" she asked over her shoulder as they walked.

He knew who she meant. "It could have been my imagination, but they seemed anxious for me to take a long journey."

She laughed. It was the first time he had heard her laughter. He decided he wanted, needed, to hear a lot more of it. They walked along a corridor. Here there were unfinished concrete walls and rubber runners on the floor. She opened one of the blue-painted steel doors and showed him into a small, stark room with institutional green-painted cinderblock walls, a scuffed-up steel table bolted to the floor, and four flimsy plastic chairs. Her paperwork and briefcase were on the table in front of one of the chairs, and she sat there and motioned to John to take a seat opposite her.

"One of them claims to be your ex-husband," John said.

"True, unfortunately."

"So you changed your name back to your maiden name?"

"No, Miller is the name of my second husband."

His heart seemed to stop for a moment. Then it sprang to life again, when she said. "He's my second divorce, also."

He grinned at her. "Are you difficult to get along with?"

"I can be, at times," she said smiling back at him. "What about you? Married?"

He hoped she was asking for the right reason. What he thought of as the right reason. "No. Never have been."

As if things had gotten too personal for her, she changed the subject quickly. "The way this works is they're going to give us as much time as we need today to talk to uncle. We'll decide on a plea and the arraignment is scheduled for tomorrow. So far, Sunny hasn't said anything to me, so I haven't even heard this side of the story, if he has one."

"What about the video tape? The D.A. says he confesses on it," John said.

"I'd be willing to show it to you, but it's very graphic as regards your friend. I don't recommend that you see it. However, I do have a transcript." She pulled some typed papers out of her briefcase, and called his attention to a particular page. He read it, and then looked up at her.

"Not really a confession, is it?" John read it out loud, "'I'm so sorry. I didn't mean for him to get hurt. I warned him. It's all my fault. All my fault.'" John looked at her. "It could be construed as exactly the opposite of a confession."

She smiled at him. "You're very observant," she said.

John said in very serious tone, "I'm an electrician, ma'am. We're paid to be observant."

She laughed again, music, wonderful music. It made this depressing little room seem like heaven to him. He hoped they would have more time alone together, but at that moment the door opened, and a policeman led Uncle Sunny in. Sunny's face positively lit up when he saw John.

"Johnny Boy!"

"Howzit, Uncle?"

This brought a big smile from Lani, which Sunny noticed. "You have aloha for each other, dass nice," Sunny said.

They both must have been red in the face, because Sunny then said, "No shame, no shame. Dass a good ting." The deputy took off the handcuffs and left them alone in the room. Sunny sat in the seat next to John and turned to look at him.

"You get one question fo' ask me," Sunny said to him.

"Why did you say you know me?"

Sunny chuckled. "I know you, alright."

"I don't understand," John said.

"When you was a little boy, you almost drown. Your father brought you to me, all blue, pretty much like one dead little kid.

So we made a prayer circle. I blow da life into you, da *ha*, da breath of life. And so you wen live. And now you stay here, fo' save my life."

John stared at Sunny, his stomach tied in a knot. Could he be making all this up, or did this man really know who John's father was? Maybe he was just mistaken. With a lump in his throat, he asked. "Did you also know my mother?"

Sunny nodded Yes.

"But how do you know that the little boy you saved all those years ago is me?"

"As soon as I see you, as soon as I wen touch your hand, I knew."

"How?"

"I just know, dass how."

Lani could see that this line of questioning was going nowhere, and she had important business to take care of. But John had one more question to ask.

"Uncle Sunny, did you kill Jimmie Putnam?"

Sunny turned to Lani. "You know me. You know I heal people, give them back their health."

"So you didn't do it?" John persisted.

Sunny looked at him and said, "Of course not. I nevah do 'em."

9

They spent the next three hours with Sunny, going through the day of the murder. He told them that Jimmie had called him that afternoon, wanted to set up a meeting. Sunny had had the impression that someone else would be there too, he didn't know who. It was Sunny who had suggested the *heiau*, because it was about halfway between the Kalonahoa Valley, where he lived, and Kahana, where Jimmie had his condominium.

"And what did you find when you got there?" Lani asked him.

"Jimmie, dead," Sunny said disconsolately. "Head all buss up."

"Why did you say you killed him?"

"I nevah say dat. I said I'm responsible, it's my fault he's dead, but I nevah kill him. Dass what they call a misunderstanding."

"But they said you had the murder weapon in your hand."

"Well, I just pick 'em up is all. Of course I wen pick 'em up. It was lying on poor Jimmie's head. I nevah like leave 'em there like dat."

"They said you were covered in blood."

"I wen pick him up, turn him over. Fo' check if he still alive. Get da blood on top me."

"Why did you say you were responsible?"

Sunny sighed deeply and closed his eyes. From the pained expression on his face, John sensed that Sunny was reliving the murder scene in his mind. "Hard fo' explain. When I see Jimmie lying there dead, I know if not for me telling him to come to dat place, he'd still be alive. Stay my fault he was dead. Was because he knew me. I felt so bad. He was a good guy, and I liked him. Was like I wen kill him. Was guilt, you know? I felt like I wen kill him myself. And I did. I wen kill him, practically."

"I still don't understand why you feel that way. It was Jimmie who set up the meeting," Lani said.

"No, there was more than dat."

"What?"

Sunny sighed again, as if this would be a long story. And it was. Sunny had been farming taro and other staples in the Kalonahoa Valley for many years. His land had been in his family for generations. It was a remote area of Maui, accessible only via a poor and dangerous road. But there was an abundant water supply, and the upper parts of the valley were perfect for taro. With Sunny's encouragement, others began to move into the valley, many of them returning to ancient family lands. The broad mouth of the valley, the lower level land leading to the sea, was owned by a Hawai'i state senator. It had been used to grow sugar cane, and later pineapple. Then this had become unprofitable, and the agricultural use had been abandoned many years before.

Starting about two years ago, someone had been trying to get the taro farmers to sell their land. There had been all kinds of offers from a series of local real estate agents. As the amounts being offered increased, a few of the farmers gave in and sold. Most were holding fast. A few months later, there was the big public announcement that Zodiac International intended to build a huge resort complex in the valley. Sunny and the rest of the holdouts now knew who was behind the land purchases. A new kind of pressure began. Lawsuits were filed over water rights and the use of the road that passed through property Zodiac now owned. The sluice in a dam upstream from the valley would get mysteriously turned off, cutting off their water supply. Land titles that had been in families for generations were being challenged. Officials from both the state and the county threatened to acquire the property in an eminent domain proceeding. The farmers had been forced to hire attorneys, and what little cash they had was fast disappearing.

About a year ago Jimmie first showed up in the valley. He said he was an American Indian, a former employee of Zodiac, tired of seeing his people pushed around on the mainland. He had made some money, and now he wanted to return to the land. But not a desert reservation somewhere where the white people wanted you out of sight and out of mind, unable to earn a living. He wanted to learn to grow things and feed himself. He had heard that in Hawai‘i there was a chance to save something for the native people, and he wanted to help. So he hung out with Sunny and his followers, some of whom were city Hawaiians who wanted to return to old traditions of subsistence living. He learned the ways of Hawai‘i and the ways of taro, the essential, life-giving staple of the ancient Hawaiians. About fifty families lived there, most of them growing taro. As those people who sold their places moved out, their houses and their taro fields were abandoned. Soon the only families left were Sunny and a few other holdouts. Then, one of the largest property owners apart from Sunny got an offer that was just too much money to turn down. This man had accumulated gambling debts on cock fighting, and he needed the money badly. He had been offered enough to pay off his debts and make a tidy profit besides. But he hated to sell, and he told Sunny about it. Sunny mentioned it to Jimmie, and Jimmie offered to buy the property for the same amount of money and to keep the land in taro. This would ensure the use of the native water rights. Plus, the man would be allowed to stay on his land. For a few more key pieces of property, it was Jimmie who stepped in with a last-minute counter offer to save the day and keep the land. Jimmie became a hero to Sunny and his followers.

Yeah, some hero, thought John. They didn't know that Jimmie still worked for Zodiac, the true buyer of the land, and that Jimmie was purchasing the land with Zodiac's money. As soon as they had what they needed, Jimmie would deed it over to Brewster. This is why Zodiac had wanted John so badly. They had wanted a genuine Hawaiian to fill the role that Jimmie had been doing. John felt sick. Jimmie had died in his place, and he had done so in a scheme of fraud and deceit.

"Uncle," he asked gently, "Did you know that Jimmie worked for the casino?"

"Not at first. We thought he was one of us."

"But then later, you knew that he worked for Zodiac?" Lani asked.

"Yeah, I knew."

So, John thought, *Sunny did have a motive for murder after all. When he figured out that Zodiac was behind it all, he would know that Jimmie had betrayed them and they could lose everything they had worked for.*

"How did you know he was working for them?" she asked.

Sunny looked surprised at this question. "How I know? He wen tell me."

"Jimmie confessed to you?" John asked in astonishment.

"Yeah. Well, not in words maybe. But I knew he was struggling with someting in his mind, someting really boddah him. Sure, I knew who he work for, he couldn't hide it from me. I just waiting for him to do da right ting. I know he going come around, 'cause he was one good boy. He going tell those Zodiac guys go to hell and he give us our land back. I know Jimmie as sure as I know you, Johnny."

John and Lani looked at each other. Could this be true? If Sunny thought that Jimmie was going to turn on his employer and give the land back to the Hawaiians, then he had no reason to kill Jimmie. Quite the contrary.

With all his heart, John wanted to believe that his friend had in the end turned against Zodiac. *Jimmie, if this is true, maybe you weren't such a bad guy after all. There were limits to what you were willing to do for money.*

Lani continued the questioning, beginning to put a possible defense together. "And that day, at that meeting, he was killed. You were supposed to be there too."

Sunny hung his head down. "I was late. Supposed to be there at six o'clock, but I didn't get there until maybe six-thirty." Sunny looked up again, tears filling his eyes. "Jimmie one good boy, brave boy. I told him I would be there. He want to help me, and they kill him for it. Stay my fault he's dead." Sunny lowered his head despondently.

Lani gave Sunny a few moments to recover before beginning again. "Uncle, I want you to think carefully about what you saw and heard on that road. You were coming from Kalonahoa, right?" she asked.

Sunny sat in deep thought for a moment. John was afraid he might have clammed up again. But finally he spoke. "No. Dass why I was late. I had to go into Lahaina, pick up a few tings. I was coming from there."

"Okay. And what did you see."

"I stay thinking, but nothing special."

"Other traffic?"

"No other cars. Was getting dark, yeah? Most of da locals home by den, and da tourists, they no like drive dat road at night." He shook his head as he tried to place himself there.

"So it was quiet out there that evening?" she asked.

"Quiet, yeah. Oh, except fo' da hunters. I forgot about dat."

"What hunters? What did they look like? Did you know them?"

"I nevah see them. I hear them shooting."

"Where was this?"

"On da road. Maybe ten minutes before I get there. I stop fo' look at da sunset, and I hear dem shooting."

"A lot of shots?"

"Just one. Dass all I hear. They hunting wild pig, probably."

There was a knock on the door, and it was opened by two deputies.

"Got to get him back to his cell for the evening count," one of them said. They cuffed Sunny and took him out. He seemed wilted and glad to go with them.

When they were gone, John asked Lani, "Would shots mean anything? I mean, Jimmie wasn't shot."

"So far as we know. What if someone shot him and then bashed his head in to cover up the cause of death?"

John thought of Jimmie being shot and bludgeoned, and it showed on his face.

"John, I'm sorry to be putting you through this," she said.

"No, I'm okay, I'm okay." He tried to make it abstract in his mind, get back to thinking analytically. "But wouldn't the police have found a bullet wound?"

"Under the circumstances, I don't think they ever would have looked for one," she said.

"I suppose you're right. I'm just thinking that the idea is a little far-fetched."

"Of course it is. Far-fetched is what we have to go on. If nothing else, it can plant a seed of doubt in a juror's mind. We're grasping at straws here."

John said, "But if what Sunny said is true, and if Zodiac knew that Jimmie was going to turn against them, then they would be the ones with a motive for murder."

"The problem is to prove it," Lani said, gathering up her papers.

10

Late that afternoon, John and Lani sat in her office. It was in a small bungalow that had been converted to an office building. John was trying to make sense of it all. Sunny thought that Jimmie had turned against the casino, but there was no proof of that. John wanted to believe it, wanted to believe in his friend. Sunny said he had heard a shot, but even if he did, it probably had nothing to do with Jimmie's murder.

Lani, on the other hand, seemed to be full of hope and energy. She had taken no notes during the interview, and now she was writing page after page of them. John thought that her memory must be phenomenal. She was ignoring John while she did this, and he hated to break her concentration. Wanting to make himself useful, and looking for some excuse to stay with her longer, he idly picked up some papers that had spilled out of a folder when she had tossed her briefcase on her desk. He was hoping she wouldn't mind.

He found himself looking at an autopsy report on Jimmie. His first instinct was to not read this grim piece of paper, but he found he was unable to ignore it. There was a brief but gruesome description of the wounds and an estimated time of death. He kept staring at the form for lack of anything else to look at. Otherwise, he knew, he would have found himself staring at Lani. At the bottom of the form there was a date and time stamp from a clock stamping machine. It was the time the body had been received by the Medical Examiner. There was a second stamp on the other side of the page. This was the time the body left the M.E.'s office, presumably to be turned over to a funeral home. Something struck him as odd. He looked up at Lani, who was still writing away.

"Excuse me, but I just noticed something."

She looked up at him, and he slid the form across the desk to her. "See these time stamps at the bottom of the form?" he said.

"What about them?" she asked.

"Look at the times."

She looked at them uncomprehendingly at first, then a smile crossed her face. "That's good, John. Very good. In at nine-ten, out at nine-twenty. A thorough autopsy."

She grabbed the phone and dialed, and when someone answered she asked for Ted Wong. She switched on the speaker phone so John could listen in. It also left her hands free to continue her furious scribbling on legal pads. Ted Wong had to be paged and located, but eventually he picked up the phone.

"Hi, hon," he said cheerily, as if taking a call from his wife.

Lani ignored this. "I'm calling in regard to Sunny Waikoloa."

"What else? I heard you spent all day with him and your new boyfriend."

She glanced at John and reddened at this.

I don't mind being thought of as her boyfriend, John thought to himself.

She said to Ted, "I want to know if the body was examined for bullet wounds."

"Bullet wounds? You've got to be kidding."

"Was it examined?"

"A thorough autopsy was performed," he said. Lani smiled at John when he said this, a shared private joke. Ted continued wearily. "Cause of death was his skull being bashed in. Gimme a break."

"Nevertheless, I want the body examined for gunshot wounds."

"Based on what evidence?"

"Based on statements by the accused."

"That's just not going to happen."

"It better happen, or else I'm going to—"

Ted interrupted her, and spoke almost mockingly. "Your threats aren't going to work on me. I'm off the case."

"As of when?"

"As of tomorrow, at the arraignment. Now that my ex-wife is appointed his attorney, I have to recuse myself from the biggest case to hit Maui in years. Thanks a lot."

"You're welcome. But as of today, you're still the D.A. of record, correct?"

"And tomorrow, the body gets shipped back to the mainland. It's all been arranged."

And I'm getting shipped out of here with it, John thought.

She said to Ted, "That's tomorrow. As of today, you're the prosecutor and I'm requesting a re-examination of the victim."

"Forget about it."

"You know me," she said teasingly. "I never forget anything."

There was a pause on the other end of the line. Now Ted was sounding more conciliatory. "Lani, you know what kind of case this is. I can't make that decision. The D.A. has to sign off on it."

"Then talk to him about it. Tell him I know some things about you that could cause him to lose his best toady."

"Lani, please. You know there aren't going to be any damn gunshot wounds."

"Look, all I'm asking you to do is your job. If you don't, and the judge finds out you ignored my request, it's going to look as if you're covering something up."

There was a deeply frustrated sign of resignation. "Gene is in Honolulu, at a banquet. I won't be able to even talk to him until morning."

"Fine. As long as the examination takes place." She hung up on him.

"Do you think they'll do it?" John asked her.

"It's almost better if they don't. If they refuse, when it comes out at trial we can make it look like a cover-up."

"You don't expect to find gunshot wounds, I take it."

She shrugged noncommittally.

"We don't have much to go on, do we?" John said. He realized it was "we" now. At least to him.

"I've had tougher ones. We need to find out who actually owned that land, Jim Putnam or Zodiac," she said rapidly scribbling more notes to herself. Now *she* was using "we." He liked the sound of it.

"What can I do to help? Sounds like I may be going home tomorrow."

"Can you stick around for the arraignment? It's at ten tomorrow morning."

"Sure, I can do that. I'm trying to figure out what I'm going to tell Jimmie's mom. Last she heard, they had their murderer in custody."

"They still think so," she said.

"But I believe he's innocent."

"If we can prove that Jimmie turned against Zodiac, that would deprive Sunny of a motive."

"How do we do that?" he asked.

"Did Jimmie say anything to you about what he was doing here?"

"We hadn't spoken in a couple of years."

She looked up at him, surprised.

"He wanted me to take this job. We argued about it. We haven't spoken since."

"What was the argument about?"

John sighed deeply before speaking. "I thought he was just caving in, letting them take advantage of his ethnicity. I would never have let them do that to me."

She looked at him thoughtfully. "You remind me of Ted. I mean before he decided to become a stooge and do whatever the establishment wanted. He used to be a man of principle."

She stopped herself. Things were getting too personal, and she hurriedly resumed her scribbling. After a while John began to feel useless and ignored. He said, "Can I take you to dinner somewhere?"

She didn't look up, but kept on writing. "Thanks, but I'll grab something later. I've got a lot of work to do tonight. You should get going to your hotel. The road's pretty dark out there at night."

He stood up. "Okay, courthouse at ten a.m. tomorrow."

"See you there."

As he turned to leave, she looked up from her pad and said, "John, I want to thank you for everything you've done. You didn't have to help. You had good reasons not to help."

John shrugged. "Just trying to do the right thing."

"*Mahalo*," she said smiling at him warmly.

He smiled back at her. "You're welcome."

As John drove toward the hotel, car windows open in the warm evening, he was thinking that, although it was only his second day here, it felt like a lifetime. And as early as tomorrow, he could be headed home. But was New Jersey really home or was this his home? If home is where the heart is, he didn't need to get on a plane.

More familiar with the hotel now, he parked his car in the self-parking area and walked into the huge open-air lobby. There was wonderful music coming from the bar area, and he was drawn to it. The same guy from the night before was playing solo guitar and singing in Hawaiian. The music was beautiful, soft, and gentle like the tropical night. While he was sure he could never have heard the tune before, it sounded so familiar. He walked over and sat down in an easy chair near the musician. The man looked up at him and smiled in recognition. When the song was over, John realized that he was the only one there. The musician said, "The band will be taking a brief intermission now. We'll be back tomorrow," and he laughed at his own joke. John got up and walked over to him.

"What was that you were playing?"

"That was 'Manuela Boy.' You don't know that one?"

"I've been away a long time. It sounded so familiar to me."

"Sure, every Hawaiian know dat song. It's one lullaby. Your mother probably sang it to you when you were a little kid."

John felt a lump in his throat, and could not speak. His mother. His real Hawaiian mother, dead all these years. If only he could remember her. But try as he might, he couldn't conjure up any image of her in his mind. The musician was staring at John, curious about him.

"Haven't heard slack key for a while, yeah?"

"Slack key?"

"Dass what we call it. We say mainland guitars have tight strings, very tense. Here, we more relaxed, loosen our strings. Slack key." Chuckling, he put his guitar in his case and said to John, "Come back again, I play more for you. I'm here every night." He left then, carrying his guitar case.

John realized he hadn't eaten anything since breakfast. He walked down the steps past an indoor waterfall, to the hotel dining room. There he treated himself to a big steak and a baked potato. Afterwards he walked through the lobby and thought about calling New Jersey. He calculated how late it would be there, and decided he had an excuse to avoid calling. He was probably going to be on his way there tomorrow anyway. He stopped to browse the hotel gift shop. It was the usual tourist stuff, plus some clothing. In one corner there were a bunch of CDs on display. He was delighted to find one by the man he had heard playing in the lobby, George Kahumoku, Jr. He picked it up and headed to the counter. Then he noticed the rack of colorful Aloha shirts. He decided that it might be nice to blend in a little more here, try to look more Hawaiian. He picked out a couple of vividly colored shirts and a pair of white shorts. He paid for everything and headed up to his room.

When he entered he saw that the message light on his phone was flashing, as he had expected it to be. There was just one message, from Angela, returning his call. Her communication was terse. She expected him home tomorrow. Period. He thought of being back in New Jersey, and marrying Angela. Now he had to wonder if he could go through with it. He hadn't been unfaithful to her, but he felt a sense of guilt as if he had.

It would have soothed his mind to listen to his new recording, but there was no CD player in his room. Nevertheless, he drifted off to sleep that night to the sound of music, a gentle Hawaiian lullaby playing in his mind, his head on his mother's lap, while she stroked his hair and tenderly sang to him those sweet Hawaiian words.

11

The main office of Zodiac International was located in Las Vegas. The headquarters for the Hawaiian branch was nominally in Honolulu. There was also an office in Wailuku, the seat of Maui County government. But the real nerve center of the operation was in the Honolua Bay Hotel, Maui's newest and most exclusive resort location. Zodiac had taken over the entire west wing on the hotel's upper floor. Merely occupying space in the most expensive and prestigious hotel on Maui had not been enough for Charles N. Brewster. A team of decorators he hired came in and looked the place over, and made a few modest suggestions. The biggest problem, as they saw it, was that his artwork would not hang properly on the existing hotel walls. Some of the larger pieces, while they would fit on the wall, required proper floor-to-ceiling spacing to be correctly displayed. This necessitated raising the ceiling an additional and all-important four inches. While they were at it, they suggested using rare and expensive koa wood for wall paneling. This would provide a way to properly set off the extensive selection of Hawaiian artifacts that Brewster had acquired in his ongoing effort to seem as supportive of Hawaiian culture as possible. The Hawaiian operation was to be the prestigious centerpiece to the Brewster empire. Among his many acquisitions here was a suitable Hawaiian trophy wife, to complement the décor.

Dick Bennett was in early to deliver some bad news to his boss of the last twelve years. He walked into Charles Brewster's office, with its sweeping views of the ocean and Molokaʻi. Brewster was seated at his desk, talking on the phone. He smiled at Bennett and motioned to him to take a seat. Even seated behind a desk, Brewster's regal bearing and patrician demeanor were apparent. Both men were attired in business suits, ties securely fastened at the neck and suit jackets buttoned in front. They were probably the only men within a 100-mile radius of Honolua to be so dressed. Charles N. Brewster did not believe in business casual or in casual business.

Brewster finished his call and turned to Bennett.

"Yes, Dick?"

"More on the murder."

Brewster sighed wearily. "Let's have it."

"I got a message from the D.A.'s office. I guess it's not a big deal, but now they want to examine the body for bullet wounds."

Brewster turned white with anger. Those few who knew him well were painfully aware that his public image concealed a foul mouth and a mean temper. "What the fuck is that about? The fucker was clubbed to death!"

"Tell me about it."

"What the hell are they thinking down there? What the fuck are they smoking, is more like it."

"Anyway, we've got the body at the funeral home, and they're going to pick it up sometime this morning. They said it should only take a few hours for the autopsy."

Grabbing his phone, Brewster said, "Goddammit, this is not going to happen." He spoke into the phone, "Tricia, get me Gene McKay on the phone, right now. No, wait a minute. Forget about it, okay?" He hung up and turned to Bennett.

"You said we have the body, right?"

"Yeah. The cops released it to us. It's at the funeral home."

"Okay, here's what you're going to do. First of all, you never got the message from the D.A. Get someone over to the funeral home now, and I mean right now, to pick up the body. Put it in a truck or something. Have them take it to the airport. Then you're going to call the pilots and get the jet ready to fly."

"To where?"

"The East Coast, New Jersey, wherever the hell Putnam was from."

"What about the D.A.?"

Brewster aped a person who doesn't know what's going on, but is trying to be helpful. "What body? They did? I didn't know. I'll try to find out. Get right back to you on that."

Bennett smiled and nodded his head in understanding. "Nobody knows anything."

"Precisely."

"But why take a chance on pissing off McKay? He's always been on our side. He's going to prosecute the hell out of Sunny Waikoloa."

"Because that woman and Putnam's friend from Jersey are going to keep digging, raising idiotic issues, delaying. We can't afford that. This murder is the best thing that ever could have happened for us. We have to take full advantage of the situation. Now get moving." He returned to some paperwork at his desk.

Bennett stood up. "Okay, done. It's just that with McKay—"

Brewster looked up at him angrily. "Are you still here?"

Bennett quickly left the office. He would, of course, follow orders. But this move was making no sense to him, no sense at all. It was going to look like they were covering something up, when they had nothing to hide. But in all the years he had worked for Charles N. Brewster, he had never seen him quite so angry. Bennett would do as he was told.

John arrived early at the courthouse for the arraignment, but the courtroom was already packed with people. Murder cases were rare on Maui, and this one involved a major issue—casino gambling, a ritual killing on a sacred site, and an accused *kahuna*. There were reporters from the two Honolulu newspapers and a Honolulu TV station, in addition to the Maui media. John stood against the wall in the rear of the courtroom. The defendant and prosecutor benches were empty. The only person on the other side of the railing was a uniformed bailiff. A few minutes passed, then there was a stir as Lani entered the courtroom dressed in a dark-blue business suit and carrying two large briefcases. She walked down the center aisle and through the gate in the railing, and set her briefcases on the defendant's table. A moment later, Ted Wong and two other men entered from a side door, nodded curtly to Lani, and sat down at the prosecution table.

And now there was a hubbub in the room as Sunny was ushered in through another doorway by two deputies, his arms handcuffed in front of him. He looked anxiously about the room until his eyes found John, and then he seemed to calm down a little. He was shown to his seat next to Lani, and the handcuffs were removed. He talked to Lani but kept looking back fretfully over his shoulder at John. Finally, the bailiff intoned, "All rise." They all stood and the judge entered. The judge was a tall, white-haired haole man in his sixties. "Circuit court of the state of Hawai'i, Judge James Paterson presiding. Case Number 03 Dash 121, the people of the state of Hawai'i vs. Kahumakawiwo'ole Kupuhea Waikoloa. Please be seated."

The judge motioned to Ted Wong, who stood and presented his case. It didn't take long. It was a cold and analytical statement of the facts, and it was damning. Sunny had been found and photographed at the scene, the victim's blood on him, the murder weapon in his hand. He had indicated his guilt, caught on video tape. He had a clear motive for the murder, protecting his land. Hearing the case laid out this way, John didn't think that anyone in the courtroom would believe that Sunny wasn't guilty. He began to have some doubts himself. Was he unknowingly helping his best friend's murderer? Then it was Lani's turn. She made a motion for dismissal of all charges based on some legal mumbo jumbo John didn't understand. It was denied. She entered a plea of not guilty for Sunny. She cited his contributions to the community and limited possibility of flight risk and asked for bail. Also denied.

Within ten minutes it was all over, and Sunny was back in handcuffs and being removed from the courtroom. The judge exited through a doorway behind the bench. John wanted to talk to Lani. But at that moment, there was a stir at the back of the courtroom as Charles N. Brewster entered, Dick Bennett at his side. John had never met Brewster in person, but he recognized him right away, as did all of the reporters in the courtroom. The man had been on the cover of *Time* magazine, not to mention *Newsweek* and *Fortune*. His sailboats, with Brewster himself at the helm, had won the last two Transpac races, and John had seen his face on TV often. Brewster smiled and shook hands with a number of people, and then Bennett announced that Mr. Brewster would like them to please step out in the hall, as he wished to make a statement. The courtroom emptied quickly, and when it did, John saw that Lani was gone, apparently having left through one of the side doors on the other side of the rail. He was disappointed, and more than that, he felt at loose ends. What was he supposed to do now? In other words, what was his excuse for staying in Hawai'i?

He exited the courtroom into the polished marble lobby. Brewster and Bennett were standing in an alcove surrounded by a milling mass of media people, the two men's faces harshly illuminated by the blazing lights of the TV crews. A cacophony of questions was directed at them by reporters trying to out-shout each other. But Brewster just stood impassively, a tolerant semi-smile on his face, waiting for complete silence. Finally the reporters seemed to get the idea that he wasn't going to say anything until they quieted down, and there was a round of shushing from their ranks. Bennett waited until you could hear a pin drop before speaking. "Mr. Brewster would now like to make a statement."

Charles N. Brewster took a step toward the proffered microphones and paused dramatically before speaking. He was dressed in a tailor-made dark-blue business suit, a crisp white cotton shirt, and a powder-blue tie that complemented his blue eyes. He stood in elegant contrast to the reporters, in their denims and sneakers and ready-to-wear garb. When he finally spoke, it was quietly, sincerely, and without notes.

"I have come here today to see for myself, personally, that justice is being done. As you know, Jim Putnam was a valued employee of Zodiac International. Much more than that . . ." Brewster paused for a moment, and when he continued, his voice was husky with emotion. "He was my friend." There was another pause as Brewster seemed to be trying to regain his composure. "Jim and I worked together for many years and on many different projects. He was a diligent, honest, and hardworking young man, and his contributions to the company will be sorely missed. I shall miss him personally. I am grateful to the Maui Police Department and the district attorney's office for their prompt and professional work in finding Jim's killer and bringing him to face the bar of justice. Thank you."

The very instant he stopped talking, there was a hair-trigger barrage of shouted questions. Bennett recognized a woman reporter with a hand gesture and the rest of them quieted down somewhat while she spoke.

"Mr. Brewster, how does this affect your plans for building a casino on Maui?"

Brewster waited for absolute silence before speaking again.

"As you know, it is up to the citizens of Hawai'i to decide whether or not they want to allow gaming in these islands. As I have often said, I see nothing but benefits for the people of this state. Should gaming be allowed at some future time, I am ready to step forward to do my part to support this form of positive economic development. Jim Putnam's death only strengthens my resolve to meet my civic responsibilities, just as he would have wanted me to do."

Instead of a shouted clamor for the next question, hands went quietly up, like obedient school children. John was impressed that in a matter of a few minutes, Brewster had managed to tame a bunch of unruly reporters. Bennett chose a reporter, who asked his question with a big smile on his face.

"How do you feel about your chances in the Transpac this year?"

Bennett started to answer for Brewster, "I hardly feel that this solemn occasion is a time to talk about . . ."

Brewster silenced him with a wave of his hand, and spoke directly to the reporter, making sure the man understood how inappropriate his question had been. "I plan on winning, and I'm going to dedicate my win to Jim Putnam's memory." He and Bennett then strode away from the microphones.

More questions were shouted out, but Brewster refused to take any more. The reporters parted for him like the Red Sea did for Moses, and he and Bennett quickly got into an elevator. The crowd let them have the elevator to themselves. John decided to take the stairway. He went down the five flights to the basement, where he had parked his car. A stretch limo, its engine running, was parked next to John's car. He was walking past the limo when a rear door opened and Dick Bennett stepped out.

"John, hi, nice to see you again. Do you have a moment to talk to Charles? He has been looking forward to meeting you."

John just stood there looking at Bennett for a long moment. *"Charles" wants to meet me? Why in hell would Charles N. Brewster want to meet me?* Bennett was holding the car door open. Reluctantly, John walked over to the limo and peered inside. Brewster, sitting in the back seat, extended a hand to him.

"John, let me say how sorry I am about the loss of your friend."

The man sounded sincere. John had to climb into the car to return the handshake. Brewster clasped his with both hands once John was seated across from him.

"Please express my heartfelt condolences to his family when you get back to New Jersey."

"Thank you, Mr. Brewster. I'll tell them."

Bennett got into the car and pulled the door closed behind him. He made a motion to the driver, and the car lurched away.

John grabbed at the door handle. "Where are you going? I've got a car parked here."

Brewster said, "John, there's something important I want to show you. It's only a few minutes from here, if you can spare the time."

John looked at him. Obviously a man like Brewster wasn't going to kidnap him. *I probably should be asking for his autograph.* He settled back into his seat, but a sense of unease was building as he watched his Malibu growing smaller in the back window of the limo.

"I guess I can spare a few minutes."

"Good! While we drive, maybe you can tell me something about Jim's family."

"Just his mother and father. If there was anyone else, he never spoke of them."

"And you knew him for how long?"

"Over twenty-five years."

"So if there had been any other family members, you would have known about it."

"I imagine so." He wondered what Brewster was getting at.

"And when was the last time you talked to Jim?"

"It's been a couple of years."

This was getting too personal, John thought.

"Oh?"

John didn't feel like telling this man anything about the fight he and Jimmie had had. It was none of his business. The phone in the car rang then, and Brewster busied himself in a conversation that lasted for the rest of their ten-minute ride. Before long they were on the airport approach road, but the driver turned off just before the terminal and went down a street that skirted the north end of the runway and curved around to the private aircraft area on the opposite side of the field. The car paused a moment for an electronic gate to open, and then they drove right onto the tarmac, passing a line of private jets. John had always had an interest in aviation, and recognized the planes as either Canadair Challengers or Gulfstream G-IVs or G-Vs. These were some of the few private jets that had the range to reach Hawai'i from the US mainland or from Asia.

At the end of the line of planes was a Boeing 737, with a portable stair mounted over a truck leading up to the front cabin door. There was a lot of activity going on around the plane, with a fuel truck and a catering truck parked next to it. John wondered what a commercial airliner was doing on this side of the field. Then he noticed that the plane had no markings, except for a small registration number on the tail. This was somebody's private jetliner. They drove up to the stairway and stopped. Brewster was off the phone now.

"This is what I wanted to show you," he said, satisfaction in his voice. "This is mine."

The chauffeur came around and opened the door and they all got out. Brewster looked up proudly at the plane. "This is the Boeing Business Jet, the 'BBJ' as we call it." He motioned toward the stairway with a genial wave. "Be my guest, John." John couldn't imagine why Brewster would want to impress *him* with his plane, but he had to admit he was interested in seeing it. They were greeted at the top of the step by a blond-haired man of about John's age dressed in a white short-sleeved shirt and an epaulette with the three bars of a first officer.

"Welcome aboard, sir," he said to John.

John stepped inside. He had not realized how big the interior of a 737 would be with just a few seats in it and with the overhead luggage compartments removed. The plane was cavernous, and he realized he was looking at just one compartment. The lower walls of the interior and the bulkheads were made of a lustrous wood, the ceiling covered with a suede-like cloth. There was sisal carpeting and the seats and sofa scattered about the interior were finished in a subtle Hawaiian print and trimmed with what looked like bamboo. The seatbelt buckles were plated with gold. It was an airborne luxury Hawaiian hotel suite.

Brewster gestured grandly about him. "All the interior wood you are looking at is koa. This aircraft has a range of 6,200 nautical miles with eight passengers, has a maximum takeoff weight of 171,000 pounds and can reach speeds of up to .82 mach." He motioned toward the front of the plane. "Latest technology glass cockpit. I have my type rating, and I pilot it myself most of the time. Let me show you the rest of the plane." He walked toward the rear, and John followed him, trailed by Bennett. John was shown the bathroom, several times the size of a commercial jet's. It had a leather-upholstered commode, a mirrored vanity, a marble sink with gold-plated fixtures, and koa wood cabinets. "The one in the rear of the plane has a shower," Brewster told him. They passed through a galley and through a wood-paneled office.

Then Brewster opened a door in the rear of the office and motioned John into what normally would have been the bedroom.

Instead of a bed though, there was a casket on a metal stand, draped with the flag of the Zodiac International Corporation. Bennett spoke to him calmly, putting a hand on John's shoulder. "Sorry to spring this on you, John. Some plans changed at the last minute, and the plane became available. We thought it might be easier for you this way. You can travel home with Jim and you won't have any hassles with security or anything. I know it's tough enough on you as it is." John felt as if the air had suddenly been sucked out of the cabin and he had to struggle to breathe. The reality of his situation, the reality of his life was now before him. Hawai'i was a dream, Lani would turn out to be a passing fancy, and soon a distant memory. Sunny was probably lying about knowing who John was, it was just too crazy to be true. He had come here to bring Jimmie home, and now he must do his duty. And he also knew that he had to do one more thing he had come to do. "Can you leave me alone with him for a few moments?" he said to Bennett.

"Sure. You're all checked out of your hotel, and your luggage is aboard. And if you'll give me your key, we'll get your rental car and return it for you." In a daze, John reached into his pocket and handed the key to Bennett. It felt as if he was surrendering his final connection to Hawai'i. Bennett patted his shoulder and walked out the door they had come through, closing the door behind him. Brewster was nowhere to be seen.

John walked slowly up to the coffin and stopped. This was going to be hard. A full minute passed before he folded the flag back where it was covering the head of the casket. The lid did not appear to be secured in any way. In all his thirty-two years, he had never seen a dead person before. What if Jimmie's head was so bashed in that he couldn't recognize him? He was filled with dread, but there was no choice now. He opened the door slowly and gasped. It was Jimmie, clearly, and he appeared to be asleep. John had the crazy idea of shaking him to wake him up.

If only he would open his eyes, everything would be okay, and they would be friends again. He realized that, without Jimmie, his life was going to be a lot bleaker from now on. He lowered the lid and began rearranging the flag on top. Then he thought about this flag and what it symbolized to him and he angrily yanked the thing off Jimmie's casket. He crunched the flag up and stuffed it under a dresser fixed to one wall.

He turned and trudged slowly back through the office and into the empty main passenger compartment where he collapsed into one of the richly upholstered chairs. Outside, the fuel truck was leaving, and the catering truck was already gone, as was the limo. His time here was growing short. He pulled out his cell phone. He needed to talk to Lani. He dialed her office and got no answer. Her voicemail picked it up and he found he didn't know what to say to her. Finally he spoke, "Lani, this is John Rossi. Charles Brewster has offered his plane to fly Jimmie home. I'm going with him. I hope you and Sunny will be okay." It was starting to sound pretty lame, so he concluded with, "I'll call you." It was around 11:00 a.m. Reluctantly, he decided to try Angela at her office. She picked up on the first ring.

"Angela, this is John."

"Tell me you're on your way home," she said, her tone suggesting that she wasn't going to like the answer.

He was starting to get a headache. "I'm on my way home," he said wearily.

This seemed to take the wind out of her sails. "Really?"

"We take off in just a few minutes. Jimmie is on board the plane with me."

"Oh Johnny, I was really worried about you. About us."

"I know. Well, I'll be there soon."

"I'll meet you at the airport."

His stomach was starting to roil. "We're not going to arrive until," he made a hasty mental calculation. Around ten hours flying time, six-hour time difference, "around three a.m., I think."

"I'll come anyway."

"But I have my car there. Also, I'm flying on Charles N. Brewster's private jet, so I don't even know where exactly the plane is going to arrive."

Finally, she reluctantly said, "Okay. But call me when you land, even if it's some crazy hour."

"I will, sweetheart. Bye for now."

He rang off and tried Lani's number again. No answer. He didn't see any point in leaving a second message. He looked outside and realized he needed to breathe some more of the heady Hawaiian air before he left these islands, probably forever. He walked to the front of the plane. He glanced into the cockpit, where the co-pilot was sitting in his seat working some switches on an overhead panel. He looked up at John.

"Everything okay, sir? Can I get you something to drink? It's a last minute flight, so we probably won't have a cabin crew."

"No thanks. I just thought I'd get some air."

"Take your time. Our clearance is delayed for a bit. Icy runways at Newark have things backed up there. Just waiting for the captain to bring us the okay."

Ice, thought John. He went through the fuselage door and stepped out on the roll-up stairway and into the bright sunlight and the warm morning. He had a clear view of Haleakalā, glistening green in the morning sun. Looking toward the end of the runway, he could see the ocean, an inviting blue-green color. Two days here and he'd never made it into the water. There was so much he hadn't seen and done. He had the urge to race down the steps and run away from this plane, which was going to be bringing him back to ice. He wanted to see the crater at the top of the volcano. He wanted to drive out to Hana. He wanted to eat more *poi*. He wanted to sit in the hotel lobby and listen to slack key guitar music. He wanted to find out if Sunny really knew his family. He wanted to be with Lani. That above all. But it was not to be. He had a duty to perform. An older man in a captain's uniform came out of the small hangar building and walked toward the plane carrying a flight bag. *I guess this is it*, he thought.

As the captain approached the bottom of the stairs, a car drove up to the plane honking its horn. The captain stopped and walked over to the car. A couple of men in shirtsleeves and ties got out and started talking to him. John couldn't hear the conversation, but it was something very earnest, and one of the men kept pointing toward the plane. The captain shrugged his shoulders, and then looked toward the hangar. He gestured to someone there to come over to the plane, and John was surprised to see Bennett come walking across the tarmac. The co-pilot appeared on the stairs behind John.

"What's going on?" John asked him.

"No idea."

Bennett started talking to the two men, and the pilot came up the steps.

"What was that about?" the co-pilot asked.

"I don't know," the pilot said. "Something about an autopsy. They want to take the body off the plane and back into town. I think Bennett has them pretty well convinced that we don't have a body on board." He winked at John, and said, "Mr. Brewster was very insistent that we get going right away."

So they hadn't done the autopsy after all, John thought. Bennett had lied to him about that. And they had sure been in a hurry to get John off the island. It all seemed so clear now. Seeing Jimmie dead, having to leave suddenly, John had been so clouded by emotion that he wasn't thinking clearly. What the hell was Brewster up to? The co-pilot went back into the cockpit, and John knew if he was going to do something, it had to be now. If Bennett could successfully con his way out of this situation, John would be on his way to Newark without knowing what he had come to Hawai'i to learn. He made his decision then. He walked quickly to the back of the plane and into the compartment containing the casket. There was a fuselage door in the compartment and John read the instructions for operating it. He hesitated a moment. Opening an airplane's cabin door seemed almost an unnatural act, something a passenger should never do except in the direst emergency. But it was now or never. He yanked up on the door handle, and a red warning light started blinking. He figured there was going to be a light showing up somewhere in the cockpit as well, and he knew he had to move quickly. He turned the handle all the way and the door popped open. He shoved it open the rest of the way and it swung out over the tarmac. He looked down to see the startled faces of Bennett and the two other men standing right beneath, looking up at him. John yelled down to them, "The casket is in here. I think you're going to need a forklift or something."

The men gave Bennett a nasty look. The co-pilot came running into the cabin. "What the hell are you doing?"

"Seeing that justice is done," John said.

John expected a bawling-out from the man. Instead, the co-pilot smiled and shrugged. "Okay, whatever. You might as well be on Brewster's shit list too."

The man started to walk back toward the cockpit.

"What happens now?" John asked him.

"I guess we're not flying today." Then the man reversed direction and walked toward the rear of the plane. "Almost forgot. Your luggage is back here. I'll go get it for you."

He disappeared though the rear door of the cabin, returned a few moments later with John's carry-on bag, and handed it to him. John thanked him, but he did not leave the plane until he had seen the casket unloaded and delivered to the safe hands of the officials. Bennett had slipped away. When the casket was finally on the ground he walked through the cabin and went down the stairs carrying his bag. When he reached the bottom and stepped onto the tarmac, he felt a wave of elation. He was staying. At least for now.

12

John walked over to the hangar. There was a small waiting area inside and a reception desk. A young woman looked up at him and smiled. "Aloha. Can I help you?"

"Looks like my flight's been delayed. Do you know what happened to my car keys?"

"Oh, was that your car? I'm sorry, they've already gone over to get it. It's probably been returned by now."

"Can you get me a taxi over to the terminal?" John asked her.

"We can do better than that. Kalani!" she called out.

Kalani appeared, a slender dark young man.

"Please take this gentleman over to the terminal."

John thanked her, and Kalani took his bag and led him outside to a white Lincoln Town Car. When you arrived on Maui in a private jet, everything was first class, John thought. Kalani opened the door for him and put John's bag in the trunk. He drove John directly to the Dollar Rent-a-Car office and dropped him there. John went inside and found that his Malibu had already been checked in. Brewster and crew had been very efficient in trying to get him out of here. The rental clerk asked him if he would like to rent the same type of car. John started to say yes, then asked if they had any convertibles available. They did, and ten minutes later he was loading his luggage into the trunk of a yellow Chrysler Sebring convertible. That's when he realized that, when they had gotten his bag from the hotel, they had forgotten to take his winter coat. He smiled at the thought. He didn't care.

Driving down the airport road with the top down, he felt as if he were in a dream. Just two days ago he had arrived here for the first time and driven down this same road. This time he knew his way around. He drove into Wailuku to Lani's office. He didn't know if he needed an excuse or not, but it seemed they would have a lot to discuss now. He didn't see her little silver Honda CRV in front, and she was not in her office. She carried a cell phone, but John didn't have that number, only her office number. He drove over to the courthouse and checked the parking area for her car. Then he went to the police station and used the lobby phone to ask for her. Not there either. He realized that she must have other clients, and she could be anywhere on the island. He had no idea where she lived or how to get in touch with her. He thought of leaving another message on her office voicemail telling her he was still here, but he really wanted an excuse to go and see her.

He drove idly around Wailuku, looking at the harbor area, spending a while watching the waves break on the rock jetties. A cruise ship came in and docked and he watched that for some time before driving back to her office. Still not there. It was getting late and he decided to make the familiar drive across the island and back to his hotel. This time as he approached Lahaina, he made the first left turn into town and drove down Front Street, through a shady residential section and then into the downtown area. It was really quite picturesque, despite the crowded sidewalks shoulder to shoulder with tourists. Many of the buildings were from the 1800s, and facing them was the Lahaina Roads anchorage, once filled with whaling vessels and now plied by fishing boats, speedboats pulling parasailing tourists, glass-bottomed boats, and pleasure craft. A few miles out to sea was the island of Lāna'i. He drove through town and out the other side into another residential area and then over a humpbacked bridge just before a shopping mall on the right-hand side.

Suddenly he smelled something delicious and realized that once again he had forgotten to eat. He pulled into a parking lot on the left side of the street and parked in front of a place called Aloha Mixed Plate. Smoke from a grill was visible, and this is what he had smelled. He went in and found that all the seating was outdoors. He took a seat at a plastic table in a patio area surrounded by hibiscus plants, blooming yellow with white centers. He had a clear view of Mala wharf and its small boat harbor just a few yards away, and of Lāna'i to the left and Moloka'i on the right. He could see boatloads of tourists out on the water, headed out for sightseeing, snorkeling, and fishing. A couple of speedboats were pulling dangling parasailers high above the water. He felt envious. He was here on business, and probably wouldn't make it into the ocean at all. When a waitress appeared, he ordered the mixed plate and a lemonade. The food was delicious: teriyaki beef and shoyu chicken, grilled mahi mahi, white rice, and macaroni salad, and he ate with gusto. Afterwards he tried Lani's number again with no luck. Dreading Angela's reaction to the news that he was not on his way, he was putting off a call to her. Back in his car, he drove north to where Front Street ended and joined Honoapi'ilani Highway, Route Thirty. Driving north on the highway he passed the police station and the turnoff for the big Kā'anapali Hotels and continued another ten miles to his hotel in Kapalua. He parked in the hotel lot and went into the lobby, disappointed that there was no music tonight. At the front desk he gave them his name.

"Yes, sir, your bill is all taken care of by Zodiac International."

"Did they make another reservation for me?"

"No sir, but we have rooms available."

"What do they cost?"

"They range from an ocean view suite at $1,700 to a garden view room at $365."

"Okay, I'll let you know."

John walked into the lobby. He could not afford to pay those rates, not for very long. Then it hit him that he didn't know how long he'd be staying. And he found that he liked the idea. He became aware that music was playing now, and he went over to the cocktail lounge area. The musician was there, and once again the lounge was nearly empty. It was like having a private concert. He ordered a Coke from the bartender and listened to the wonderful sounds. It was hard to put into words the feelings he had when he heard this music. It seemed to speak to his very soul. He listened to the whole set, and when the musician took a break, John walked over to him.

"That was beautiful."

"Tanks, bruddah. It's the music of aloha."

"That's the way it feels to me."

"You been here before, yeah?"

"I have', yes," John said.

"Nice hotel."

"Yeah. I wish I could afford it."

"Expensive, yeah? So where you staying now?"

"I'm currently homeless," John joked. "I'll probably drive down to Kā'anapali and look for a room."

"If you need one place not too expensive, you can try da Mauian. No mo' TV, no mo' phone. But right on da beach, real nice place ovah there. Hawaiian family own 'em."

"How far away is it?"

"Stay right down da road, half mile or so. Just drive out da parking lot, like two hotels down, on da right. Tell 'em George Kahumoku sent you."

John stuck out his hand and they shook.

"Thank you, George. Oh, I bought your CD. Haven't had a chance to listen to it yet."

"Bring it by one evening. I'll autograph it for you."

"Thank you, I'll do that."

Leaving the hotel, John retrieved his car from the parking area and drove to the Mauian. He found it easily, nestled in a grove of mango and palm trees. There was a small office with a sliding glass window. A pretty, smiling woman wearing a muumuu slid the glass open when she saw him walk up.

"Aloha," she said cheerfully.

"Aloha. George Kahumoku, from the Kapalua Bay Hotel, suggested your hotel to me. Do you have any rooms available?"

"Yes, we do."

It was a two-story hotel with only around forty rooms. John took the least expensive accommodation, a "garden room," very reasonably priced. There was a small pool and extensive and beautiful landscaping. But the real attraction was the beach right in front of the hotel. Napili Bay formed a beautiful, quiet little cove. Hotels ringed the bay, but unlike Kāʻanapali , they were all low-rise, beneath the level of the palm trees.

His room was very Hawaiian in decor. There was no air-conditioning, but between the sea breeze coming in off the bay and a ceiling fan, John found that he was quite comfortable. There was even a small kitchen area. Homeless no more, John silently thanked George Kahumoku for the recommendation.

13

The next morning John woke up early. He had phone calls to make. He was supposed to have been in New Jersey by now, and he knew that Angela would be frantic. There was a good excuse for not being there, but no excuse for not calling. He picked up his cell phone, but the signal was intermittent. He had noticed a phone booth near the pool area. Pulling on shorts and a T-shirt, he grabbed his wallet and room key and stepped outside. It was another glorious morning, and he decided to have a look at the bay before making the call. The water looked so inviting, and he had not had a chance to go in since he arrived. He couldn't resist and went right back to his room, where he changed into a swimsuit. He found a beach towel in the closet, grabbed it, and walked down the sidewalk and onto the sand. Almost no one was in the water at this hour, and he had the whole bay practically to himself. He dropped his towel and walked in. It was a little cool, but a perfect temperature for swimming. He paddled out slowly to get a feel for things, then let loose with powerful strokes, swimming the bay from one side to the other. It felt wonderful. Swimming had always come naturally to him. The last time he had gone swimming alone had been one evening in his high school's pool when he had had the place all to himself. The high school free-style champion had shown up and seen that John was pretty fast, and had challenged him to a race. John had won. Maybe there was something in his genes about swimming, something having to do with being born on an island.

Another lap of the bay would have felt great, but he had to make his phone call. He went back to his room, showered and dressed quickly in his new Hawaiian clothes, then walked over to the phone booth. It was around noon on the east coast, and Angela would be at work. She answered the phone breathlessly.

"Hi sweetheart, it's me."

"John, where are you?" she demanded

"I'm still in Hawai'i."

"What?" she said, her voice full of angry disbelief.

"They wouldn't release Jimmie's body, and the plane never took off."

"Why didn't you call me?"

John struggled to answer this one. "There were a lot of delays, and my cell phone doesn't always work here."

She wasn't going for it. "You could have found some way to call me."

"Honestly, I hated to call with the bad news. And I hoped to find out when they would release him, so I would be able to tell you when I'd be on my way."

"And when *will* you be coming home?"

"I don't know. I've been calling the lawyer, but she hasn't been around."

"What lawyer?"

Now John was feeling guilty. *And you should feel guilty*, he told himself. Had Angela heard him say "she?"

"There's a lawyer handling things at this end."

"A woman lawyer. Is she young and pretty?"

Women are incredible, John thought. *You can't hide a damn thing from them.*

"Angela . . ."

"Yes, I'm being silly," she sighed. "Are you coming home today?"

"They were going to do an autopsy yesterday. Supposedly, it takes just a few hours. So I should be able to leave today. It's still early here, so I don't have any information yet. How's everything back there?"

"Oh, the usual. It's been cold." John was about to tell her about Maui, but she said, "No, don't bother to tell me how wonderful the weather is over there."

"Okay, I won't."

"I went by your apartment this morning. I thought you would be there."

"Yeah," he said flatly.

"Your mail was piling up in the box, so I put it inside. You had a letter from a James Putnam: Isn't that your friend Jimmie?"

John was stunned. He hadn't had a word from Jimmie in two years. And now there was a letter from him?

"Can you go and get it and read it to me?"

"I have it right here. I thought it might be important."

"Please, Angela. Open it and read it to me."

"Okay, hold on."

He could hear fumbling and rattling of paper. He realized he had been holding his breath in anticipation. He waited for her to read it to him.

"Well, it doesn't say much."

She was obviously reading it to herself. After a moment she read it out loud to him. "'John. If you ever make it to Hawai'i some day, be sure and look up my friend Joe in the . . .'" She stumbled as she read the next word. "'Kalonahoa Valley. Ask him to show you where we used to go for a quick belt.' And it's signed, 'Jimmie.' "

John had her read it to him again, and it still meant nothing to him. *Of all the times to write, and all the things to write about, why this?*

"Weird, huh?"

"Yes, it is."

"Maybe it's some kind of joke."

"What is the postmark on the envelope?"

"Hold on . . . It's January 11."

John felt his stomach tighten. By the end of that day, Jimmie was dead. This letter sounded casual, but it had to mean something. And John knew that he would be heading for the Kalonahoa Valley today to look for someone named Joe.

"Angela, I'm going to look into this. I promise to call you back later today."

"This is what I was afraid was going to happen."

"You know I'm coming back. I will be bringing Jimmie home."

She seemed a little reassured by this, and they rang off. He was about to call Jimmie's mom, but he thought he should get more information first. The government offices wouldn't open for a while. In the meantime he would go out to the Kalonahoa Valley, wherever that was. He walked toward the hotel lobby. The woman who had checked him in was working in the hotel reception area, and he decided to ask her for directions. She smiled brightly at him when he walked up and slid back the glass window.

"Good morning. How can I help you?"

"Can you tell me how to get to the Kalonahoa Valley?"

The hotel manager had walked into the office at that moment and overheard the conversation.

"Kalonahoa? Why do you want to go there?"

"I need to talk to somebody there. Why? Is there a problem?"

"The road is very bad, very dangerous. Your rental car contract probably won't allow you to go out there anyway."

"I really have to go, though."

"Also, there's been some trouble out there lately. Not a good time to make the trip."

"What kind of trouble?"

The manager seemed reluctant to talk about it, but John waited until he spoke.

"A man was killed a few days ago. They're kind of on the warpath, those guys."

"I know about that. It was my friend who was killed."

There were immediate and sincere groans of sympathy from the manager and the woman then, and they expressed their condolences. John said he had to go there, and they reluctantly gave him directions. It was pretty simple. Drive out to the Honoapi'ilani Highway, hang a left toward Kapalua and drive until the pavement gave out. Keep on going until he reached the pink fruit stand, and then ask for directions.

John went out to his car. He had been parked under plumeria trees, and the car was festooned with white-and-pink blossoms. He raised the wiper blades and brushed the flowers off the windshield. It occurred to him that had he been in New Jersey this morning, he'd be scraping ice off the windows instead. Driving south on Lower Honoapi'ilani Road, he made the left turn toward the mountains on a street that took him past the Napili shopping center and then turned north on the highway at the traffic light. In front of him was the island of Moloka'i. It suddenly hit him that he was driving a convertible. He pulled over and pressed the button to lower the top, then got back on the road. The highway made a sweeping right turn as it followed the contours of the island and passed a golf course. The road then narrowed and began to wind along a cliff. There was only an occasional house now, and there were pineapple fields stretching up the slope to his right, a steep rocky shoreline off to the left. He glanced across the channel at Moloka'i. The clouds he had seen earlier were gone, and the full mountain skyline was visible, green in the bright morning light. The curves on the road became tighter, with yellow signs marking them for ten miles per hour.

Then there were additional signs saying Honk Horn, and John realized that it had been some time since he had seen another car.

He rounded a curve and suddenly there was a spectacular view in front of him, jagged rock formations and huge brown cliffs reaching down to the sea, where rollers were hitting the rocks raising enormous plumes of sea spray. At that moment the pavement ended, and the road turned to gravel. He drove around the edge of the cliff and started down the road into a valley. There was room for just one car here, and he hoped he wouldn't meet someone coming up. He got to the base of the valley and went over a tiny one-lane concrete bridge. The road made a sharp left turn and started climbing again. Two feet to his left was a sheer cliff down to the water, a 200-foot drop. And seemingly at his right elbow, the cliff wall rose almost straight up. He drove up the steep road, rounded a bend to the right, and here was another valley, similar to the last. There were no farms here, no houses, just cliffs. He marveled that a road had been built at all.

When he reached the top of the next cliff, he noticed that there was a field to his right, strewn with rock rubble. In some places, the rocks were piled up, forming a kind of platform. It was a *heiau*, John knew, a rock temple. He thought with a shudder that Jimmie had been murdered at such a place. The field dropped away, and again there was the road going down along a cliff and back up on the other side of the valley. As he went over yet another narrow bridge, he could see that there was a metal gate and a rough dirt path leading up from the road. Apparently people were living out here.

Two valleys later, he emerged to an even more impressive sight, another valley, much wider than the ones he had seen before. This one had a beautiful white sand beach lined with palm trees. There were large open fields, and as he descended down the side of the cliff he saw a small pink structure along the road. As he approached it, he could see that it was a fruit stand.

He slowed, but there was no one there. Just past the stand John stopped at a road leading up into the valley. There was a swinging metal gate there, with a sign reading PRIVATE PROPERTY. Two men in police uniforms were sitting in a Jeep parked next to the gate. John stopped his car next to the Jeep.

"Good morning," he said to them.

"Morning," they both replied politely.

"Is this the Kalonahoa Valley?"

"You're looking at it, brah."

"I'm looking for a guy named Joe."

"Joe? You mean Joe Kalia?"

"I don't know his last name."

The men looked at each other and shrugged.

John said, "Okay, let's say it's Joe Kalia. Does he live up this road?"

The men looked uneasy. "What you want with Joe?" one of them asked.

"I just need to talk to him. It's important."

"Nobody's allowed up this road, Mr. Brewster says."

"Charles Brewster?"

"That's the one."

John had to think of some way to get past these guys and up this road. He was not going to be turned away.

He smiled at them. "You ever been on his plane?"

The men chuckled at this. "Nevah been invited," one of them said.

"Charles showed me around it yesterday. You know he has that whole interior finished in koa? And gold-trimmed seatbelt buckles. Unbelievable."

The men looked at each other again, unsure of what to do. "What you said your name was?"

"John Rossi."

"You get one ID you can show us?"

John fished his wallet out of his pants, pulled out his driver's license, and handed it over. The man showed it to his partner, who took a clipboard from the dashboard of the Jeep and carefully wrote down every piece of information on the license. They handed it back, and one of the men got out of the Jeep and opened the gate for him.

"You maybe not going get past the next bunch. They're not too happy fo' see strangers."

John drove through the gate, and said, "Mahalo" to the guard who opened it for him.

"Tell Joe, Kenny says howzit."

So this was the road to Joe. It was the valley where Jimmie had been going for the past few months. Sunny's valley. As the land sloped upwards, the road entered tall grass, five or six feet high. Occasionally there would be a clearing, and John could see the beach and the ocean on one side, and green mountains rising up on the other. As the road got to higher and higher elevations, there were trees, and the vegetation became more lush. The higher he got, the bigger the trees and the greener the terrain. And the rougher the road. He had to slow to a few miles an hour to pick his way through without bottoming out the car. Now he could at first hear, and then see a waterfall, 200 or 300 feet high, a narrow band of water coming down from the side of the cliff. He stopped to look, then turned to look at the ocean a mile or two below. This had to be one of the most beautiful places on Earth. He continued on then, and as he climbed, the valley walls were narrowing. He came around a bend in the road and skidded to a stop. The road was blocked by an old pickup truck. A half-dozen Hawaiian men were hanging around near the truck. A couple of them had shaved heads, and were wearing only loincloths and carrying spears and clubs. They had head leis and wore woven sandals. They were heavily tattooed with what looked to John like South Pacific markings. These were Hawaiian warriors, and evidently he had driven into the middle of a war zone. They did not look pleased to see him. They walked up to the car, eying him suspiciously.

"What you doing up here, man?"

"I need to talk to Joe."

"Joe's not here. Now you turn around and go back."

"It's very important that I talk to him. It's about the guy who got murdered."

"What about him?"

"He was a friend of mine."

Now they really looked angry. One of them pointed his spear at John. "Get out of the car."

John turned off the engine and got out. The pit of his stomach was churning. If he didn't need to be here, wasn't determined to find out what had happened to Jimmie, he would have turned around and driven right back to the road. Absurdly, he also felt self-conscious standing there in his resort clothes, the clean white shorts, white socks, and tennis shoes, and the festive Aloha shirt he had bought at the hotel gift shop, trying to look more Hawaiian. The guys who weren't in war paint were wearing shorts, T-shirts, and rubber slippers.

"So Jimmie one friend of yours?"

"Yes, and I've been working with Lani Miller on Uncle Sunny's defense."

The men exchanged a look. Then one of them nodded his head to the other, and the second man reached under the belt of his loincloth and produced a bright-yellow plastic walkie-talkie. He spoke into it."

"Charley, dis Henry, ovah."

After a moment there was a response that John could not make out.

"Get one guy down heah, one frien' of Jimmie, wants to talk to Joe."

There was more static and a muffled response.

"Yeah, dass what I wen tell him. Buggah says he knows Lani Miller."

There was another response, and the man asked him, "What's your name, brah?" John told him, and the man passed it on. There was a final response, and the man put the walkie-talkie back under his loincloth and spoke to John.

"They said fo' wait."

So John leaned against his car and waited, watched warily by the Hawaiians.

14

About twenty minutes later, John heard the distinctive sound of a four-wheel-drive vehicle in low gear making its way down from somewhere above. It came into view through the trees, and he could see that it was a silver CRV, similar to Lani's. As it got closer, he could see that it *was* Lani. She stopped on the other side of the pickup truck, shut down the engine, and came around to talk to him. She was dressed casually, in a tank top and shorts, and he admired her long, lovely legs. It just added to his delight in seeing her. The surprise on her face was clear.

"What are you doing here? I thought you were long gone."

"I was on the plane, and we were ready to go. Some guys showed up at the last minute. It turns out they hadn't done the second autopsy."

"Those bastards! Still, I'm surprised they couldn't talk their way out of it."

"They tried to. I kind of disabled the plane," he said looking sheepishly at his shoes.

She smiled approvingly at him. "Did you?"

He was feeling a bit embarrassed. "Didn't you get my messages?" he asked her.

"I've been up here since yesterday. My cell doesn't work here. I just got the message that you were leaving. On Brewster's plane."

"They more or less abducted me. I didn't know what the hell to do. They had Jimmie. They had even packed my suitcase and put it on board."

"Nice of them," she said sarcastically. "But why are you here? What's this about Joe?"

"I got a letter from Jimmie sent to New Jersey. They read it to me. He told me to come here and talk to Joe," he told her. "It was mailed on the day he died."

She looked at him and nodded. "Yes, okay, I can see why you came." She motioned toward his car. "You'll never get up there in that thing. Park it off the road, and I'll drive you up." He got back in and maneuvered his car off the road. Before he shut it down, she called out to him, "And put up the top. It rains here." He raised the electric top and closed and locked the doors. Observed closely by the Hawaiian men, he followed Lani past the pickup truck blocking the road, and they got in her car. She started it up and managed to get it turned around in the small space available, and they ground up the hill. The road was full of rocks, and in several places they had to ford small streams.

"A lot of water up here."

"Yes, water. Water is the key to taro, and if you lose the taro, you lose everything. It is the basis for all life."

She saw him looking at her as she made this solemn pronouncement. "That's what we Hawaiians believe. Of course most people can't stand poi."

"I love poi," he said matter-of-factly.

It was her turn to shoot him a look.

They arrived in an open area and parked next to a small stream. In front of them terraced pools of brown muddy water filled with taro stepped up the hillside. She led him up a narrow, complicated path, cutting one way and then another around the taro patches. Some contained miniature plants that looked like they had just been planted. Others had more mature plants, some of them several feet tall. Finally they reached the first of a number of small wooden houses. They were freshly painted in green with white trim. All around them, things were growing, ornamental plants as well as vegetables and herb gardens.

John followed Lani up a path lined with lava rocks to one of the houses, where they went up a set of steep wooden steps to a porch that overlooked the valley. From there, they could see over the tops of the trees and all the way to the ocean. It was idyllic. John thought of what it might be like to live in such a place, growing your own food, going down to the ocean to fish. A smile broadened on his face as he thought about this. Lani was looking at him, apparently reading his thoughts once again. "So what do you think? Even better than being an electrician in New Jersey?" she asked him.

"I don't know, it's a tough choice. But I'm beginning to waver."

She laughed, and it was music to his ears.

"Who lives here?"

"This is Jimmie's place."

He looked at her, startled. "I didn't know Jimmie lived here." Then he started looking around the place.

"Part of the time. He also had a condo in Kahana." She motioned toward the door. "Go on in, if you like."

He opened a screen door and went inside the house. Jimmie's house. The simple wood paneled interior was painted white. Screened windows were open on three sides of the house, allowing the breezes to flow through. There was a small, fairly modern kitchen with a propane stove and a propane-powered refrigerator. The furniture was mostly rattan, with green Hawaiian upholstery. There was a second room, a small bedroom containing a white-painted dresser, a mirror, and a bed with an orange-and-white Hawaiian quilt. John opened one of the dresser drawers and found that it was full of clothing.

He called out to Lani, "Is all this stuff Jimmie's?"

In a moment she appeared at the door. "Those are his," she said. "You might want to think about borrowing some of them."

"So I don't look like I'm on my way to play golf at the Ritz-Carlton?"

She smiled. "You said it, I didn't." She left the room and went back out onto the porch. He stripped down to his undershorts and pulled on a worn pair of blue shorts from the drawer. He looked through a drawer full of T-shirts and found a faded white one, with a picture of a can of Spam on the front. He had heard that Hawaiians eat more Spam per capita than anyone else, so it seemed like a good choice. He stowed his shoes and socks in a corner and folded his resort clothes and put them on the bed. He walked out on the porch barefooted, and Lani looked at him approvingly. "That's more like it. There are some rubber slippers downstairs."

"And the transformation will be complete," he intoned.

She laughed, and it seemed that every time she did, his feelings for her deepened. It kind of scared him. He was too old for puppy love and crushes. And he certainly did not know her well enough to call this feeling "love." She was beautiful, and he was in Hawai'i for the first time, and his emotions were all tangled up. It must be the romance of the place, he decided. Maybe.

"Where do we find Joe?" he asked her.

"He went out hunting this morning. They're looking for him."

"Hunting for what?'

"Wild pig."

"So you know this place pretty well?"

"I'd never been up here before yesterday. I know places like it. I grew up in a similar place, but on the Big Island."

"I'd like to see it some day. I'd like to see all the islands."

"You should do that. You never had any urge to come here before?"

John smiled, as he thought about being thirteen years old, and wanting to come here more than anything else in the world. He told her about this, and as they waited for Joe he told her many other things about himself. She was a good listener, seemed fascinated by his story, and had a lot of questions. Then he had one for her.

"Do you think Sunny really knows who my parents were?"

She thought about this for a while. "I think he's sincere. I think he believes that he knows you."

"But does he, really?"

"It's possible, I guess. Is there something about you that he might have recognized? Some scar or birthmark?"

"Not that I know of."

"You know that *kahuna* have mysterious powers."

"I've heard."

"I believe it. I'm an educated person, and I'm not superstitious. But you have to have respect for them, take my word for it."

"If he does know something, will he ever tell me?"

"Yes, I think he intends to. He's using his knowledge to keep you here."

"But why? How can I help him?"

"You already have. His friends think he's abandoned them and everything they thought he stood for. They think Sunny found out that Jim was Brewster's spy and killed him. And because of that they could lose their land and their way of life. They can't understand what he did and why he did it. You and I are about all Sunny has right now."

They were interrupted by a shout from below, and a tall, muscular man in a red T-shirt and black shorts lumbered up the path toward the house. Joe. He shed his slippers at the base of the stairs and climbed up to meet them. He reached the top of the stairs and regarded them cautiously. His face reflected Hawaiian openness and friendliness as well as a certain amount of suspicion. John held out his hand, and they shook.

"John Rossi. One of the cops down on the road asked me to say hello. Kenny."

"My brother-in-law stay down there? How you figgah?"

Lani motioned to him to take a seat and offered him a glass of water, which he gratefully accepted and drank right down. Then he looked John over. "So you're John. Jimmie told me about you. Said you would never come to Hawai'i."

"I didn't expect to."

"Jimmie and I were good friends, I thought. We nevah know who he stay working for."

"I know."

"But Sunny found out."

"Do you think Sunny killed him?"

Joe thought about this for a while. "Sunny is a healer. He wen heal Jimmie, you knew that?"

"No. When was this?"

"A couple weeks ago. Jimmie got real sick, he had one high fever. Middle of the night, too late to get him to the hospital. We thought he was going to die. Sunny wen wrap him in ti leaves, prayed like crazy for him, plenny old kine Hawaiian healing chants." He caught himself spouting superstition. "If you believe in that kind of thing. Anyway, Jimmie wen pull through."

"So you don't believe that Sunny killed him."

"It's more that I nevah like believe he do 'em. But the cops have all this evidence. Who else could have done 'em?"

"That's what we intend to find out," Lani said.

"Jimmie wrote to me, on the day he died," John said.

"Yeah? No kidding?"

"He asked me to come here and see you."

Joe sat up, interested. "Me? How come?"

"He said to ask you to show me where you and he used to go for a quick belt."

Joe laughed, a deep belly laugh. "Quick belt. That was Jimmie's word for it. Yeah, Sunny doesn't like drinking ovah here. But Jimmie and I used to like to take a belt once in a while. Later, Sunny got Jimmie to give 'em up."

"Was there some special place you used to go?"

"Not really, usually my house, or this one, after Jimmie bought it."

John's heart sank. A dead end. "So you don't know what he meant by that."

Joe thought for a while.

"Well, when he first got here, we used to go up to this little place up in the trees, kind of one tree house. Nobody else ever wen use 'em. Jimmie kept a bottle stashed up there. I neveh go up there for long time, though."

"Can you show us where it is?"

"Sure."

He led them down the steps, and John found a worn pair of rubber slippers. He wiggled into them, enjoying the strange feeling of the rubber between his toes. They walked a short way down the stone-lined path, and then cut off to the right onto a smaller path that led them into a ravine. As they went down, the sound of rushing water grew louder. At the bottom of the ravine was a small but strong-running stream, crossed by a wide split log. They followed Joe across it and up the other side, stopping at the base of a large tree. About twenty feet up, they could see a small wooden platform. Joe climbed up to it while John and Lani waited below. They could hear him shuffling around for a few moments, and when he climbed down, he was holding a thickly stuffed letter-sized envelope. He handed it to John. It was addressed: "John Rossi. Eyes Only." John had to smile. This was an old joke. Years before, the two friends had gone together to see a James Bond movie, and for the next several months every letter, document, package, every piece of paper Jimmie had handed John said "Eyes Only" on it.

At that moment it started to rain, and the ink on the envelope began to smear and run. He quickly stuffed it inside his shirt.

They went back to Jimmie's house, scrambling up the now muddy slope from the ravine, and then up the steps to the house. John put the envelope on the porch table, and went in to wash his hands before opening it. When he returned, Lani and Joe were sitting at the table, staring at the envelope. The three of them sat for a moment around the table looking at the thing, before John snatched it up and opened it. There was a stationery-store will inside, with some other papers. John shuddered involuntarily. Jimmie had expected to die.

He handed the will to Lani. *Might as well have a lawyer look at it, as long as there's one handy.* There was another paper, in Jimmie's handwriting, and addressed to John. He unfolded it and read it silently to himself while Lani looked over the will.

Johnny,
If you are reading this the worst has probably happened. Wow, I just realized that I'm now dead. Of course it's going to be me reading this thing and chuckling at my overactive imagination, before I toss it. If you don't mind, that's what I'm thinking now. It will help me get through this. I sent you a second letter, which I know you'll receive in NJ, so that you could find this one. I didn't want to look too stupid, in case nothing happens to me, that's why I made it kind of cryptic. Hey, if you're reading this, that means you finally made it to HI. What do you think? Isn't it marvelous? Here I feel a contentment (wow, there's a word that I never thought would apply to me) I have never known, never even knew that I wanted. I love it here, and I think you will too. Anyway, I wanted you to know something important: You were right. I've been a jerk. Maybe my whole life. Certainly my whole career. But I also wanted you to know that I have never wanted

to hurt anyone. But I know now that I've done some very bad things to people. Especially my own people.

I wish I could say that I listened to you two years ago and began to change, but I didn't. It just made me mad at you. Now, when it's too late, I finally see that it was facing the truth that made me so angry. I guess that's why, when this job in Hawai'i came up, I jumped at it. It was going to be my own independent operation, away from that snake Bennett and His Royal Highness Charles N. Brewster. Many promises were made. I thought I'd be free from my role as the token Indian and be a real executive in a high position. That's what they told me, and I believed them. Come to HI, do your thing, promotion to Vice President of Operations, $100,000 bonus, yada yada. And best of all, even though you may not believe this, I was thinking that now I can prove to you that I am more than just the token Indian. This means a lot to me, Johnny, more than you can ever know. I was giddy with anticipation of how this would change my life.

When I got here, I find out there's no executive position, no office for me, I can't bring my Porsche over, I can't even say I work for Zodiac. I've got to pretend to be a disgruntled ex-employee of Zodiac to con the locals out of their land. Another job for the brown man. It was a stunning and gut-wrenching blow.

A better man (like you) would have quit. I wish I had done it. I could afford it. Lord knows I've made plenty over the years, but it didn't seem like enough. Is it ever? I had "walking away" money, in other words, but I didn't have "fuck you" money. And that's what I wanted to tell these guys when I quit. So I went along, as always.

But things got even worse. To insinuate myself here I attended Hawai'i independence rallies to start with, and I found that I was in sympathy with these people. I fell in love with Hawai'i and with the Hawaiians. I was supposed to masquerade as someone to help them keep their land, as Zodiac applied the pressure through lawsuits, quiet title proceedings, shutting off water, closing roads, etc. They would sell to me, their supposed friend, who bought the land out of the goodness of his heart so that they could continue living there. This is land that has been in their families for generations, land that is productive, and yields them a living. I gained their trust and sold my soul as I acquired their land, supposedly to help them keep Zodiac at bay.

But Sunny and the others won't ever budge from their land, and of course my heart wasn't into talking them out of it. Brewster isn't used to someone who won't sell out. To them, the land is their life. To him, it's just real estate. He needs their land because he needs their water. He has to have millions of gallons per day to get a permit, or he can't build a damn thing. That means he has to kick out the taro farmers. He's tried to buy them out, sue them out, block their roads. At our last meeting, I told Brewster that the situation was impossible, these guys weren't ever going to leave. I told him he should forget about this place, get some land somewhere else. But for some reason he seems to be fixated on this valley. Then he made threats. He said he'd fire me, expose me, even have me killed if I didn't do my job. Hell, I'm a corporate guy, a suit, and he's talking like we're the goddam mafia. I know it sounds crazy, but it has me scared for my life. I have been thinking of sneaking away and hiding out somewhere for a few years.

Then, a couple of weeks ago something happened. Uncle Sunny got me out of a nasty situation. I had a high fever. I think I would have died if he hadn't helped me. Ask Joe about it. Sunny has special powers, he can see things other people can't. Anyway, I've decided not to flee with my tail between my legs. I'm going to try to set up a meeting between Uncle Sunny and Zodiac. I think if anyone can convince Zodiac that this valley is a bad place for a casino, it's Sunny. Of course, then Sunny will know that I still work for them, so my cover will be blown. To tell you the truth I feel certain that he already knows.

I don't know how Brewster will react: He can be pretty damn creepy. There are a lot of stories about how he has dealt with people who cross him. I used to think that it was just stuff he concocted to frighten the opposition. Now that I'm the opposition, I'm no longer that certain. The man has incredible wealth and power. I would just like my old job back, and I'd like to drive my Porsche again. The hell with the title and the bonus. But if the shithead gets nasty, I have a little press release I wrote—a copy is enclosed. Please publish this, if you feel it's necessary.

Okay, I'm feeling better now that I've written this. I'm probably reading it to myself. Hi, Jimmie, aren't you feeling foolish, you dummy?

But just in case, Johnny, I want you to know that you're the one person in my life that I've always admired and respected, despite what I may have said and done. You have always had integrity. I admire it, even if I've never had the guts to emulate it. For me, for your friends, for your family (which doesn't deserve you, as I've often said), you're Mr. Dependable. Come to think of it, that's why I know that, if something has happened to me, you'll come here, and be reading this. I love you, my brother. Never doubt that I've always considered you to be my best friend. I'll be your friend forever.

Jimmie
PS: I thought I should have a will. It is enclosed. I'm leaving my savings to my folks, but all my property here goes to you, Johnny. Congratulations. You finally have your little piece of Hawai'i.

John put the letter down on the table, stunned, tears in his eyes. Lani and Joe looked at him. He simply handed it over to her. He picked up the remaining papers from the envelope. There were a dozen copies of an official looking press release done on Zodiac corporate stationery. It read:

> For immediate release:
>
> James E. Putnam, Vice President of Hawai'i Operations for Zodiac International, has announced his resignation. He has stated that he believes that Zodiac has been perpetrating a fraud

> on the people of Hawai'i, and he can no longer participate in such actions. He believes that his life is in danger, not from the good taro farmers of Kalonahoa Valley, but from persons in the employ of Zodiac International, for whom he has labored loyally and steadfastly for the last eight years. He wishes the people of Hawai'i to know that he regrets having participated in the recent actions by Zodiac to deprive native Hawaiians of their water and their land.

Each copy bore James Putnam's signature. When Lani handed Jimmie's letter over to Joe, there was a tear in her eye as well. She perused the press release and set it on the table, and looked at John, then reached over and took his hand.

"I can't begin to imagine what it would be like to receive a letter like that, especially under these circumstances."

Joe had finished reading the letter. "So what the hell does this mean? Brewster wen kill Jimmie?"

"Those kinds of guys never do their own killing. They get someone else to do it," John said.

"Bennett?" Lani asked.

"The cobra? Maybe. I don't know," John said.

Joe said, "I figured if wasn't Sunny, had to be one of us. Somebody who found out who Jimmie was working for. I mean, the fishhook and everything."

"How did you know about that?" Lani wanted to know.

"You know, people talk," Joe said.

"What fishhook?" John asked

Lani thought for a long moment before speaking. "In an ongoing police investigation, an officer of the court is not supposed to reveal confidential information to the public."

Joe scoffed. "Everybody knows about it."

She turned to John. "This is going to be hard for you to hear." She hesitated for a brief moment before continuing. "Jimmie was bludgeoned to death. He was placed face down on the rock and hit repeatedly with a stone club from behind. It was the ritual way of killing an enemy. And there was an old Hawaiian fish-hook through his cheek."

"Dass the way they used to deal with a traitor. Treat 'em like one fish they caught," Joe said.

"I'm sorry, John, I had hoped you would be spared these details," Lani said.

John thought this over. "So whoever killed him knew about all this cultural stuff. It doesn't sound like Brewster, does it?"

Lani said, "No, but anyone could know about it if they did any reading on the subject."

"So where does this leave us?" John asked her.

Lani thought about it for a while, and then a smile began to form. "Jimmie was V.P. of Operations. That was the title they gave him. It turned out not to mean anything to them or to him, but as an executive, he would be authorized to issue a press release."

"You mean we release it, even though he's dead?" John asked.

"Not just release it. We call a press conference," she said.

John was smiling too, now. "Yes, I like that. Let's see what Brewster does about it."

"Does anyone have a working phone here?" she asked Joe.

"Yeah, Oliver get one."

They got up quickly and gathered the papers together, and walked down the hill to Oliver's house. He was glad to let them use his phone, and Lani made a series of calls to set up the press conference for the following day. Afterwards, she and John walked toward her car.

John said, "Not much to do until tomorrow, I guess."

She seemed lost in thought for a few moments, then said to him, “Would you like to go for a drive with me?” She looked as if she thought he might say no. There was not a chance of that.

15

They drove in her car all the way down to the highway. It was a tough drive, and she had to cut this way and that to avoid rocks, deep potholes, and high spots on the road. He kept quiet, admiring her expert rough-road driving skills. He glanced over at her from time to time, enjoying the intense look of concentration on her pretty face, and a shapely leg stabbing at the clutch. They finally got down to the main highway, and she turned back toward the Lahaina side. He didn't ask where they were going, didn't care, happy to be in her company. She drove a short distance and pulled over in front of the pink fruit stand. "Let's see if we can get something for lunch," she said.

A dark, skinny man had been dozing in a chair behind a counter loaded with pineapples, bananas, mangoes, guavas, and papayas. He stood up and smiled at them.

"Aloha."

"Aloha," Lani returned the greeting.

To John, he said, "Howzit, bruddah?" John sensed that something was different now, and it took him a moment to figure it out. Without the aloha resort wear, without the shoes and socks, he looked like a local. And he found that he enjoyed it. He didn't want to spoil the effect by opening his mouth and sounding like he just got off the plane from New Jersey, so he just smiled and nodded at the man and let Lani do the talking. She asked if they sold anything besides fruit, and the man told her his wife had made *laulaus* that morning, and he went across the road to a small house John hadn't noticed before.

"I guess you have to know what to ask for," he said.

"You never know what they're going to have," she told him.

The man came right back carrying a plastic shopping bag and handed it to John. "I put a couple papah plates and some chopsticks in there fo' you."

John said, "Mahalo," in the best pidgin accent he could muster.

Lani already had her wallet out and paid the man, over John's objections. They got into the car and went a short distance on the highway to where a gravel road led down to the beach. She turned there and drove as far as she could without getting stuck in the sand before she parked. She got a couple of rolled-up straw mats out of the car and they set themselves up in the shade of a palm tree. John didn't know what a *laulau* was. Lani explained that it was fish and vegetables wrapped in *ti* leaves and tied up, then cooked in an outdoor cooker. He found it delicious, and they dived into the food.

"Maybe we can find a shave ice stand someplace for dessert."

"I hope so. I'd really like to try that some time."

She laughed. "You really are amazing."

"Why do you say that?"

"Dressed like that, you look like a *Kamaʻāina*, a *kanaka*, like you've lived here all your life. And you've never had a shave ice." Then she mused, "I wonder how many I've had since I was a little girl."

"You grew up on the Big Island?"

"My family is from Puna. They're farmers."

"But you left the farm."

"I'm an only child. There was no son to run the farm, and I was free to choose my own path."

"Did you always want to be a lawyer?"

Lani gazed out to sea. "No. When I was in high school, I wanted to be a doctor. I wanted to be helping my people. But I think that when it comes to Western medicine, Hawaiians like to go to a *haole* doctor. Stupid prejudice. I don't know, maybe I'm the same way myself. But there are very few lawyers out there who understand Hawai'i and Hawaiians. So I decided to study law, to defend my people."

"Defend them against what?"

"People like Brewster. People who want to take what is left of our land. They already have nearly all of it. Then they want to come to an unspoiled place like this and help themselves to the rest."

"How do you stop them?"

"With the one tool that has been left to us: water rights. Hawaiians believe that a private property owner has no more rights to water than they have to the sunshine. The Hawaiian constitution guarantees our rights to practice our culture, including the growing of taro."

"But if Brewster owns the land . . ."

"He owns most of the valley, right up to where Sunny is farming. His problem is that he needs water."

"There seems to be plenty of it here."

"Plenty for taro farming. But do you know what Brewster wants to build here?"

"No."

"He has plans to put up a hotel with two twenty-story towers. He wants to build a casino, as big as anything in Las Vegas. The most exclusive gambling resort in the world. He'd become the biggest private employer in the state. But there's one thing that's stopping him. Water. He needs to be able to pump enough water out of these mountains to support a small city. And Sunny and his friends have been able to keep him from getting the permits he needs to get to that water, because if he takes the millions of gallons he wants, they won't have enough left to grow taro. He's been battling these guys for two years. First he tried to buy their land. Then he tried to block the road leading up there. Now he's suing in federal court, forcing these guys to hire lawyers, trying to bankrupt them."

"But I thought gambling isn't legal here."

"It isn't, at least not yet. But he's been ferrying members of the legislature on his private jet to junkets at his mainland casinos, to Asian gambling locations, anywhere they want to go."

John had a guilty thought about nearly having flown on this plane himself.

Lani's discourse was becoming heated now. "They claim they're doing all this for the good of Hawaiian people, to boost the economy, to provide jobs. Always jobs. It's like wrapping yourself in the flag. They try to make it sound like the sole purpose of the place is to provide employment. They never talk about how much richer they're going to become. And you know, I don't care about that, but they want to do it by turning this place into another Waikiki, with slot machines."

She suddenly seemed to realize how strident she sounded, and looked a bit abashed. She got up then and collected the plates, and John shook the sand off their mats before rolling them up. "Can you picture this place after Brewster gets done with it?" Lani asked.

John looked around at the beautiful, untouched valley and the pristine beach, and tried to picture high-rise buildings, the sound of slot machines. "It's hard to even imagine. But what can we do to stop it?"

"If Sunny is convicted of this murder, probably nothing. He's the spiritual leader of the taro farmers, and without him, they won't be able to stick it out. And Brewster's been working even harder since Sunny's arrest to get these guys kicked off their land. If people think it's a question of supporting some kind of Hawaiian cultural extremists versus the possibility of creating thousands of new jobs, it can and will turn the tide for Brewster. He is taking full advantage of Jimmie's murder to turn public sentiment to support for gambling. All it takes is a vote of the legislature."

They got into the car, and John was surprised when she asked him to drive. Instead of going back to the valley, she asked him to go the other way, toward Wailuku. They drove for miles on the winding road, along cliffs, the ocean breaking against the dark rocks far below. While John directed all of his attention to the narrow road, she was craning her neck, at every turn, looking carefully at the scenery. When they came to a lone house near the roadside, she asked him to stop and wait in the car. She knocked on the door of the house and spent a minute or two talking to a woman who answered the door before coming back to the car.

John said, "I assume you weren't asking for directions."

She smiled. "I was asking about last Monday evening, if anyone there heard a car come by."

John realized that she had had more in mind than a picnic on the beach and a pleasant drive. "What did she say?"

"They weren't home then."

"You think whoever killed Jimmie came by this way?"

"Had to," she said. "Otherwise the tour bus driver would have seen someone. I already asked them, and there were no cars coming that way. I know this is a long shot, but if someone else was at the *heiau* that night they might have gone back this way to avoid the cops coming out from Lahaina. The folks here know the local cars. Maybe they saw a strange one."

They were still miles from Wailuku, but the closer they came to the city the more houses there were near the road. For a while she had him stop at every one. At many of them, no one was home. Sometimes she found someone to talk to, but not a single person could recall seeing or hearing anything that night. Eventually, as they approached the outskirts of the town, they found themselves in an area that was no longer rural. A passing car here would be a normal event that would not be noticed by the residents. She asked him to stop and turn back to the valley. Before he could find a spot to turn around, a school bus went by, coming from Wailuku. John finally made the U-turn and they followed the bus as it ground slowly along the road without making any stops. There was no safe place to pass. Lani seemed discouraged, and he tried to cheer her up with stories about growing up Hawaiian in New Jersey. He wanted to hear her laugh at least once more before they got back to the valley and went their separate ways.

The bus finally stopped in front of a small, closed-up shave ice stand by the road. An old man was waiting there. A couple of young boys wearing knapsacks got off the bus and were greeted by their grandfather. This was apparently the last stop on the route. While John and Lani waited to get by, the bus made a U-turn on the narrow road, then drove back toward Wailuku. The old man waved at the driver as the bus moved off. Lani asked John to pull over. "Aloha, uncle," she said from her open car window.

"Aloha," he said, returning her smile.

"Is this your stand?" she asked him.

"Yeah. But we stay closed now."

"Uncle, were you out here at sunset last Monday?"

"No, I wen shut down before dat."

"Can you see the cars on the road from your house?"

"Can. We can see anyone who goes by."

"Any traffic last Monday?"

The old man scratched his head. "Hard fo' remember, you know?"

"You don't get many cars coming by at night do you? This would have been just after dark."

The old man just shrugged.

"This guy would have been going toward Wailuku," Lani said. "Probably would have been in a big hurry."

This obviously stirred a memory. "You know, there was one car wen come by real fast, just after dark. Headed Wailuku too."

"Was this on Monday?"

"Could be."

"You were in your house?"

"Watching TV. We saw this car go by, buggah was smokin'. We were thinking this guy not going make it all the way to Wailuku, driving like dat."

"What show were you watching, do you remember?"

"Yeah, because I went fo' see the car, and missed the ending. It was *Columbo.* One re-run, you know. Pretty sure dass on Monday."

Lani jotted down a note to double-check for the day and time of the show. "What about the car? What did it look like?"

"It was yellow. Don't know what kind. Was loud. Dass why we wen notice it. Bright-yellow car."

"But you don't know what kind?"

The old man looked embarrassed. "No, don't really know about cars."

A yellow car, unknown type, probably on Monday. Not much to go on, John thought.

Lani thanked the old man for his help. They were getting ready to drive off when one of the grandchildren, a boy of about nine years old walked up to their car and peered in at them.

"Hey, mister."

"Howzit?"

"I saw the car."

"Do you know what kind of car it was?"

"My brother has one," the boy said

"One what?" John asked him.

"One car like that one I saw."

Lani and John smiled at each other. "Your little brother owns a car?" he asked.

The boy called out to his younger brother, who was standing shyly with his grandfather, and came over to the car only reluctantly.

"Show them your cars," the boy said to his little brother.

The younger boy took off his knapsack and placed it on the hood of Lani's Honda. John and Lani got out of her car. The kid opened a zipper, reached in, and started pulling out his prized collection of hot wheels cars. He had over a dozen. They were NASCAR racing cars, and John and Lani exchanged a smile at the serious care he used in handling them. Obviously, there weren't any racing cars passing by last Monday, but they enjoyed watching the boy, even if this wasn't going to help them. He arranged them one by one carefully on the hood of the CRV. As each car was set down, the older brother announced the brand and year of the cars. John was impressed at how well the kid knew his automobiles. Finally the younger boy pulled out a small red car and set it down on the hood. His older brother picked it up and handed it to John. "This one."

John said, "But you said it was a yellow car."

The boy looked at them, exasperated at their lack of comprehension. "It was yellow, but just like this."

Lani asked, "What kind of car is that?"

John looked it over and recognized the distinctive shape. Before he could answer her question, the boy spoke up, as if addressing a not too bright person, or maybe just a girl. "Dodge Viper."

Lani smiled at him. "It is? What kind of car is this?" she asked him, indicating her own car.

"Honda CRV," the kid said without hesitation.

Lani nodded at him, clearly impressed. John gave him back the toy Viper. "This is what you saw going by last Monday?"

The boy nodded solemnly, and handed the car back to his little brother, who proceeded to carefully collect his other cars from the hood and place them meticulously back in his knapsack, one at a time. The older boy took his younger brother by the hand and led him across the road to where their grandfather was waiting for them. They opened the gate and walked through, closing it behind them and went up the hill to their house.

Lani said, "He seems to know about cars"

"He was dead-on with every one of the models. How many yellow Dodge Vipers do you figure there are on Maui?"

"I never paid much attention. It's pretty unusual looking. Not very many, I wouldn't think," Lani said.

John had a gleam in his eye. "Think maybe Zodiac International owns one?" He took out his phone and called the number Sam had given him. He caught the detective just as he was leaving the office.

Sam said, "I heard that you got uncle talking."

"He's talking, but he's not saying much. Has your investigation uncovered anything new?"

"What investigation? The case is marked closed."

"Can you do something for me?" John asked.

There was a long pause at the end of the line, and John had the feeling that Sam was sitting back down at his desk. "Look, John, I told you what I think, but that's just my hunch, nothing more. It carries no weight in a case like this. I have to account for all my time, which investigations I'm on. So the answer is no, I can't do anything for you."

There was a long pause, and John waited it out. "Okay, what?" Sam finally said.

"Can you find out who owns a yellow Dodge Viper?"

"I can tell you that right now. There are only a couple of them on the island. They're rentals. Don't know which agencies, offhand."

John was very disappointed. Still, maybe the murderer had rented one of them. "Can you find out for me?"

Sam sighed. "Yeah, I can do that. Just takes a few minutes. I've got to go now, but I can call you in the morning."

John thanked him, gave him his cell phone number, and asked him to leave a message if there was no answer.

"Sam will let me know in the morning," he told Lani.

"How'd you get him to do that?"

"It must be my native New Jersey charm."

He was treated to another of her marvelous laughs, as she checked her own cell phone to see if she had a signal. "Let's find out if we have any autopsy results yet." She called the D.A.'s office and was shuffled around until she got to the Maui County Medical Examiner. John watched her as she listened for a while before saying, "You checked specifically for a bullet wound? . . . So you're saying you found nothing? . . . Inconclusive? That's not the same as finding nothing . . . I understand that there was extensive tissue damage. We both knew that going in. Okay, tell you what. I'm going to have another expert examine the body. And you'd better not release him to anyone this time."

She hung up the phone. "They find what they want to find. I'm sorry, but Jimmie can't go home just yet."

"I understand," John said.

She started out across the road. "I want to get the kid's statement, and his name and phone number."

"If you don't mind, I'll stay here and make some calls."

When she had crossed the road and let herself through the gate, John started dialing. He called his brother at the office in New Jersey to let him know he was going to be delayed getting back. His brother had already left for the day. The six hours of time difference was making it hard to stay in touch. He left a message. Then he made the difficult call to Jimmie's mom. He explained the situation as succinctly as he could.

"Do you think they have the right guy?" she asked him.

"In my heart, no, I don't."

"And when can I have Jimmie back?"

"I don't know. There's been another delay now." John wasn't going to talk to her about autopsies.

"Johnny, you've done everything I asked you to do and more. I can't ask you to stay there any longer. You have a job, a fiancée . . ."

"I need to find out for myself, Mrs. Putnam. I'm going to stay here until I do."

Her voice sounded teary. "I'm so grateful to you Johnny. I feel so helpless."

"I'll find out what happened, and I'll bring him home to you."

They said their goodbyes, and he called Angela at home. "Hi, sweetheart. Did I wake you?"

She went directly to her argument tone of voice. "Are you ever coming home or what?"

"There's been another delay."

"And tomorrow they'll be still another."

"It's possible. I just don't know."

"Don't think I don't know what's really going on over there. You just don't want to come back, I can hear it in your voice. Probably have a girlfriend already."

John decided that he needed to tell her the truth. "Angela, I—"

"I don't want to hear it! I don't want to hear it!" she shouted and there was a heavy click in his ear as her phone was slammed down.

Lani returned to the car a few minutes later, carrying her legal pad. She smiled at him as she slid behind the wheel. He had the same feeling he got whenever she had been gone and he saw her again. She simply took his breath away.

"What?" she asked him.

"No, nothing," he said smiling at her. He had known Lani for two days. What kind of future could they have together? She was educated, she was beautiful, and she was deeply Hawaiian. He was a coconut, a tradesman from Jersey. There was a good possibility that his feelings for her would never be returned. And now he was thinking about burning bridges behind him on the mainland. He was beginning to realize how vulnerable he was leaving himself.

She was looking up at the sky. "I think we'd better get back and get your car out of there. It looks like rain, and that road can probably flood pretty easily."

She started the car and they drove along the cliff road under darkening skies. Their conversation was subdued. John kept thinking about Angela, about his East Coast life. If she hadn't hung up on him, he might have broken off his engagement right then and there. Instead, he hadn't been straight with her. He knew she would be angry, and so would her father. Her father was not a man you wanted to have mad at you. On the other hand, breaking an engagement was not something he wanted to do over the phone. How would it be when he finally got back to New Jersey? Would he ever be able to forget all that was happening to him here? Would he want to?

They got to the gate up to the valley at about four in the afternoon. The roads were wet. It had already been raining there. Kenny and his partner let them in with a smile and a wave. Brewster had hired them to keep people out, but when your brother-in-law was one of the ringleaders, you weren't going to do a really great job blocking the road.

It was a tough, muddy drive up to the second gate, and even with her car in four-wheel drive, they barely made it to where his car was parked. They'd had to drive through some fast-running streambeds that had been nearly dry earlier in the day, but the skies were clearing and there was a huge rainbow across the entire valley. The waterfall was running spectacularly. Joe was waiting for them at the pickup. He walked over to John's side of the car. "Didn't think you guys was going make it."

"We almost didn't," John said.

"Well, you never going get out of here tonight."

"Why not? Looks like it's clearing up," John said.

"Here, it is." He pointed up into the mountains. "Up there been raining for hours. In another ten minutes those streams you just drove through going be rivers. Anyway, come up. We're going to have one luau tonight. I wen shot one pig this morning, he stay in the *imu*."

John looked at Lani. He had a feeling that it wasn't just the weather. Joe really wanted them to stay. "Looks like we're stuck."

Joe said to him, "You better park 'em, never going make it up dat hill."

16

Lani pulled the CRV off the road behind John's car, and they got into the truck that had been used to block the road. It was an old Dodge Power Wagon, sitting up high on huge wheels and tires. They drove up the hill, and before long John could see that Joe had not exaggerated. The road was strewn with boulders that had washed down with the rain, and they had to pass through streams that were nearly up to the door sills of the big truck. They would never have made it in Lani's little car. By the time they got to the clearing near Jimmie's house, there was bright sunshine coming through the leaves, but the little stream next to the road was now a thundering torrent. A couple of men were sitting by what looked like a ring of stones lying on the ground. Joe parked the truck and led John and Lani there. He pointed at the ring and said, "Got one pig, two turkeys, ten chickens, and plenny sweet potato in there." He went over and put his hand palm down on the ground in several places inside the stone ring, holding it there for a few moments each time.

"Stay ready Joe?" one of the men asked him.

Joe stood up and said, "Let's do 'em." The men reached down and pulled up two corners of a canvas tarp that had been buried under the dirt. As the tarp was slowly lifted, steam came out from underneath, along with a delicious smell of cooking food. They pulled the tarp off carefully, keeping dirt out of the *imu*, the underground oven. Beneath the tarp were layers of broad banana leaves. These they removed layer by layer. With each layer removed, the wonderful aromas grew, and John was really getting hungry. He grinned at Lani, who was also enjoying the show. Finally there were the pig and chicken and turkeys, all wrapped tightly in leaves. Joe had unloaded several folding tables from his truck, and people from the valley, attracted by the smell of the food, were starting to arrive. There were men, women, and children. They were bringing food of their own in coolers, pots, and plastic containers. A few of them brought guitars and ukuleles. As the evening sun slanted through the trees, they set themselves up with blankets and folding chairs on the grass near the river.

Lani was helping some of the women put out their food, and John made himself useful helping Joe carry the pig from the *imu* to the tables, where Joe showed him how to shred the pork in the traditional Hawaiian way. He found himself behind the table serving up the food onto paper plates Joe had produced from the back of his truck. Some of the people looked at him with curiosity, and whenever Joe caught it he would bellow out, "Dis Keoni, one friend of mine." *Keoni*, John thought. What Sunny had called him. For all he knew, some of these people could be his relatives. He wondered if his mom or dad had had any sisters or brothers. He wondered if Sunny was ever going to tell him, or if he even knew.

As darkness set in, people started to light kerosene lanterns they had brought down from their houses. John tried all the food, much of it new to him. Some of the people had brought fish also, and he tried to memorize the names, *Uhu*, *Ono*, *Opakapaka*, *Manini*. Lani was circulating around talking to just about everyone. People had lots of questions for her about Sunny, about the investigation, about his chances. Meanwhile, people ate and ate. Joe said to him, "We Hawaiians don't eat until we full. We eat until we tired." John laughed. He looked around and found Lani sitting on a blanket with a couple of young women with their children. He walked over to where they were sitting. Lani introduced him as John, but he told them to call him "Keoni." Lani smiled at this.

The woman said, "She said you one friend of Jimmie."

"Yes. I've known him since we were kids."

A girl of about seven had been listening to John. "Mommy, he talks funny."

Her mother was obviously embarrassed. "Shh," she said to her daughter. "Now you trying fo' help uncle, she said," the woman said to him.

"Yes," John said.

"So you think uncle nevah do 'em."

"No, I don't."

"I nevah think so either. Not uncle. Maybe somebody else ovah here, they find out Jimmie work for da kine, for da gamblers, then they want kill him. Not uncle."

"That's what I think too."

"Dass a good ting, you help out uncle."

"I'll do my best."

He spoke to many others that evening. The police and the media had done a good job of convincing everyone that the evidence against Sunny was overwhelming. Many had been angry at him. Those who weren't seemed to be confused and hurt, even while maintaining their loyalty to their leader. They were not violent people, and they didn't think it was necessary to use violence. They had also been angry at Jimmie, who they thought was a friend and turned out to work for the developer trying to kick them off their land. He and Lani tried to help them understand the truth. John couldn't tell whether he had reached them or not.

After a while someone started playing an ukulele, and then was joined by a man on the guitar playing a bass line. Another man started singing a song in Hawaiian, and before long, a woman who had to be at least in her seventies got up and started dancing a hula. She was soon joined by a couple of her grandchildren, girls about seven or eight years old. John was astonished at the simple elegance of the dance, at how gracefully they did it, whether young or old, thin or fat. A circle of people formed around the dancers, and the ukulele was passed to other hands. John and Lani sat on opposite sides of the circle. Once he thought he saw her looking at him, and then she seemed to look away shyly when he caught her glance.

He realized that everyone was expected to play an instrument or sing or dance. He had learned some Hawaiian songs and played his ukulele often, but that had been more than twenty years ago.

When it was Lani's turn to participate, she got up and danced a hula. To his eyes, it was as perfectly done as he had ever seen, and he wondered how long she had been doing this, how she had learned. Her hips swayed sinuously, and her hands seemed to flow. He could see how the hula could tell a story, why it was important to Hawaiians. She sat down to a round of applause for the newcomer. He felt a nudge, and someone was handing him an ukulele. He tried strumming it, attempting to remember a few chords, trying to think of a simple tune he could play. He could remember a song called "Lovely Hula Hands," and after sounding out a few chords, he finally got the hang of it again. Someone recognized the tune. An older woman starting singing along with him. Then the guitarist joined in, playing bass, and a couple of the women got up and danced. The last time he had played the ukulele, he had been sitting alone in his room, playing only when he was sure that no one else was in the house. He would never have imagined that he would be playing it again here, with these people, his own people. He glanced across at Lani's smiling face, and even the mosquitoes he had to slap at occasionally could not dampen the pure joy he felt in his heart.

Joe had been cleaning up and putting things away, but there was a clamor for him to join the party. He started dancing to "Lovely Hula Hands" with the women. This was evidently not a male hula, and there was much laughter from the audience as Joe mimicked the movements of the women. John had never seen a man dance the hula before, didn't even know it was done. And he found that this large man, while perhaps a bit more energetic, was every bit as graceful as the women. The song finished, and John handed back the uke, to claps on the back and a round of applause. Now Joe took up a guitar, and sat on a log playing a song John recognized from an old recording he had listened to as a child: "Henehene kou 'aka." Joe's guitar playing was as energetic as his hula, and instead of tapping a toe in time with the music, he bounced both feet, wiggled his hips and waved the neck of the guitar, his eyes closed, a big smile on his face. The song was mostly in Hawaiian, but there was a line in English that went, "Our eyes have met, our lips not yet." And at that moment his eyes locked for a long moment with Lani sitting across the circle from him. He felt a wave of feelings for her wash over him, turning him to jelly. Was he in love? He had known her for only a few days. He thought of love as what he had experienced with Angela, something that grew out of knowing a person for years, knowing what the person was really like. He hardly knew Lani. But somehow he felt that she was perfect for him. He knew this was dangerous and foolish. He was not a teenager anymore. He told himself these things, tried to turn it off, but he couldn't do it. He resolved to try not to get too close to her for a while, afraid that he would make a fool of himself.

The party broke up at around 10:00 p.m. These were farmers, early risers. As he helped Joe and the others fold up the tables, it occurred to John that he didn't have a place to sleep. But then he remembered with a start that he had a house here. They got the things put away, and he looked around for Lani. She was nowhere to be seen. It had been a magical afternoon and evening for him, and he was disappointed and even a little hurt that she had gone off without even saying good night. As he walked up the hill to "his" house in bright moonlight, he wondered where she would be spending the night. She seemed to have made lot of friends here, and he figured she'd have some place to stay. As he approached Jimmie's house, he could hear the sound of the outdoor shower. He took off his slippers and started up the steps. He was surprised to hear Lani's voice coming from the shower.

"I hope you don't mind. I got kind of sweaty dancing."

"No, not a problem, help yourself. How's the water?"

"Cold, but it feels good. You should try it."

For a moment he fantasized taking a shower with her, and he got an instant erection. But then he heard her turn the water off. He sat down on the steps and spoke to her as she dried herself in the shower. "Are you all set for a place to stay? Where did you stay last night?"

"I stayed here. But this is your house now."

"Good, then I can invite you to stay here again tonight."

"There's just the one bed."

A lot of cute sexist rejoinders popped into his head, but he realized that he cared too much for this woman to treat her that way. He said, "There's that big chair in the living room. Looks pretty comfortable. I'll take that."

She didn't respond to that. She stepped out of the shower, barefoot and wrapped in a big bath towel, her long dark hair hanging down damply. She looked so beautiful in the moonlight, he wanted to take her in his arms and kiss her. But he didn't know what her feelings for him were, and didn't want to seem as if he were taking advantage. At least that's what his mind was telling him, even if the throbbing between his legs was telling him something else. She smiled and brushed past him up the steps, saying, "I'll turn on a light."

He decided that a cold shower was exactly what he needed. He walked over to the shower. It was a simple affair, a concrete pad with a drain in the middle and a lattice of teak boards set over it. There were head-high wooden walls on three sides, with the steep hillside forming the fourth wall. There was soap in a soap dish and inside a cupboard were some towels. He stripped off his clothing and turned on the water. There was a cold water tap only, but it really did feel good. He finished the shower and toweled himself off, then went up the steps wrapped in the towel. Lani had lit a kerosene lantern, and it illuminated the living room. She came out of the bedroom, barefoot and wrapped in the bath towel, brushing her long hair. "Are you sure you don't want the bed? You're too big for that chair."

"I'll be fine."

An awkward moment of silence followed. He felt that the two of them were teetering on the edge of something. Did she want him too? It would be so easy to take those few steps across the room and scoop her into his arms and find out. But then he thought of talking to her afterwards, getting to know each other. When she found out he was engaged to someone else, he could lose her forever. That he would not be able to bear. Finally she spoke.

"Okay, then. See you in the morning." She turned and walked into the bedroom, closing the door softly behind her.

He awakened to the sound of pounding. Sunlight was streaming in the window. He got out of his chair and walked stiffly to the window. Joe was down below looking up at him. "Good morning!" he yelled up at John. "Sorry, I didn't know you were going to sleep late."

"What time is it?" John asked.

"Six-thirty."

He dressed quickly, and by the time he was finished Lani came out of the bedroom, dressed and ready to go. "You're up. I didn't want to wake you," she said.

"Everybody's up early," John said.

"Today's a big day," she said. "Did you sleep okay?"

John shrugged. "Not really."

"Me either," she said looking into his eyes.

He knew he had to take a chance. "Look, Lani, there are some things—"

"Thank you."

"For what?"

"For being a gentleman. For not taking advantage of the situation."

"It was hard not to."

"Not just for you," she said. Then, to his surprise, she crossed the room and kissed him gently on the lips. "You're a good man, John Rossi. I like you."

He embraced her gently and said huskily, "I like you too. More than I can say."

She pulled away from him and said, "Come to my house tonight. I'll make dinner."

"I'll be there," he said, and gently kissed her forehead.

They looked at each other for a moment, and then she said, "We'd better get going."

They walked down the steps together.

"I've got a press conference scheduled for noon on the steps of the courthouse. I expect a pretty good turnout for that," she said.

"I'll follow you over there in my car."

"I was thinking that it might be better if you went back to the other side and checked on that Dodge Viper."

"Yeah, I suppose."

"You could check out of your hotel, if you want to move into Jimmie's place in Kahana. It will save you some money. It's your place now."

"I don't have the address or the keys."

"I can get those for you."

"Good. I'll see you soon."

"Turn on a TV at noon. I'm probably going to be on all the local news stations."

"In person, I mean."

"Yes, tonight. Around seven."

She took a notepad and pen out of her pocket and wrote down the address for him. She handed the paper to him. He was already counting the minutes, and had a big grin on his face. They walked down to the truck side by side, close together, almost touching. Joe was there tidying up after last night. He smiled at them, apparently assuming they had slept together.

"Sleep well?" he said with a mischievous grin, not expecting a response and not getting one. "I'll drive you down to your cars."

They got into the truck and Joe said to John, "Can you do me one big favor?"

"Sure."

"Give me one ride to Lahaina. I no like take my truck on da highway. I get one ride home later, with Kenny."

"Okay, glad to do it."

They bounced down the bumpy road. Water levels had dropped considerably, and it was a relatively easy drive. When they got to the cars, Joe pretended to busy himself with something on his truck, as John and Lani said goodbye. She drove down the hill in her CRV, and John and Joe followed in his car. With her four-wheel drive and high ground clearance, she was able to make a lot better time on the road, and by the time they reached the lower gate she was gone.

17

John and Joe drove toward Lahaina in his convertible. John couldn't seem to wipe the silly grin off his face. She liked him, she really did. They had touched. They had kissed. He would be with her tonight. Life was glorious this morning. After they passed by a couple of the steep northern valleys, they came to the open rock field that John had noticed before. John wanted to know and he didn't want to know, but in the end he asked Joe, "Is this the place where—?" He couldn't quite form the words.

"Yeah, this is where it wen happen. You like take a look?"

John didn't answer, but he pulled over and parked in the wide spot in the road where stone steps led up to the field. The blissful mood of the morning was quickly fading. John sat silently in the car, trying to decide if he wanted to go up or not.

"Up to you, brah. I understand if you no like see," Joe said.

Finally John made up his mind, and he and Joe got out of the car and walked up the steps. The area was about half the size of a football field, and littered with lava rocks. Across the blue-water channel, where waves were beginning to chop up white in a morning wind, stood the mountains of Moloka'i. He looked across the field. Just one corner of the *heiau* was still standing. John knew that originally it had been a stone platform with thatched grass structures on top. Joe led him to the spot where Jimmie had been found, Sunny standing over him with the murder weapon in his hand. From here he could see two of the coastal valleys in the direction of Lahaina. He could make out the thin brown line where the road was cut into the rock face of the cliff. He looked out over the water. It was starting to cloud up now, and the top of Moloka'i was disappearing in the mist. There was no sound except for the gusting wind and the waves thumping on the rocks below. He could not keep himself from imagining what had happened at this place at sunset, just one week ago. And how it had changed his life completely.

Back in the car, they drove along the cliffs until they came around a bend and hit the paved road. John picked up his cell phone and had a signal, so he called Sam Peters. Sam gave him the name of two rental car agencies, both in Lahaina, that rented Dodge Vipers. John had Joe write them down. Before he rang off, Sam reminded him, "You didn't get this from me." John put the phone down and asked Joe, "Can you give me directions to these places?"

"I go with you."

"I hate to take up your time."

"I like see what wen happen, same like you."

As they passed by Kapalua, Joe had him make a turn off the highway, and they drove down a newly paved two-lane blacktop past a driving range and a restaurant. It was starting to rain. Joe directed him to make a right turn into a parking lot and they pulled up in front of an old-looking plantation style building with a sign identifying it as "The Honolua Store."

"Breakfast," Joe said simply.

"My treat," John said.

They ran through heavy rain and into the store. It was an old building with a worn wooden floor. The front part of the store sold golfing clothes and tourist stuff. Through a large doorway, the back part was sort of an old-fashioned grocery store, and at one end there was a counter where plate lunches and Hawaiian-style breakfasts were offered. The menu was painted on boards on the wall, and John asked Joe many questions: What's a loco-moco? What is Portuguese sausage? Joe placed his order and went to a machine to get some coffee, while John tried to figure out what he wanted. Finally he realized that after the big meal last night, he wasn't even that hungry. He asked if they had poi, and he ordered a double serving of that. He browsed through the glass-doored refrigerators and found his favorite drink, and they took their food to the counter near the front door, where John paid. They sat at picnic tables on the lanai outside and ate. The rain was coming down in buckets, running off the tin roof over their heads and bringing out another set of fragrances from the pine trees and the damp earth. John breathed it all in. Rain or shine, he loved it here.

"What you stay drinking?" Joe asked him.

John held up the small yellow bottle. "Yoo Hoo."

"Yoo Hoo and poi. You one crazy mixed-up dude, brah."

John grinned at him and thought of seeing Lani in a few more hours. His happy mood returned as he sucked the poi from his fingers and washed it down with Yoo Hoo.

They got back into the car and drove toward Lahaina. As they headed south the skies began to clear, and soon the roads were dry as well. It hadn't rained there at all. Joe explained that in Lahaina, it rains like a son of a bitch about two times a year. The rest of the time it's hot and dry.

The first rental car place was easy to find, right on the highway north of town. Outside were parked a yellow Plymouth Prowler, a two-seater, with its distinct bicycle fenders, and a red Ferrari, like the one from the TV show *Magnum P.I.* Apparently some tourists liked to pretend to be Tom Selleck while they were in Hawai'i.

They parked the car and went in to inquire about a yellow Viper. They were told that they only had a red Viper, but it was rented out. Wouldn't they like to take the Prowler? It was yellow. Apparently there was a mistake. They had never had a yellow Viper.

They left disappointed and drove into Lahaina. It was packed with tourists, and a large cruise ship moored in the channel had added its load to the usual crush on the sidewalks. They parked in a lot and walked a couple of blocks to the address they were given. It was a small rental agency that specialized in Harley-Davidsons, but right in front a yellow Dodge Viper was on display, apparently the only one on Maui. John found himself growing increasingly excited. He didn't actually know if this car had anything to do with Jimmie's murder, but it was a lead, something of substance. They walked into the small office. The *haole* guy behind the counter was dressed in typical dealing-with-tourists attire, black long pants, black shoes and socks, and a reverse print Aloha shirt, tucked in at the waist. He smiled and looked up as the door opened, then his expression changed as he saw the two Hawaiian guys in T-shirts, rubber slippers, and shorts walk in. *It's pretty obvious we're not customers*, John thought. They walked up to the counter.

"Howzit," John said.

"Hi, how you doing?"

"I wanted to ask you about that Viper in front."

The guy visibly brightened. Customers after all?

"You rent that out a lot?" John asked.

"You bet. It's a very popular car. If you want it, I suggest you snatch it up before it's gone."

"Can you tell me who you had it rented to last Monday evening?"

The guy looked at them suspiciously now. "Why do you want to know that?"

John tried to sound as official as he could. "This is in connection with a police investigation."

"You guys are cops?"

"We're working with the police, yes."

"Got some ID?"

John realized that pulling out a New Jersey driver's license would get him nowhere. "We're trying to do this informally. If you don't talk to us, you'll just have to deal with the police later."

"Listen, I don't know what this is about, but I need to see a court order, or something. At least a badge."

Joe was getting exasperated. "Why can't you just tell us, brah. What's the big deal?"

The guy didn't like this tone, and he was starting to get his back up now. "That kind of information is confidential. Maybe you guys are trying to find out something about a customer of mine. Maybe it's a divorce case or something. I can't just tell anybody who walks in here what people were doing with my cars. No, no way. A cop walks in here, maybe. But not you guys."

There didn't seem to be much point in arguing, so they left the office and walked out into the bright sunlight. The yellow Viper sat there in front of them, a taunting, frustrating challenge. *Where were you last Monday evening?* John wanted to ask it.

"Why don't you call your cop friend?" Joe asked.

"I'll call him. But he may not be able to help. Supposedly there's no investigation going on. They have their murderer."

He pulled out his cell phone to call Sam, but they were interrupted by a brown-skinned man dressed in coveralls who came out of the garage next to the office wiping his hands on a blue shop towel.

"Hey, Joe!" he called out.

Joe smiled and walked up to him and they shook hands in the Hawaiian way and then clapped each other warmly on the back. Joe introduced him to John.

"John, this my frien' Garrett."

John extended his hand. "Hi, Garrett, nice to meet you." John caught the disconcerted look he was getting used to, a Hawaiian guy sounding like a tourist from the East Coast.

Joe spoke to Garrett. "What, you stay working here now?"

"Motorcycle mechanic. Pretty good job."

"Your boss one real tight-ass, yeah?"

Garrett laughed. "Yeah, he da nervous type. What you doing here, anyway?"

Joe pointed toward the Viper. "Trying to find out who wen rent this car. Guy no like tell us notting."

"Figures," Garrett said.

"Can you help us out or what, brah, maybe take a look at the records, give us a call?"

Garrett looked dubious.

John said, "We don't want to get you fired or anything."

"No, dass okay," Garrett said after a moment. "I wait until he stay at lunch or someting. Gimme yoah numbah."

He pulled a pad and pencil from the pocket of his overalls and took down John's cell phone number.

"What dates you like know about?" Garrett asked.

"January 11."

Joe added, "We like know da name of the person who wen rent it. Plus any other information, address, phone, driver's license, you know."

Garrett wrote it down. "January 11, okay, I go take a look and let you know." He thought for a moment. "Hey, dass just last week, yeah?"

"Monday," John said.

"No need look at da records. Dat car was heah all day," Garrett told him.

"Are you sure about the day?"

"Car was heah all *week*, brah."

"That guy in the office said it's rented all the time." John said.

Garrett laughed. "Bullshit. He tell any kine fo' rent dat car."

"Maybe somebody took it in the evening?"

Garrett shook his head. "I wen work late on Monday, until ten o'clock, fixing one bike some tourist ran off da road. Dat yellow car was sitting there da whole time, guarans, brah."

John and Joe thanked Garrett and walked back toward their car. John was feeling completely deflated. It was turning into a real up-and-down day. He realized that he had pinned too much hope on the kid with the toy cars. He should have known better, but after all, they were grasping at straws. They were going to have to come up with something really substantial or Sunny was going to spend the rest of his life in prison. And the real murderer was going to get away with it. They got into the car, and he saw that it was nearly noon. "Where can we find a TV?" he asked Joe. "I want to see the press conference."

Joe directed him to a small barbeque joint on Front Street, just a little north of town. John parked the car in what he figured had to be one of the most scenic parking lots on Earth, surrounded by palm trees and facing the harbor. Inside the restaurant there was a TV set over the bar. Many of the tables were occupied, but no one else was at the bar, and they asked the bartender to tune it to the local news channel. They sat down and ordered a coke and a beer. John had to admit, he wasn't sure if it was the conference or Lani that he so wanted to see. To his surprise, the news opened right up with a "breaking news" graphic and went directly to the courthouse. This was indeed a big story on Maui. And there was Lani standing in front of a group of reporters on the steps of the courthouse. He was nuts about this beautiful woman, and, amazingly, she liked him. It was staggering. It was unbelievable. She seemed very at ease despite all the microphones and cameras pointed at her, and he felt proud of her. She identified herself as counsel for Sunny Waikoloa and announced that she had a brief statement to make, but first she wanted to read an official press release from James E. Putnam, "Recent murder victim and Vice President of Zodiac International." She went on to read the release that Jimmie had written, then made her statement.

"I have had no desire to try this case in the press," she said. "But those who wish to see my client convicted have been doing exactly that. I felt it necessary to respond. The points I wish to make clear are these: Number one, my client, Sunny Waikoloa had no motive, no motive whatsoever, for killing Mr. Putnam. Number two, James Putnam feared for his life, not from Sunny Waikoloa, but from his own employer, Zodiac International. That's all I have to say, and I would prefer not to answer any questions at this time." She tried to step away, but they had her cornered.

A reporter asked, "What was the date of this press release?"

Lani said, "January 10, the day before Mr. Putnam was murdered. It was never announced officially by Zodiac, I think for obvious reasons. But it is an official press release by an executive of the corporation who was authorized to issue press releases. We felt that the public has the right to know of its existence."

The first reporter asked her, "What does Zodiac have to say about it?"

"You'll have to ask them," Lani told him.

She took no more questions, despite the persistence of reporters, who followed her down the steps and across the plaza until they reached the end of their cables. The camera switched to a reporter on the scene, who said, "Well, there you have it, a highly unusual statement for a defense attorney to make. But then this whole case has been unusual."

She was interrupted by the anchors in the studio, who now appeared in an inset on the screen. "Tricia, has there been any response from Zodiac International?"

"No, Herb," Tricia said into her microphone. "It's too early for that. I expect that we'll be hearing from them before long, though."

18

Charles Brewster, sitting in his office at the Honolua Bay hotel, switched off the set. He was glad he was alone for a change. He had to think things through. A few days ago the situation couldn't have been better. Sunny Waikoloa, the one guy who could stop his project, had been arrested for the murder of a key Zodiac employee. Brewster couldn't believe his luck. It was a public relations coup. Sunny wasn't even denying that he had killed Putnam. And after confessing the crime on videotape in front of witnesses, he had clammed up and wouldn't even talk to his lawyer. It was perfect, just perfect.

As soon as the news had hit, he had started his calls, first to Hawai'i state senator Alfred Toguchi. Toguchi agreed that this incident could turn the tide in favor of the casino project and of legalized gambling in Hawai'i. Toguchi had seemed a little put off by Brewster's obvious glee at the situation, considering that one of his own longtime employees had just been killed. Brewster didn't care. A ripe plum had fallen in his lap, and he was going to enjoy eating it. Of course, Toguchi wanted him to wait a few days before exploiting the situation. That was Hawai'i for you. They were never in a hurry for anything here. On the mainland, he could have the police, maybe even the national guard, up there in the valley making arrests. This was an opportunity to implicate them all in the murder. This handful of people, this brown bunch of taro farmers, their feet in the mud, who had been responsible for stopping a project of this importance for two long years, were finally going to get their comeuppance.

Then this Rossi clown from New Jersey showed up, and everything changed. The D.A., who had made three gambling junkets on the BBJ, was keeping Brewster informed. The defense wanted to look for bullet wounds, for God's sake. And now this damned press conference.

There was a quiet knock on the door and Bennett came in.

"You saw that?" Bennett asked him, motioning toward the TV.

Brewster nodded his head.

Bennett said, "Putnam, that son of a bitch. He deserved to die, got what he deserved. Fucking traitor."

"So you believe that press release was real?" Brewster asked with a sneer.

"Wasn't it? I mean, we knew that he was sympathetic to those guys."

"We knew, no one else did," Brewster said. He thought for a moment before a nasty smile creased his face. He suddenly stood up and slapped the top of his desk. "So here's what we're going to do: First, we prepare our own press release. We deny that Putnam's is authentic. Second, we get the judge to impose an immediate gag order. No more trial by press. Third, we deal with this woman attorney. I want the D.A. to look into disbarment proceedings. Misuse of the press."

"I don't know that that's grounds for disbarment."

"Doesn't matter. All we have to do is leak it that she's being investigated."

"I'll call McKay," Bennett said. "What about a press conference of our own?"

"I wouldn't give them the satisfaction. Publicly we respond in a low-key manner, but I want action on this. Now!"

Bennett scurried out the door.

19

After they finished their lunch, John and Joe went out to the car. "Where can I drop you?" John asked him.

"I gotta find one friend of mine. You think you can take me over to the Ace Hardware in town? I need to pick up some stuff and I'll call him from there."

As John got ready to start the car, his cell phone rang. A Hawaiian man's voice asked to speak to Joe. John handed him the phone. Joe listened for a few moments, then said, "Okay, I'll tell him. Tanks, eh?" He handed the phone back to John.

"Dat was my cousin, Garrett."

"From the car rental place."

"Yeah. He wanted to know if we just wanted to know about rental Vipers or privately owned too."

"Any one."

"Well, one of the other guys at the shop says he saw one last week."

Another Viper. "Where?"

"On one flatbed truck. Like just came in from the port."

"Where was this?"

"Kapalua."

So maybe the car had just come in and wasn't registered yet, John thought. "Okay, I'm going to go up there and check it out."

"Kapalua one pretty big place. Could be anywhere. Could be inside one garage."

"The thing is, if Garrett's friend is right, we now know there's another Viper somewhere on this island." The question was, how were they going to find it?

They drove back into Lahaina and John dropped Joe off at the Ace Hardware store. It seemed to be getting hotter and hotter in town. Before leaving the parking lot, John put up the convertible top and turned on the air-conditioning. He had a lot of time to kill before meeting Lani. He cruised down Front Street and saw a sign for a public library. A rare parking space was opening up at the curb, and he waited patiently while a tourist in a large rental car pulled out of the tight space. He parked there and went around to the front door of the library. The building was in an incredibly beautiful location facing the harbor. Inside, browsing the stacks specializing in Hawaiian books, a memory came flooding back: When he was thirteen years old he would sneak off to the public library in Bloomfield to read about Hawai'i.

But he had not come in here to read about the islands. He went over and found a seat in front of a computer connected to the internet. Jimmie once told him that Brewster had allowed himself to be interviewed by a journalist for an alternative press magazine, perhaps thinking he could get himself a more hip image. The reporter had asked some annoying questions. Jimmie had actually been there when security guards not so gently escorted the man from the office. An unflattering article followed. John wanted to read what the man had written. It took several attempts with a search engine, but he finally found the article, in a magazine called *Appleseed*. He scanned through what started out as an ordinary sounding interview until he found the place where the reporter asked about Brewster's widely reported doctoral degree from Princeton.

I told him, "Perhaps I should be calling you Dr. Brewster." Charles Brewster looked almost embarrassed, and his voice was full of modesty. We had the following exchange then. I'm giving it to you verbatim here, as I tape-recorded it."

Brewster: Dr. Brewster sounds so stuffy. I generally ask people not to call me that.

Me: And your doctorate is in what area of study?

Brewster: Philosophy.

Me: Interestingly enough, I checked with Princeton, sir, and they tell me that while you took several graduate level courses there, they have no record of a degree being issued. Perhaps you could clarify that for me.

Brewster: Princeton? Who said anything about Princeton?

Me: You did, sir.

Brewster: No, I believe you were the one who said that.

Me: Could you tell me then, sir, what university is your doctorate from?

Brewster: As I told you, I never asked anyone to call me doctor.

Me: But are you saying—

Brewster: My graduate degrees are a matter of public record, and I have nothing more for you on that subject.

Me: Very well then, sir, perhaps we could discuss your military record. You have often talked about

> flying with the Marines in combat in Viet Nam. If I am not mistaken, that model on your desk is a replica of the F-4 Phantom jet you flew. I noticed that it even has a decal with your name on it next to the cockpit.
>
> Brewster: Some of us were patriotic and served our country well. Some people fled to Canada with their tails between their legs.
>
> I have to admit, I was impressed. Brewster had done his homework. I had spent the war years in Canada, I'm proud to say. In any case, that was the end of the interview. Two uniformed and armed guards suddenly appeared in the office to escort me out of the building. I would have liked to hear Brewster's response to my inquiry with the United States Marine Corps, which had him listed as a former mess officer at Miramar Naval Air Station. While there, he had probably seen a Phantom jet, but had never flown one, and he never left the country during the war. Among many other questions, I didn't get an opportunity to ask him about the time he claims to have played Bobby Fischer to a draw in a pickup chess game in a park in New York City. I couldn't reach Mr. Fischer, but a little research showed that he was in Europe at the time of the supposed match. Maybe Brewster was a little off on the time. Or maybe the man is a pathological liar.

The rest of the article went on to describe Brewster's efforts to get the reporter fired. When that didn't work, he attempted unsuccessfully to buy the outstanding debt of the publication to shut it down. This was followed by sudden and mysterious, perhaps unrelated, visits from the fire department and health department, and an auditor from the State Franchise Tax Bureau. In the end, he failed to prevent publication, but who ever heard of *Appleseed* anyway?

John printed off copies of relevant pages, paid the librarian, and got back into his car to drive north. He decided to have a look at the resort of Kāʻanapali , which he had passed several times in the last couple of days. Driving north on the highway, he made the left turn into the Kāʻanapali area. The road on the beach side was lined with high-rise hotels. There was not even a glimpse of the beach or the ocean from the road. The other side of the road was golf courses. He thought it strange that people would come to a place like this, with its splendid scenery and beaches, and play golf, something they could do back home in Michigan or wherever. There was a public parking garage, and he left the car there. A shopping center next to the garage featured stores with expensive brand names such as Versace, Gucci, and Prada. He wondered what these stores were doing here, why people would want to come to Hawaiʻi to shop at a store they could find in any big city. It made no sense to him. On the beachfront, he walked along the pathway between the beach and the hotels. He traveled the concrete sidewalk from the Sheraton Hotel at the north end to the Hyatt at the other. The place was packed with tourists, the swimming pools lined with wall-to-wall chaise lounges placed inches apart with identical hotel towels and their sunburned occupants. He thought with deep sadness of the pristine Kalonahoa Valley, lined with high-rises, the ringing of slot machines from casino floors audible on the beach. Was it really necessary for every beach on the island to be "developed"? Couldn't some small part of Hawaiʻi remain untouched?

20

Charles N. Brewster didn't think so. In his display room were several tables containing the architectural models of the development at Kalonahoa. It was where he went when he needed to recharge the batteries, restore his spirits. He seemed to be needing to do that more and more lately.

His venture had all started with such promise. He'd long had his eye on Hawai'i as a place for a major investment. He had met his fourth wife, Wainani, in Atlantic City, just after the Miss America contest had concluded. She was there representing her state as Miss Hawai'i. With her dark good looks, she stood out among all the blonde beauties. And there was another thing he knew about her. She was an heir to the throne of the Kingdom of Hawai'i. The last reigning monarch was Queen Lili'uokalani in the late 1800s. She had died leaving no children. But Wainani could trace her heritage back to the first king to unite the islands, Kamehameha the Great. There were various sovereignty movements trying to restore Hawai'i to independent nation status along with the monarchy, and most of them recognized Wainani as the heir apparent.

Not that this was going to happen anytime soon, but if it did, and he happened to be married to her, he would be the king. The goddam king! And with casino gambling legalized, he would be the king of one of the wealthiest monarchies on earth. Even if Hawai'i remained a state, he could be its most powerful citizen. He knew that Hawai'i was perfectly positioned to draw off wealthy Asian gamblers who would otherwise have to go to the seedy casinos of Macao or fly all the way to Las Vegas. In the Kalonahoa Valley, he would begin his new empire. He had sold the idea to the legislature, the labor unions, and the public as "limited" casino gambling. But what the limits were, was not clear. The implication was that it would be limited to the one remote valley, which would be accessible initially only by hovercraft and helicopter, and soon after by a new road cut through the West Maui mountains. But for Brewster, there were no limits. He knew that, once gambling was legal, he would be able to put casinos everywhere on the islands, and draw in not just the high-rollers but the average tourist, and indeed the average Hawaiian. These people loved to gamble, it was in their blood. There were all kinds of illegal betting going on already—cockfights, Pai Gow, you name it. All it needed was one man to take control.

He looked over his model of the casino. Eighty thousand square feet. Three hundred artificial palm trees indoors, each costing over fifty grand. The recorded sound of the ocean piped into the building. The Hawaiian night sky with twinkling lights painted on the ceiling. Fully air-conditioned to overcome the daytime heat of the valley, simulating a pleasant evening in paradise. Hawai'i as it could be, should be. No one would ever have to go outside. It was better than Disneyland. He was a goddam genius. And what a tremendous benefit it would be to Hawaiians. Six thousand new jobs. To get the legislature to consider enacting gambling, he'd agreed to pay $100 million for his operating license, enough money to put every Hawaiian high school graduate through four years of college. This fact had been trumpeted in a series of "public service" TV ads, showing the fresh, smiling faces of jubilant young people in cap and gown. Of course the $100 million was nothing compared to the profits that he would be taking out of here. He was surprised and delighted that his friends in the legislature were willing to settle for so little. Not that he expected to ever come up with the money, really. Business was like sex: promise anything to get what you want, but once you've gotten it, there's no need to follow through afterwards.

The phone in the room buzzed. Everyone knew he was not to be disturbed when he was in here, so it had to be something urgent. He left the room, his revived spirits already beginning to sour. Bennett was waiting for him in his office.

"Sorry to disturb you, Charles, but I heard from the D.A. They did another autopsy. There was no evidence of a bullet wound."

"Of course not."

"But the defense attorney is insisting that the body be examined by the Honolulu coroner. I don't think that Rossi is going to go home until the body does."

"Great," Brewster said bitterly.

"Also, the D.A. wants to talk to you really badly about that press release. I told him it was bogus, but he insists."

"Have we heard from the judge about the gag order?"

"Bud talked to him. He's on a case in Honolulu today. He'll be back tomorrow, and he promises a ruling by noon."

Brewster sat down heavily on a sofa. He had to find some way to turn all this in the right direction. Everything he had been setting up for years was at risk. He found himself gazing at a portrait of his beautiful Hawaiian wife on the wall across the room. On a credenza below the portrait was a good sized scale model of his personal Boeing jet. A smile crossed his lips as he turned to Bennett. "Call the D.A. and tell him we're going to have a press conference at six this evening."

"A press conference? What are we going to say?"

Brewster's smile broadened. "Let's do it in the same place, on the courthouse steps. Have Agnes call the media, tell them there's going to be an important announcement."

With that, he dismissed Bennett with a wave of his hand.

21

John finished his self-guided tour of Kāʻanapali and drove north to Napili, to the address he had gotten from Lani. She wasn't supposed to be there for another forty-five minutes, but he couldn't wait. Her house was on a potholed street that went up the hill from Lower Honoapiilani road. He found it almost at the top of the hill, set back behind a vacant lot. It was a green, freshly painted little plantation type cottage raised a few feet above ground level, with large overhanging eaves and a lanai stretching around three sides of the house. Behind the house was a gully leading down from the mountains above. Looking up that way as far as he could see, the land was planted in pineapple. There were some comfortable-looking rattan chairs on the lanai, and John went up the porch steps and took a seat to wait for her. From here he had glimpses of the sea, and good views of both Lānaʻi and Molokaʻi. An hour passed, and he began to imagine that their impulsive moments of last night and this morning had not been real, or that she had reconsidered and would not be happy to see him there. When she drove up a few minutes later, her smile and a tender embrace dispelled all doubts, and simply melted him. He could hardly think of anything to say.

"You did great on TV," he finally said.

"That's going to give me trouble. I'm going to catch hell from the judge."

"It was the only thing you could have done."

"Brewster is doing a press conference at six. That's why I'm running late. I was trying to find out what it's about, but I couldn't get anything. We'll have to watch it on TV like everyone else."

She opened the door with her key and they walked in. It was a neat and cozy little place, with polished wood floors and white wood-paneled walls. The rustic rattan furniture was upholstered with colorful Hawaiian prints. Pictures from old Hawai'i hung in koa wood frames. She picked up a remote control from a small wooden table and switched on the TV set.

"John, I had in mind to cook a meal, but I haven't had time to shop. Would you mind if we just order a pizza or something? I'll give you a rain check on the home cooking."

All John could think about was that now he had still another date lined up with her. "Sounds great," he said.

She dialed her phone and placed the order, while the news program came on. John turned up the volume, and she came and sat by his side on the sofa. It was a small sofa, and he was acutely aware that they were nearly touching.

Brewster's news conference was the opening item, and the scene quickly switched from the studio to the steps of the courthouse where a podium and microphones had been set up. Brewster was there, as was Bennett. At Brewster's side was a very pretty young Hawaiian woman. John had expected to see Brewster in some extravagant koa-paneled room in a fancy hotel. Instead, he was in the exact same place where Lani had been at noon. It seemed ominous. It was. Bennett took the microphone. "Mr. Brewster would like to make a statement."

He handed the mic to Brewster, who stood there waiting for absolute silence before continuing. He seemed to have shadows under his eyes, as if he hadn't been sleeping. Lani noticed this.

"He needs better makeup."

John said, "It probably *is* makeup."

Finally Brewster spoke. There was a waver in his voice, a man undergoing some great emotion. John figured it was a crock, some kind of act, like the haggard look.

"At noon today, as you already know, the defense team representing Mr. Sunny Waikoloa made a statement implicating my company, Zodiac International, and by inference, me, in the murder of our close friend and associate Jim Putnam."

He paused for a moment, as if it were difficult to go on.

John said, "Defense team? Who are the other members, I wonder?"

Lani seemed to be taking it all seriously. "Shh," she said.

Brewster continued, "When I arrived in Hawai'i, I experienced the warm welcome known here in the islands as 'aloha.' It made me want to strive to do the best for folks here. I knew that I would be providing thousands of jobs for the people of Hawai'i, but I wanted to do more. That is why I insisted on my Education For All program to provide a full, four-year college education for any high school graduate who wished to attend university. That is why I have worked closely with local interests to promote the planting of taro. That is why I directed that funding be provided for the Brewster Center for Cultural Research, which I had the pleasure of dedicating last month at the University of Hawai'i at Manoa."

He stopped for a moment, as if deep in thought. "But my project, which I had hoped would be nothing but a positive for the good people of Hawai'i, has resulted in the death of someone I cared about deeply. And now, these terrible accusations, have wounded my wife and me grievously. I could never have envisioned such an outcome in a work that started out so wonderfully. I am not sorry I came to Hawai'i, but I am truly sorry if I have been in any way responsible, however remotely, for introducing friction and sorrow to these islands, the home of my lovely wife, Wainani."

He paused, choked up, unable to go on. He looked at his wife, and she smiled up at him and gave him an encouraging hug, as if he needed it to be able to speak. John mimed a violin playing, and Lani give him a playful elbow. "Accordingly, it is with great sadness that I announce that I will discontinue my business activities on Maui and Wainani and I will leave Hawai'i immediately after this press conference terminates."

There was a murmur from the crowd, and Brewster waited for silence.

Lani suddenly sat up straight. "No!" she said. John noticed that even Bennett seemed to be stunned. Brewster continued, "So Hawai'i, I bid you a fond aloha. Despite the tragic circumstances, I will always remember with warm affection the many friends I have made here."

He and his wife waved to the crowd, Brewster with moist eyes and a heartbreaking attempt at a smile on his face. "Aloha, Hawai'i. Aloha," they called out to the crowd as they stepped away from the microphones and walked hand and hand followed by a shouting gang of reporters to a waiting limousine and drove off.

Lani was upset. "Dammit, he's getting away!"

John wasn't buying it. "He's not going anywhere. It's a pack of lies."

"John, he's on his way to the airport right now," she said. "He's going to get away with murder. Why would he stay?"

John had no answer to this. He just knew in his heart that Brewster was a consummate con artist and he believed nothing the man said. But as the TV cameras zoomed in on the departing taillights of Brewster's limo, he had to admit, it was a helluva performance.

It had been a bravura performance, Brewster thought, as the limo drove toward the airport. He looked across at Bennett in the jump seat facing him, caught his stricken expression, and laughed out loud, startling both his wife and Bennett.

"You might have told me about this," Bennett said resentfully.

"If I had, they wouldn't have seen the startled expression on your face. You were an integral part of the show, Dick." Brewster laughed again. "You were great."

"Well, I don't see what's so funny about making a business decision of this magnitude without consulting me. What am I supposed to do now?"

Brewster reached into his inside suit pocket and pulled out a sheaf of papers and handed them to Bennett.

"What is this?" Bennett asked him.

"Operation Clamor. I worked it out with Agnes this afternoon."

"While you had me rushing around doing meaningless errands?"

"Dick, to have my right hand man look as surprised as everyone else, well, that was something I needed."

Wainani had been listening to all this. "You mean this has all been another act? We're not really leaving?"

"Oh, we're leaving, all right," said Brewster. "But Operation Clamor is going to cause us to reconsider." He pointed to the papers in Bennett's hand. "By tomorrow labor unions are going to be on the courthouse steps demanding that the D.A. clarify his position on whether Zodiac International had anything to do with Putnam's murder. Agnes had a great idea, listen to this: The Coalition for 6,000 Jobs. They'll be screaming for justice. State legislators will be clamoring for my return. Their phone numbers are all in there. I predict I'll be back in two, maybe three days."

"He is risen," Wainani said sarcastically.

Brewster shot her a dirty look, and then went on while she fumbled in the limo's bar and poured herself a stiff drink. Brewster's happy look returned as he spoke to Bennett. Bennett's smile was widening. "I can't believe I didn't see this coming, after all the years I've known you. You old dog. I knew you wouldn't just pull out." Brewster smiled in satisfaction.

Brewster said, "Have a look at page eight. My masterstroke. I'm having Agnes bring in a half dozen actresses from California, dark, pretty young girls. She's going to set up media interviews outside several high schools here. There will be tears in their eyes as they wonder how they're ever going to be able to afford college, now that the Education For All program is going away.

Wainani had heard enough. "You creep," she murmured. "You fucking creep."

Brewster's hand moved with stunning swiftness as he punched her hard in the stomach, knocking the drink out of her hand. He would have slapped her face, but he needed her to look good in case there were cameras at the airport. She groaned and doubled over in pain. He spoke to her coldly. "Try to stay sober enough to make it up the steps of the plane, will you, dearest?"

Lani and John sat at her kitchen table and ate their pizza. John thought it was awful stuff, compared to New Jersey pizza, but he was hungry and wolfed it down. He told Lani about his reading at the library, and even though they had watched the TV as Brewster and his wife boarded the jet, waved from the door, and then flew away, he insisted that it had to be an act. They were interrupted by the ringing of John's cell phone. It was Joe, calling from Oliver's place in the valley.

"Hey, is it really true? Is Brewster out of here?" Joe asked him.

"I wouldn't bet on it. What do the people up there think?"

"You can still hear them cheering outside. You think he's gone for good?"

"I hate to spoil the party, braddah, but no, I don't think so. We'll see."

He switched off the call and noticed Lani looking at him tenderly. "You've made a lot of friends in a short time. You really care about people. That's a wonderful quality."

He smiled at her. "Honestly, I don't know that I've always been that way. This place has changed me. I really like these Hawaiian friends I've made. I'd sure like to help them out if I can."

"You know, Hawaiians are by nature friendly and welcoming. It's part of our culture. But there's sometimes a dark side too. You need to be aware of that. And be careful."

"What do you mean?" he asked her.

"You know that I've been looking into all possibilities, any others who might have been involved in Jimmie's murder."

John considered this puzzling statement. "I don't know what you're getting at."

"You know that besides Sunny, besides someone from the casino, there's also the possibility that someone else from the valley is involved. After all, Jimmie had betrayed them all. Or so they would have thought."

"I guess that's true."

"And one person in particular was Jimmie's special friend."

He thought about this for a moment, then looked at her in surprise. "You mean Joe?"

"He became a fast friend, didn't he? He's been sticking pretty close to you, keeping tabs on what you're up to."

"I can't believe he'd let Sunny go to jail."

"People will do almost anything to stay out of prison. Especially if they already know what it's like there."

"Are you saying that Joe is a criminal?"

She sighed and looked at him. "I know you want to see the good in people, especially the taro farmers, but there's something about Joe that you don't know." She looked away and hesitated a moment before continuing. "In 1981, Joe got into a fight with his best friend. They had both been on a beach, drinking. Joe hit his friend on the head with a piece of wood. The man later died, and Joe was convicted of manslaughter. He served ten years in prison."

Lani saw the upset look on John's face. "Look, I know that was over twenty years ago. It was an entirely different situation. I'm just asking you to watch out for yourself. Will you do that for me?"

"Okay, you're right. I'll be more cautious from now on." He looked into her dark eyes, as deep and shimmering and full of mystery as pools beneath a gentle Hawaiian waterfall. "But not with you. You I trust completely."

Their eyes locked on each other for a moment. He desperately wanted to kiss her, but thoughts of the unfinished business with Angela churned his stomach with guilt. He said to her, "Would like to hear some really nice music? I'd like to play a CD for you."

She smiled, and said, "It's getting late."

"You have to go to work tomorrow."

"And you have to go to Jimmie's place."

"Jimmie's place?"

"His condo in Kahana."

She got up and went to her purse and came back with a piece of paper and a key ring. She handed it to him. "Here's the address. These are Jimmie's keys. I got the police to give them to me."

John stood up and put the keys and the paper in his pocket.

"Maybe afterwards you can come to my office and we can have lunch together," Lani said.

"I'd like that," he said.

They walked to the door together. A warm embrace later and he was out the door getting into his car. She watched him leave, standing in the open doorway, backlit by the living room lights. In the rearview mirror, he could see her shadow on the lanai all the way down to the intersection with Lower Honoapiilani Road, where he turned the corner to the hotel. He hadn't been away from her for a minute, and he couldn't wait to see her again tomorrow.

22

The next morning he arose early and enjoyed a long swim in Napili Bay. The hotel served a sort of tropical continental breakfast, including papaya, sweet pineapple, taro rolls, and various fruit juices. He sat outside by the pool, still in his bathing suit, and enjoyed the warm sun on his back and the sight of Moloka'i lit by the morning light. Afterwards, he showered and dressed, and drove about ten minutes south to the condo in Kahana, a ten-story building called Kahana Hako, right on the beach. He took the elevator to the top floor and walked to the end of the hall to unit 1001. He opened the door and walked in.

Yes, he thought, *this is Jimmie's kind of place*. The decor was new and ultra-modern. Unlike the house in the valley, he could easily picture Jimmie living here. Then John was nearly overcome with sadness thinking that Jimmie would never again come home to this place. He walked into the living room and took it all in. There was a fabulous view of the ocean and the island of Lāna'i through a glass door leading onto a balcony overlooking the ocean. The place was spotless, obviously still being cleaned regularly by a maid service. A week's mail was stacked neatly on a kitchen counter. He looked through the mail to see if there was anything of significance. He found nothing that looked useful. There was a copy of a magazine called *Maui Business*, with a full-page photo of Charles Brewster on the cover. He picked out a couple of bills from the pile of letters. If Jimmie's will was substantiated, John was now the owner of this place. He'd have to find a way to keep things in shape for a sale, because if it was really his, he had no intention of living here. Even if he had a place, he wanted it to be more Hawaiian in feel, like Lani's house or the place in the valley. In the meantime, there was the usual detritus of death to take care of, bills to pay, a body still to be buried. After a thorough search of the place to see if Jimmie had left any additional clues to his murder, John left, carrying just the bills and the magazine. He resolved to find out all he could about Brewster. *Know your enemy.*

It was only 10:00 a.m., but he couldn't wait to see Lani. He drove across the island to her office and parked in front. She was with a client, a Polynesian-looking woman and her daughter. He sat in the waiting room and picked up the morning's *Maui News*. On the front page there was a picture of Brewster and his wife waving goodbye on the top step of his plane. The caption read, 'Aloha, Mr. Brewster, Aloha.' According to the article, Brewster's staff would be closing down operations for him. The loss of jobs was outlined, and the loss of "one of Maui's best friends ever." According to the article, Lani was going to be investigated for making public Jimmie's press release. It implied that she had acted unethically, if not illegally. What really made John angry was the full-page ad placed by the Zodiac Corporation, bidding farewell to Hawai'i and claiming innocence of any wrongdoing. It was cleverly worded and professionally laid out. John figured this whole tearful departure thing had to have been carefully orchestrated. And there had to be a reason.

He put the paper down in disgust and read the *Maui Business* magazine article about Brewster. It was a puff piece, outlining Brewster's plans for limited casino gambling and his already impressive contributions to the economy and culture. Besides the big stuff, like university buildings, Brewster had been busy making friends locally. He frequently used his jet to ferry cancer victims from outlying islands to Honolulu for treatment. He had paid for a new facility for a local canoe club. He bought ancient Hawaiian artifacts from private collectors and donated them to the Bishop Museum in Honolulu, and he put up the money to restore an old temple. When a Maui high school's band equipment was destroyed when their van caught fire during a trip to a football game, Brewster bought them a new van and brand-new, top-quality instruments. *Probably started the fire in the first place, you bastard*, John thought. The article favorably compared Brewster to Walt Disney for his imagination and to Andrew Carnegie for his generosity. He was listed in *Fortune* as one of the 400 richest people in America, with over $100 million in assets. The article described in some detail the intense screening to which he had been subjected by Maui's Department of Business Development, as Hawai'i's first potential casino licensee.

Finally Lani's clients left, and John went into her office. She was visibly upset. "Did you read the paper?"

"Yes."

"He's getting away with murder, and they're investigating *me*. I called the D.A. this morning and asked him to look for the yellow Viper, and you know what he said? 'Haven't you done enough to that man?' Instead of doing something about Brewster, they're talking about disbarment proceedings."

He looked at her, remembering the first time he'd laid eyes on her. She'd been angry then, and still she was beautiful. John said, "Well, I still like you."

She looked at him for a long moment, and then smiled and said softly, "Will you please get out of here so I can get some work done?"

"I'm bored," he said making a sour face and imitating a petulant child.

She laughed and said, "Go find something to do. The Bailey House Museum is right near by."

"I don't like museums. I think I'll go investigate somebody."

"Yes, good, you go investigate, have fun. Come back at one o'clock and we'll have lunch," she said, as she picked up her phone to make a call.

He left her office, taking the *Maui Business* magazine with him, and drove over to the Maui County office building. There was no place to park in the lot, and he realized he could easily have walked from Lani's office. He found a spot on a quiet street a couple of blocks away and walked to the building. In the lobby directory he found the name he was looking for, and he took the elevator to the fifth floor. There was no one at the reception desk, so he went directly to the office number from the directory. The door was open. Behind the desk sat Bill Rodgers, a fiftyish *haole* in a short-sleeved dress shirt and tie. Opposite him sat an extremely large young man with very dark skin and a black, bushy head of hair. They both looked up at him. John said, "I'm terribly sorry for the interruption." He held up the issue of *Maui Business*. "Are you the Bill Rodgers in this magazine?"

This proved to be the right thing to say, as Rodgers seemed to warm immediately. Apparently, he liked the recognition. John saw how he could play this.

"Yeah, that's me, alright. My fifteen minutes of fame."

John went over to the desk and stuck out his hand, as if meeting his favorite rock star. "John Rossi. *Very* pleased to meet you. Sounds like you did a really thorough job investigating Zodiac. I don't think I've ever read of a more disciplined, comprehensive, and methodical examination of an American corporation."

Each added adjective seemed to light up Rodgers's face a notch more. He smiled and motioned John to the empty chair next to the large young man, who sat completely impassively, looking at him.

"Yeah, well, the situation called for it, so we had to be thorough. Dot all the t's and cross the i's," he said.

John laughed as if he'd just heard the world's funniest joke. There was no reaction whatsoever from the other man.

"Of course, I can't take all the credit. Maka here did most of the work. He's a graduate of Wharton, you know."

John turned and smiled and shook hands with Maka, who did not smile or show any other emotion.

"Wharton, wow, no wonder the work was so meticulous and systematic."

Adjectives did not seem to work on Maka, who just looked at John with eyes barely visible in the folds of his huge face. Obviously, John's snow job might be working on Rodgers, but Maka wasn't buying it.

"Yeah, I'm lucky to have the big guy on my team. He earned himself a nice raise with his work on that report," Rodgers said.

"I'm not surprised. You know, the way this report is described, I'd sure love to have a look at it. Maybe show it to some of my classmates at business school."

This seemed to take Rodgers aback a little. "Well, you know we don't generally make copies of this kind of confidential information available."

"Oh? I thought it was a matter of public record."

Rodgers was getting a bit flustered. "Technically, yes. Well, I suppose it's okay." He motioned to Maka to come with him. "Maka, let's see if we can find a copy of that report for mister—what was your name sir?"

"Rossi, John Rossi."

The two of them left the office and John sat and waited for several minutes. He realized he shouldn't have given them his real name, in case Rodgers was checking up on him. He stood up and went to the office door, and glanced over the tops of the cubicles. Sure enough, there was Rodgers talking on the phone in an office on the other side of the room. John sat down again, wondering what excuse Rodgers would eventually have for not giving him the report. Rodgers walked in a minute later, not surprisingly empty-handed. Maka was nowhere to be seen.

"Sorry to keep you waiting Mr. Rossi. It seems we have already distributed all of our copies of the report."

"Can't you make another copy?"

"It's over a hundred pages long, you see, and we're pretty backed up on our copying right now. Maybe you can check back with us in a few days, and we'll have one for you then."

John knew it was a pack of lies, but he thought he should consult with Lani before making enemies here. He grabbed Rodgers hand and shook it vigorously.

"Okay, I'll give you a call next week then, see if it's ready. It was a genuine pleasure to meet you, sir."

He left the building and walked down the street toward his car. He had hoped to be able to study the report this morning, keep out of Lani's hair. *Lani's hair*, he thought dreamily, wishing he could just pop back in at the office, push her hair back and kiss her neck. These pleasant thoughts were disturbed by the sight of his car, which seemed to be sitting a little lower than he remembered. As he approached, he could see the reason. All of the tires were deflated. He quickly looked around for a culprit, but he had been absent for nearly forty-five minutes, and whoever did it could be long gone. He went over to the car and examined the tires. They had been slashed, not just had the air let out of them. Was this a common problem on Maui or had he been targeted? He checked the passenger door; it was still locked. He unlocked it and opened the glove box to get out his rental contract. There in the glove box was the answer to his question. A piece of bright red paper was marked with heavy black letters: "GO HOME."

He took the rental contract and the piece of paper and locked the car, then walked toward Lani's office. He didn't know if he should contact the police first, or the car rental agency. She would know the best way to handle it. If this was Brewster's work it was pretty juvenile for him. But, as he found himself constantly glancing over his shoulder, he realized it might be juvenile, but it was effective. He was walking between two buildings when he thought he heard a sound behind him. He turned quickly to look, but scanning down both sides of the street he could see that there was no one there. Now he was being silly, he decided, and he turned around then jumped back a step as he found his way blocked by Maka's huge form. They just stared at each other for a moment, before John said, "Why did you slash my tires?"

Maka almost smiled at him, then said, "Who are you, bruddah?" His voice was amazingly gentle for such a giant of a man. He sounded like some little accountant. Which he was, except for the "little" part.

"I told you. John Rossi."

"Somebody doesn't like you so much. Do you know who?" Maka asked.

"If I had to guess, I would say Charles N. Brewster," John said.

"I thought so, the way Bill was acting," Maka said. "Why do you want to see that report?"

John thought for a moment about how to answer this question. He decided that Maka was probably taking a chance talking to him, and John could take a chance on Maka. "I think Brewster, or more likely someone he hired, killed my best friend."

Maka nodded. It was obviously the kind of answer he'd hoped to hear. "James Putnam. I heard about it, of course. You think Brewster would do a thing like that?"

"Yes, I do," John answered.

"He might do something to you too. Tire slashing is kid stuff. You'd better start watching your back," Maka said.

"I intend to."

"And what do you expect to find in the report?"

"Lies."

Maka smiled at him, his huge cheeks nearly obscuring his eyes. He handed John a package he had been carrying. "I included some additional materials that may clear things up. Also, my home phone number is there, if you have any questions."

John took the package from him. "Why are you doing this?"

Maka said, "I'm a Certified Public Accountant. C.P.A. I take pride in what I do. My report is accurate, but they changed all my conclusions around. I could take my boss changing things. He's the boss, it's his signature, and it's his prerogative. But he sat in there and told you I'm responsible. He put my name on it when he did that, and that's not right. It's time someone heard the truth."

Maka turned then and started to walk away.

"And what is the truth?" John called after him.

Maka turned to him and said, "There's no way Brewster can just leave Hawai'i. If he does, he's going to lose everything. You can expect to see him again, and soon." Just before turning and walking away, he chuckled and added, "The fact is, I have more money than Brewster has. That man is flat broke."

23

John took the package back to Lani's office. She was with another client, so he sat on the sofa in her outer office, opened the brown paper wrapper, and started reading through the material. It was full of technical accounting jargon about reserves, methods of depreciation, and other terminology. He had to admit to himself, he couldn't really follow it. He guessed that Bill Rodgers probably couldn't either. Rodgers had undoubtedly been ordered to go through the report process and make sure Brewster got a clean bill of health, and that is exactly what he had done.

Far more illuminating than the report itself were the analysis and conclusion that Maka had prepared. These had never seen the light of day, and John could understand why. According to Maka, for years Brewster had been simply taking out one loan to pay off another. Most of his mainland operations were losing money. Brewster had made projections of revenues that invariably showed them becoming profitable next year, but these were only estimates and there was no indication of how or why they would swing from a loss to a profit. He had agreements from various banks to borrow an additional $200 million to construct the hotel and casino in Hawai'i. But buried in the financial statements was the information that half of that money would be going to pay off old loans on out-of-state debt.

Included were copies of letters Maka had sent out to Zodiac, their accountants and their attorneys, politely but firmly requesting explanations. Their responses were indignant letters from big Wall Street firms, from well-known law firms, and from Brewster's own staff. They claimed that all of his operations would soon be in the black, that most of the losses were mere paper losses taking advantage of tax write-offs, and that the casinos were much more profitable than they appeared. In the end, the opinion of a junior CPA hadn't counted for much and the way was cleared for Brewster to get a casino license, pending the passing of the appropriate enabling legislation.

The material confirmed everything John thought about Brewster, and added more. Now he knew why Jimmie had to die. Jimmie had gone native. Had he gone public with what he knew about Zodiac's scam of the taro farmers, he would have seriously damaged Brewster's chance of getting gambling approved by the legislature. Brewster was on the brink of financial disaster; inside revelations might have pushed him over. And now Brewster had pulled his disappearing act. Had he approved Jimmie's murder and wanted to escape prosecution or was there some other ploy involved?

Lani's office door opened. She saw her clients out, watching them get into their car. Only her Honda was still in the small parking lot.

"Where's your car?"

"I've had an interesting morning," he said. "Let's go for a little drive."

He grabbed Maka's package and his car rental papers and they got into her car. He directed her to the street where his car was parked. As they drove up the opposite side of the street, they could see that a policeman was there looking over the car. Lani gasped when she saw it.

"Do you think this was directed at you?" she asked him.

He handed her the threatening note, and she looked at him, concern in her eyes.

"John, someone's already killed Jimmie," she said.

"Jimmie didn't see it coming."

"He did. He made a will, and he wrote to you."

"Well, I don't think he really believed that they were capable of murder. I've got my eyes wide open." He saw the dubious look on her face.

The policeman saw them there and walked over to their car. "This your car?" he asked Lani, pointing to John's Malibu.

John got out and walked over to him. "It's mine," he said. He handed the cop the rental agreement.

"Show him the note too," Lani said.

John handed him the note. The cop looked at it and said, "Where did this come from?"

"It was in the glove box," John told him.

The policeman motioned to John to come over to his patrol car. He got a clipboard from the front seat and had John answer questions while he filled out a multi-part report form. Lani came over and listened to their conversation. After he finished with the form, the cop had one last question.

"Do you have any idea who might have done this?" he wanted to know.

John was about to answer, but Lani said, "No, we don't." This surprised John, and after the cop left he asked her about it.

"It won't do any good to accuse Brewster right now. And we don't want them to come back at us with a charge of libel, or filing a false police report," she said.

"They can do that?"

"I know they would. We're the bad guys right now in the eyes of the establishment."

John called Dollar to come and collect the car. Lani said that she thought she could get Jimmie's car out of the police impound lot where it had been towed after the murder, and it would save John the cost of renting another car. They went to lunch then, and over iced tea and burgers, John told her about the package from Maka. She thought it could provide good material for Sunny's case, but they still didn't have much of a defense against the murder charge itself.

"But we've got a lot of stuff," he protested.

"Think about it," she told him. "We've got an analysis that says Brewster is broke. But that's not necessarily a motive for murder, and they'll have their own analysis by their own accountants that says it isn't true anyway. We have a ten-year-old boy who claims to have seen and recognized a car, in the dark. But we don't have the car, not even a record of one. Even if it exists, even if it belongs to Brewster himself, it's no proof of his involvement in murder. There's no proof that Jimmie was going to turn against the casino except for the letter and the press release. It's just a couple of pieces of paper, and the prosecution will claim they're faked. What we have would be good evidence if the D.A. didn't have a video tape of Sunny at the crime scene, confessing to the crime, covered in blood, murder weapon in his hand, and with a possible motive, depending on who you want to believe."

John said, "It's almost like he's a political prisoner."

"It's a lot like that, John. And it's going to get worse. You should hear the reactions of the politicians to Brewster's departure. He's pumped millions into their campaigns, into their districts. The gravy train has departed, and they're seething mad at guess who? Sunny, the purported murderer."

John slumped in his seat. They could slash his tires and get away with it if they wanted to. Hell, they had probably killed his best friend. Now Joe and his friends were probably going to lose their valley and their homes. And Uncle Sunny stood to lose much, much more.

24

After lunch Lani drove John to the police impound lot near the airport. Jimmie's car was a red late-model Jeep Wrangler. She left John to process the paperwork for the car's release, and they agreed to meet at the jail afterwards.

As she drove to the jail, she thought about the slashing of John's car tires, and the note. John had become a threat to someone. If that someone had killed Jimmie, they might be willing to kill John too. And that she could not bear. She had fallen in love with him so quickly that it scared her. She had made two mistakes before: Ted, an Asian man, and Mike, her *haole* second husband. She had never met anyone of her own race who appealed to her. And along came this strong and handsome Hawaiian man who sounded like a *haole* from New Jersey. She couldn't fathom her own heart, why she had fallen so quickly. She just knew that she loved him, loved his honesty and integrity, loved seeing his stumbling efforts to be Hawaiian again. As a Hawaiian, she knew the value of *'ohana*, of family. She was determined now to help him find his, and she knew where she had to start.

She arrived at the jail for her interview with Sunny. A deputy brought Sunny into the interview room, removing the handcuffs and closing the door. She could read on his face his disappointment that John wasn't with her.

"Johnny Boy not coming?" he asked.

"He'll be here soon."

"He one good boy, Johnny. Always one great little kid. I knew he going turn out good, no matter where he grow up."

"Uncle, I need to ask you about that."

He sat in silence for a while. "Yes, you like know about him now dat you have aloha for him."

"It's not right to keep him in the dark."

"You know at first I nevah like tell him 'cause I was afraid he going leave. It was not just for me that it was important for him to stay, it was for him too." He reached over to raise her chin and look directly into her eyes. "And now for you too, I think."

She reddened, but didn't respond. He said, "You pure Hawaiian, yeah?"

"Yes."

"I thought so. He is too."

"Uncle, how do you know that he is the same little boy you knew thirty years ago."

Sunny smiled at her. "Because he look exactly like his father. Exactly. And I wen know his father well."

"Who is his father?"

Sunny sat deep in thought for a few moments. "If I tell you about this, you gotta promise not to tell Johnny about it."

"You know I can't do that."

"There's a reason. All this wen happen thirty years ago. The people from that time scatter all ovah the islands, and lots of them to the mainland. I nevah know who's dead and who's alive. You can see that he belongs here, not the mainland. I know he like stay here. I think it going break his spirit to get him thinking he can find his *'ohana* here when maybe they all dead now. I going tell you about them only if you promise to find out first if any of them are living. Then, if nothing turns up, I just tell him I wen make mistake."

Lani thought about this, and decided that Sunny was right. Why get John's hopes up and then dash them? "Okay, you have my word."

Sunny seemed satisfied with this, and he sat back in his chair and closed his eyes, taking himself back to thirty years ago. "This was in Makena, before they wen build all those big hotels ovah there," he began. He described an idyllic life, a group of families in small houses near the beach. They were fishermen there, and they knew where to find *uhu*, *aku*, *manini*, and they caught them in abundance. Some of the old *ahupua'a* system had somehow survived, and on the slopes above the beach Hawaiian farmers were growing taro, breadfruit, bananas, and other staples. They gave these to the fishermen in exchange for fish. When the *ahi* were running in the wintertime, if the prices were good, they were able to get enough cash to last them through the rest of the year. Not that they needed much. Between what they could grow and what they could trade, no one went hungry. Sunny had grown up there, and had been identified by the elders at an early age as one having the special powers. They took him under their wing and taught him the ancient prayers and the healing arts.

Of course, some in the little community did not believe in this Hawaiian hocus-pocus. There was a little wooden church, a Catholic church. The priest there was a *haole* from the mainland, Father Tom, who had lived in Hawai'i for many years. He was a charismatic man, and among his followers were the families of the man and woman who would become John's parents.

Lani interrupted him. "Can you tell me their names?"

"His mother was Aileen Kalakana, and his father was Keoni Punahuloa. I knew them well, saw them grow up together."

She wrote the names down on her legal pad.

Sunny continued with the story. When Aileen and Keoni were around seventeen years old, Sunny saw them together on the beach one day, and from the way they looked at each other, he could tell that they had become lovers. He also knew that Keoni was very attracted to the church and was deeply influenced by Father Tom. When Keoni graduated from high school, Father Tom offered him an opportunity to go into the seminary on the mainland, and Keoni accepted. Keoni had always craved adventure, and this would be the only chance he would get to travel and see some of the world. So he'd left Aileen behind, and about nine months later she gave birth to a son, whom she named Keoni, after his father. She did not tell anyone who the father was. Not that everyone didn't know. Everyone, that is, except Father Tom, who didn't want to see the truth of it. It was almost four years before anyone saw Keoni again, when he returned to the islands as a fully ordained priest. Father Tom proudly asked him to serve Sunday mass at the little church. He had decided to surprise the congregation with Keoni's arrival, and it was indeed a surprise.

When Keoni looked out into the congregation that day and saw Aileen and her little boy, he knew the boy had to be his. As soon as he could after the mass, he took Aileen aside, and she confirmed what he already knew. Spiritually, Keoni was rent asunder by the discovery that he was a father. He had returned to the islands in high spirits, thinking of all the good he would do as a pure Hawaiian priest. And now this, an illegitimate child. But Keoni was also a decent man, and he felt responsibility. He thought it would be right for him to get to know the boy. Aileen felt the same way. She could see the changes in Keoni brought by his years on the mainland. He was a stranger to her now, in his priest's cassock. They no longer had much in common, and she had no desire to live with him, even if he had been willing to give up the priesthood. But she did not want to deprive him of knowing his son, so when he asked to take little Johnny fishing in a borrowed canoe, she was glad.

They went out that day a little ways into the channel, and dropped their hand lines. And while Keoni was distracted with a fish on his line, Johnny somehow slipped overboard. It was several moments before Keoni noticed that the child was gone. He dived into the water and began a frantic search. It took two frenzied minutes before he found his son, tangled in a line under the boat. Little Johnny was blue and was not breathing. Keoni got him into the canoe and tried everything he knew to revive him, but the boy would not breathe. The young priest paddled frantically to the shore, praying feverishly. Sunny had been walking on the beach and saw Keoni coming in, saw that something was wrong. He waded out to meet the canoe. Keoni, his Catholic prayers unanswered, sat sobbing in the boat.

"My son, my son! I've killed my son!"

By this time others, including Aileen, had heard the commotion and came running down to the water. Keoni suddenly leaped out of the canoe and starting running up and down the beach, wailing and beating his chest.

Sunny stood over the still blue boy and began his healing chants, infusing the *ha*, the breath of life into little Johnny. He touched the boy's face, his chest, working to restore life. He asked others to join hands around him and the boy. Sunny continued his prayers in Hawaiian, while Aileen held her son's small hand and wept. And after a minute or two the boy began to retch, and then to take rasping breaths, and his color began to come back.

Keoni heard the cries of joy and rushed up to Aileen, his face a mask of bewilderment and rage. He scared her, and she scooped Johnny up and held him tightly to her breast. Seeing that the old Hawaiian prayers had worked and his own Catholic ones had not, he fell to his knees and pounded on the sand screaming and crying, before leaping up and trying to tear the little boy from her arms. While the people on the beach restrained him, Aileen ran with the child to her house. All that afternoon and through the night, she sat holding her boy, afraid that Keoni would come for him. As she later told Sunny, the more she thought about it the more she convinced herself that the near-drowning was not an accident.

All this happened at a time when Makena was changing. The people who had lived there for generations were about to be displaced by new hotel construction. As they had no clear legal title to their property, the entire community would be forced to leave. Aileen and her family were about to be evicted, penniless, from the only life they had ever known.

Father Tom had invested years in Keoni, his Hawaiian protégé. He couldn't bear to lose him now. But he was frightened by Keoni's frame of mind. He had seemed to go mad. What if Aileen was right, and the close call with the boy had not been an accident? The old priest couldn't bring himself to truly believe this, but he knew that he had to keep Keoni close to him, to help him regain his balance and his faith. But he couldn't take any risks with the little boy.

And so Father Tom hatched a plan. He told Aileen that Keoni was out of his mind and might try to kill Johnny again. The priest had connections on the mainland and would find a place where Johnny would be safe, where Keoni couldn't get to him. He would be well cared for by a wealthy Catholic family, just for a while, until things settled down. To protect him, only Father Tom would know where Johnny was.

Aileen at first refused. It was Keoni who should be sent away, not Johnny. Father Tom said he couldn't force Keoni to go. And besides, this was only temporary, just for a short time. Soon little Johnny would be back home, and he would be safe. Faced with poverty and uncertainty, given the danger to her boy, and trusting this priest she had known all her life, Aileen had agreed to send her son away for a little while. A couple of days later, he was gone. And a few weeks after that the bulldozers arrived, and the little houses were knocked down. Sunny decided to return to old family land in the Kalonahoa Valley and grow taro.

In the thirty years since these events, Sunny had left the valley only occasionally, and had rarely seen any of the people from Makena. He had heard that Father Tom died soon afterwards, and did not know if John's parents were dead or alive.

"Johnny says they told him his parents are dead," Lani said.

"Maybe, maybe," Sunny said, leaning back in his chair. Then he looked pointedly at Lani. "Or maybe they like fo' him to believe dat."

She didn't get time to think about this possibility. At that moment, the door opened and a jailor let John in. As usual, Sunny lit up when he saw him. And it was John whose face lit up when he saw Lani.

Sunny saw it immediately. "Something different, I think."

"What do you mean?" John asked him

"You two stay in love, now. You weren't before, but you are now."

Lani found herself blushing, and John smiled, just a little uncomfortable.

Sunny stood and hugged John. "I think you come looking for Hawai'i, Johnny Boy, but instead you wen find your own self."

"Yeah," John sighed, looking over at Lani.

She suddenly had the image of Johnny as a little boy, growing up in Makena. She longed to tell him the story, and she would tell him, but she wanted to find out about his family first. His parents, young as they were when he was born, would only be in their early fifties now. The priest, Keoni Punahuloa, shouldn't be that hard to locate through the church. The mother, even if she were still alive, might be tougher. She could have married and changed her name. She could be on any one of the islands or gone from the islands. The last name, Kalakana, was a fairly common one. Maybe if she made some calls she would find someone who was a relative. If his mother had passed away, maybe she could at least find a gravesite for John to visit.

She watched the two of them as John sat down next to Sunny. She sensed that Sunny was relieved to have unburdened himself to her. But what was he going to tell John if he asked about his mother and father? And ultimately, what would she be able to tell John about his parents?

John and Lani left the police station together, and as they walked in silence across the parking lot, he took Lani's hand. She squeezed his hand tightly in return. They did not look at each other, but simply walked hand in hand to her car. He was surprised how erotic the effect of just touching her was, and he felt himself getting hard. He hoped she wouldn't notice. They arrived at her Honda, and she turned to face him. They stood there looking at each other, still holding hands.

"I have to go back to my office for a while," she said. "Do you want to come?"

"Actually, I have some business to take care of. Maybe I can meet you later."

"Come to my house tonight. This time I'm really going to fix dinner for you."

"Okay." He smiled at her and lightly touched her face. She smiled at him, and got into her car and drove off. John watched her until her car was out of sight, then walked over to his Jeep. He climbed in and sat in thought. He loved Lani, there was no denying it. Even Sunny could see it. Maybe she loved him too. But he was living a lie. There was no putting it off any more, he would have to get things straight with Angela. He dreaded the conversation and her reaction. He didn't like doing it on the phone instead of in person. He was also more than a little worried about her father's reaction. You don't run out on the daughter of a mafia don. But one thing he knew: He couldn't let one more day, one more hour go by without facing up to it. He pulled out his cell phone and found that he had a good signal. A man and woman came walking past his car in an animated conversation that he could hear quite clearly in his open Jeep. He decided to drive to a more private place. He started the Jeep and drove out of the parking lot, heading toward the harbor. About ten minutes later he found a quiet spot off the main road. A big apartment block was on one side of the road, and on the other side was an empty lot and beyond that the sea. He pulled into the open area and parked near the water. It was 5:00 p.m. in Maui, so it would be 11:00 at night in New Jersey. He dialed Angela's home number. She answered sleepily.

"Hello?"

"Angela, it's John."

There was a moment of hesitation, and he was afraid she might have hung up on him. "Yeah, now what?" she finally said with a yawn he could hear clearly.

"I'm sorry about what happened last time we talked."

"Yeah, me too," she said in a tone that seemed almost bored. She sounded more than just drowsy. More like drugged or drunk.

"Angela, there's something important I need to tell you."

"Uh huh," was all she said.

He said, "Angela, I can't be engaged to you anymore. I'm so sorry," and waited for the explosion.

"Yeah, that's what I figured you were going to say," she said calmly.

"I'm sorry."

"You keep saying that." He could hear the rising anger in her voice. "Okay, just stay there. Don't bother coming back. I was getting along just fine before, and I don't need you now. When I think that I was willing to get married to someone like you just to make my father happy."

"But that's the way I've been feeling about it too. Like we're doing it for my parents, and for your father."

Her tone of voice turned threatening. "Well he's not going to be too happy when I tell him about this. That's something you'd better think about, John." Her tone was almost gleeful.

"Well, it's just something I have to do."

"Don't try that shit with me. I'm the one who's dumping you, don't try to turn it around. The fucking engagement is off!"

The connection clicked off, and John sat there in the silent car. He was burning his bridges behind him. He felt a sense of loss, but also of exhilaration. He wondered how Angela's father was going to take this. And his own family.

He knew it was late, but he dialed his sister's number. "Hello?"

"Aloha," John said.

It took her a moment, to figure out that it wasn't a crank call, before she responded in her smiling voice. "Johnny, I'm so glad you called. I wanted to tell you how sorry I am about Jimmie."

"Thanks, Lizzie."

"How are you coping?"

"It's been hard. I'm trying to find out what happened to Jimmie. But I've met some nice people here."

"How is Hawai'i ? Do you remember when we were kids, and you told me all about Hawai'i ? You even played the ukulele for me a few times."

"You remember that?"

"You had stars in your eyes. You wanted to go there so badly."

"I know."

"You finally made it. So how is it for you?"

"It's hard to describe. It's—it's everything, the whole place, the people, the way the air smells and feels. This is going to sound crazy, but it feels like . . . home. Lizzie, this is hard for me to say to you, as close as we've always been. I hope you won't take this the wrong way, but until I came here I never realized how lonely I was."

Lizzie was silent for a long moment before she spoke. "You're thinking about staying?"

"It's hard not to think about it."

"What about Angela?"

"We broke up."

There was surprise in her voice. "When did this happen?"

"Just now. It was no good, I can see that now."

"Finally!"

Her comment caught John by surprise. "I thought you liked Angela."

"I do. But I like you more. I know why you were going to marry her. For the same reason you've done practically everything in your life. For Mom and Dad."

"Lizzie, I would feel terrible to just abandon them, the business, you."

"Listen, between Mike and Louise, Rossi & Son will do just fine, despite Tony. Who knows, maybe if he doesn't have you to lean on even my brother will manage to get his act together. Mom did the best she could to love you as a son, but you know and I know that it wasn't what it should have been."

"I don't begrudge her anything."

"I know you don't. Maybe you should. I don't know. I think if I had been in your place, I would have run away from them years ago." She paused for a moment before continuing. "Johnny, there is one thing I would like you to do for me."

"Name it."

"Think of yourself and your own happiness for a change. It's okay to do that. It's allowed. Everyone else in the family has been doing that for years. Now it's your turn."

"Thanks, Lizzie. I love you."

"I love you too, big brother. Take care."

25

John drove back across the island to his hotel. Before long he was stuck in traffic, a steady stream of cars headed by a big, slow-moving yellow pineapple truck. He didn't care. Yet another magnificent sunset was taking place through his windshield. He thought of that trite bumper-sticker saying, "This is the first day of the rest of your life." But that's just what he was feeling, that a whole new life beckoned to him. A life here, a life with Lani in it. Making his way through Lahaina and Kā'anapali, he got to his hotel just as the sun touched the horizon. In minutes he had changed into a bathing suit. He trotted onto the beach and down into the warm water of Napili Bay. After swimming four full laps of the bay, a good two miles, he hauled himself onto the sand, tired but refreshed by the vigorous exercise. He sat in a beach chair and let the balmy warmth of the summer-like evening dry his skin. The sun had dipped below the horizon, but the clouds were still lit up pink and orange behind Moloka'i, a glorious sight. The pinks had begun to fade to gray before he went back to his room and showered and dressed. He walked through the quiet, scented night air to his Jeep in the hotel parking lot. Five minutes later he rolled to a stop in the driveway behind Lani's Honda. He walked up her steps. In the darkened living room the TV was on. He knocked on the screen door, and he heard Lani call out, "In here!" The front door was open and he let himself in.

She was sitting on the sofa watching the TV, clearly angry about something. She said, "Have you seen what's been going on?" She motioned to the TV set.

"No TV at the hotel," he said.

"That's right, I forgot. Well look at this." He sat down next to her. In a series of interviews outside the legislature, several politicians talked about the importance of luring Zodiac back to the islands, the best way being by immediately passing legislation to allow casino gambling. Only they called it "gaming."

"Gaming," Lani muttered. "A word invented by the gambling industry."

She was just getting warmed up. "All they talk about is jobs and education, like it's all benefits and no shortcomings. Brewster has poured millions into election campaigns for these guys. You think he doesn't expect something in return? You know how many of them have made junkets on his jet? You ever hear anybody talk about the hundreds of millions Brewster's going to make from this?"

One Hawaiian senator was saying, "How can we say no to a guy who comes to Hawai'i and is willing to hand us a hundred million dollars, and that's just for the license? Do you want to be the one to tell thousands of our children that they can't get the decent education that this money would provide?"

Just one person opposed to legalized gambling was interviewed, a willowy, middle-aged woman who spoke calmly and plainly. "Think about where all that money is coming from. It's from folks who are losing it. Our people have it bad enough already, without taking so much of their money that they only make some wealthy casino owner even richer. Hawai'i is a special place, made even more special by the fact that we don't allow casinos here. We don't have to destroy our island paradise. We can do better than being croupiers and blackjack dealers."

"You tell 'em, lady!" Lani said.

"I like her," John said.

When they got finished talking to the politicians, the scene shifted to another reporter standing on a sidewalk outside a high school. He interviewed a couple of unusually pretty young girls. One of them actually had tears in her dark-brown eyes—the camera moving in for a close-up—as she spoke forlornly about how she had been hoping to be able to go to college, but that was going to be impossible now, because the funding provided by the casinos would not be there.

Lani looked at John and said, "Does she sound Hawaiian to you?"

"I don't know. Kind of Mexican, maybe."

"Yeah, that's what I thought."

The station took a commercial break, and John took Lani's hand.

"John, I'm sorry. I shouldn't let this stuff get to me. I know I'm not being very good company right now."

"There's nowhere else I'd rather be," he said gently, looking into her eyes.

He took her hand and squeezed it, and she squeezed his back. The station came back from the commercial, but before the news anchor said anything she took her hand out of his, scooped up the remote control and shut the set off.

"Are you hungry?" she asked him.

"Starving."

"Let's go eat."

They sat at the kitchen table and ate the meal she had prepared. He was expecting some kind of Hawaiian dish. Instead she had cooked a French recipe with chicken sautéed with various spices, and a sauce made from the juices in the pan. Served on a bed of saffron rice, it was delicious. She had seemed to anticipate his hearty appetite and had made a lot of it. She had already finished, and just sat across from him smiling, watching him polish off the last piece of chicken.

"Sorry, I realize I'm making a pig of myself," he said.

"I like watching you eat," she said. And after a moment, a glisten in her eyes, she added, "I like watching you."

He reached across the table for her hand, and held it as he gazed at her.

She lowered her eyes and said uncertainly, "You know I've been married twice. I fall in love much too quickly. I didn't want to ever do that again."

She raised her head and looked at him. Words failed him, and he stood up and pulled her into his arms and did what he had dreamed of doing since that first day he saw her in the police station. He touched her hair and her cheeks, then took her lovely face gently in both hands and kissed her forehead and her hair, her cheeks, her eyes. Finally he kissed her mouth, and she immediately opened for him. He wanted to drink her in, and he felt her push her body into his. Without a word, she guided him into the bedroom, still kissing deeply. She fumbled with the buttons on his shirt, finally got them open, and it slid off his shoulders. They broke their kiss long enough for him to pull her dress over her head. He gasped when he saw that she had been naked beneath it. He quickly lowered his pants and shorts and pulled her urgently to the bed. He felt the back of his legs hit the edge of the bed, and he sat down, pulling her onto his lap, her legs on either side of him. She pressed eagerly against him, and feeling his hardness, she took him into her hand and guided him to her wet and open lips. He thrust himself inside her and she gasped in delight, working her hips around him. She broke the kiss and threw her head back, and he bent down and kissed her breasts, sucking on the nipples, switching from one to the other.

She was panting and crying out, then she suddenly kissed him and they came together.

As they both calmed down, she continued working her hips, kissing his face, his mouth, his ears. He was amazed that he didn't completely lose his hardness, and as she kissed him deeply again, he began to grow inside her once more. She felt it happening and thrust against him eagerly as he reached his full length and hardness. Suddenly she was coming again, and then his own release was upon him and he groaned in pleasure as he spent himself inside her. They stayed that way, kissing each other, loving each other, until he finally slipped wetly out of her. Suddenly shy with each other, they moved back up into the bed, still embracing. She put her head on the pillow and turned her back to him, pushing up against him. He wrapped his arms around her and took a breast in each hand. She murmured in pleasure at his touch, and wiggled her buttocks into his groin. He buried his face in her hair, and kissed the back of her neck and her ears. They spoke in whispers.

"It may be the wrong thing to say right now, but I have loved you since the first moment I saw you. Or at least, I was thunderstruck," he told her.

She sighed. "Not me. It wasn't until you opened your mouth and I heard that Joisey accent."

"Really? It didn't turn you awf?" He spoke with an exaggerated eastern pronunciation and she laughed. "And the first time I heard you laugh, I was a goner," he said

"You should have been. It's my sexiest quality."

John ran his fingers over her hardened nipples, and said, "I don't know about that."

She giggled and said, "You know, I didn't expect that I would have a chance to ask you, but that night in the valley, when they were singing that song . . ."

John sang a little bit of the lyric. "Our eyes have met, our lips not yet."

"Yeah, I thought we made a connection there. Of course, as soon as you started playing the ukulele, I was a goner myself."

They laughed together, and went on laughing and talking for another hour before they finally fell asleep, nestled together. John awoke during the night and found himself hard once more, pressed against her bottom. He realized that she was awake too, and she raised her leg and guided him into her softness, and he stroked over and over until they both were spent once again.

26

John woke up with a start. It was pitch dark in the room, and nestled against Lani's back he could feel and hear her breathing as she slept peacefully beside him. Glancing at her alarm clock on the night stand he saw that it was 4:00 a.m. He had a vaguely unsettling feeling that something had awakened him, although the night seemed quiet and still. Just awake enough for his mind to start working on his slashed tires, and Jimmie's fate, he found himself unable to go back to sleep. He got out of bed, being careful not to rouse Lani, and slipped on his T-shirt and shorts. He padded through the living room and carefully and quietly opened the front door and stepped outside. It was a dark night, and he took a few minutes to let his eyes adjust to the darkness. He walked over to where their two cars were parked in her driveway. There was no sign they had been touched. His overworked mind couldn't help wondering if he needed to be worrying about a bomb in the ignition.

Then he glanced up and saw something he'd never before witnessed—the entire sky was filled with stars. There were so many stars, it was as if he had been living on another planet before this. It was a spectacular sight. Wide awake now, he wanted to get away from the street lights for a better view. He slipped back into the house, and finding Lani still fast asleep, he took her house key from the kitchen table and went back outside, quietly closing and locking the door behind himself.

He walked up to the hill to where her street dead-ended at a park that fronted the highway on the other side. In the darkness of the park, even more stars were visible. There were so many of them that they seemed to form a white cloud. In the stillness of the night, he heard the noise, and at that moment he realized what had awakened him. Up on the Honoapiilani Highway there was a lot of traffic, and it sounded like heavy trucks. It could be anything, of course. Maybe they were moving equipment at night for a new road project. It could be the normal traffic of pineapple trucks. Perhaps they were getting ready to harvest a nearby field. Yet some instinct told him this wasn't anything routine and ordinary. Knowing he wouldn't be able to sleep again until he had had a look, he crossed the park and took up a position next to a tree beside the highway. Whatever had passed by was long gone by now, but he decided to wait for a while and see what would happen, if anything.

The night was completely quiet, and there wasn't a truck in sight anywhere. Fifteen minutes later not a single vehicle had passed, and he decided he must have been hearing things. Just then he saw two sets of headlights, probably two miles away, coming from the direction of Lahaina. He waited for them to approach. As they got closer he could see that they were large trucks. They slowed as they neared him, and then made a left turn off the highway and onto a dirt road that seemed to go up the hill into pineapple fields. There was a huge dump truck and a semi with a flatbed trailer. Chained down on the trailer was an enormous yellow bulldozer. Both trucks went up the dirt road about a quarter-mile and then disappeared where the road dropped down into a ravine.

He knew he should just go back to Lani's house and get into bed. He was wishing he had left her a note. What was he doing out here in the middle of the night, anyway? He had just about decided to leave, when more headlights appeared down the highway. This time it was three trucks, a couple of big dump trucks and a semi carrying a large backhoe. And just behind them, a new white Ford pickup truck. As the pickup made it's turn into the field, he could see the logo on the door: Zodiac International.

He just had to check this out. Crouched next to a tree, John waited for them to go up the road into the field and out of sight in the ravine. He strained to look up the highway. There was no more traffic coming. He looked at the dirt road leading into the pineapples. He figured he should have a minimum of four to five minutes to get up the road before another truck might show up. After making one last check of the highway, he ran across and into the fields. He jogged quickly up the dirt road, aware that if any vehicles came in either direction, he would have no place to hide. A sugar cane field would have provided good cover, but pineapples were too low to the ground. The stars and a rising quarter-moon gave him just enough light to see the road in front of him. After about 200 yards, the road made a sharp turn and dropped into a deep ravine. He could see a couple of old warehouse buildings next to a large cleared area. Parked in the area were about a dozen semis, their flat bed trailers loaded with bulldozers, backhoes, and graders. There were about twice as many dump trucks, mostly large ones.

He started edging closer. Just then he heard an engine start, and the headlights came on in the big white Ford pickup truck. The truck turned in his direction, headed for the highway. He turned quickly and ran back down the road as fast as he could, hearing the truck rapidly gaining ground behind him. He got to the highway and sprinted across, and threw himself into the grass in the park just as the truck got to the road and turned back toward Lahaina. He waited for it to pass before getting up and brushing himself off.

He walked back toward Lani's house. Zodiac was sneaking construction equipment around in the middle of the night. There was only one reason he could think of for that. When he arrived at Lani's house, he could see that there were lights on inside the house. He let himself in and startled her in the kitchen, where she almost dropped a mug of tea she had just prepared. She went to him and hugged him, tears in her eyes. "Don't you ever do that again."

He realized he should have left her a note. "I'm sorry," he said.

"I was so worried. I woke up and you weren't there."

"I heard noises."

"What noises?"

He told her what he had heard and seen. She confirmed that there were no big construction projects in the area that she knew of, and that the equipment he described did not sound like what would be used for any agricultural purpose.

John said, "I think that Brewster is staging equipment for a move on the valley, and it's going to be soon."

"We need to let Joe and the others know."

"I would like to find out for sure before I panic everybody out there."

"If that's what they're up to, they sure aren't going to tell you anything if you go over there and ask," she said.

"We need to think of something."

Lani went back to bed, but John knew he'd never be able to get back to sleep now. He wandered around the house, thinking. She had a spare bedroom that she was using as an office. He went in to switch on the computer. He had never looked to see if Zodiac had a web site, and he was curious about how they were presenting this current crisis in their company. Probably the usual pack of lies, he told himself. He never got around to checking out the website in any detail, because as soon as he connected to it and the Zodiac International logo appeared on the screen, he had an idea.

The next time he woke up it was morning. He was facing toward the window and couldn't see her. He had a sudden, terrible fear that it had all been a dream, and he quickly turned over to find her lying awake, gazing at him, and just that was enough to start yet another erection. They looked into each other's eyes, and he thought, *This is how it should be.* He remembered waking up many times after sex, with many different women, and feeling uncomfortable, wondering how quickly he could make his getaway. He knew that he wanted to wake up with this woman for the rest of his life. He reached out and pulled her to him, their naked bodies nestling together. They began kissing, more and more ardently with each passing moment. Suddenly she moaned and rolled on top of him and spread her legs. She sank herself onto his hardness, then leaned down and kissed him deeply as she raised and lowered her hips upon his. It didn't take long. Once again, they seemed to come together, as she gasped and collapsed upon him and they lay there pressed together, her weight pressed gloriously upon him. Finally she said, "We're behaving like a couple of hormonal teenagers."

"And I'm liking it."

She rolled off him and faced him. "So what do we do now?"

"We keep on loving each other for the rest of our lives."

"But what about New Jersey? Don't you have a lot of attachments back there?"

He thought guiltily of Angela. The engagement was off. But still, he knew he hadn't been completely honest with Lani.

"Not like the attachments I have here," he said, leaning over to take a nipple into his mouth.

Finally she pushed him away. "You'd better stop that or I'll never get out of here. I have to go to work, you know."

She got out of bed and John admired her naked body for a moment before she slipped into a light bathrobe and headed for the kitchen. He heard her clinking dishes there and running some water. A soft breeze rustled the curtains in the room, and he could feel the gentle morning air wash over him. He put his head back on the pillow and closed his eyes.

Lani came back into the room twenty minutes later, showered and ready to dress for work. John was sound asleep. She liked watching him sleep, liked having him in her bed. Johnny Boy, the young kid Sunny had rescued. Or maybe not. The search for his parents was definitely going to be a priority today. She dressed quietly, never taking her eyes off him. When she was done, she walked into the kitchen to get a cup of coffee. As she walked past the open door to her office, she saw that the computer was on. And there, sitting on her desk, was an authentic-looking Zodiac International Corporation ID card, with John's picture and the name Jack Richards. She smiled. He had been busy. She realized that he must have used her scanner to get the picture from his New Jersey driver's license, and pieced together the ID from graphics from the internet. Impressed with his creativity and his intelligence, she was more than a little worried about how he planned to use his phony ID.

A few minutes later she awakened him with tender kisses on his face. He opened his eyes and smiled at her, then pulled her into the bed with him.

"Hey, I've got to get to work!" she laughed.

"Me too."

"Uh huh. I saw your little creation in there. Exactly what are you planning to do with it?"

"Go over to that field, see if I can get somebody to talk to me."

"You think that ID will be enough?"

"I also spent a little time at the Caterpillar website, learning about construction equipment used for site grading."

"You're amazing," she said.

"I am, aren't I?"

They laughed, and she kissed him one last time and climbed out of bed, smoothing her clothing.

"There's a key to my house hidden under a stone next to the steps. Oh, and I left something for you in the office," she said as she left the room.

"What?"

"You'll see. Call me at the office later."

She went out the door, carrying her briefcase.

He got up a few minutes later and went into the office to get his Zodiac ID. He found that Lani had slid the ID card into a case on the end of a lanyard that he could hang around his neck. This would be much better than having to take an ID out of a wallet. She had also left him a clipboard with some forms attached to it. Another good idea. He and Lani. They made a great team. A hard hat would have completed the picture perfectly, but he found a plain white baseball type cap in her closet and he decided it would have to do. He dressed quickly, and drove back to the hotel. He showered and then dressed in the dark slacks and black shoes he had worn on the plane trip over. That seemed like eons ago, another life. After the freedom of the rubber slipper, the socks and tight leather lace-ups felt like having his feet in a strait-jacket. He put on one of the aloha shirts he had purchased in the hotel and tucked it in at the waist.

He got in his Jeep wearing his ID and the hat, and drove out to the highway. When the light changed he crossed the road and stopped. The construction equipment was completely out of view from the highway. Hopefully, it was still there. He took a couple of deep breaths and thought about what he was going to say, an actor rehearsing his lines. Construction job sites were familiar places to him. The key was to appear confident, even bossy. This should be one occasion where the East Coast accent would come in handy. He decided he was ready and stepped on the gas, driving quickly up the road, raising a cloud of dust behind him. As he came over a rise and descended into the ravine, he saw that there was even more equipment than before. A couple of men in hard hats, jeans, and work boots were standing next to a pickup truck. They looked up as he approached. He drove right over to them and pulled to a stop, immediately getting out, clipboard in hand. Before they had a chance to say anything, he said, "Have you got that 143H out here yet?"

The men looked at each other, then at John. A guy dressed like Aloha Friday in downtown Honolulu, sporting a Zodiac badge, and with a mainland accent. As John had hoped, they seemed to be momentarily thrown.

"A 143H? Everything we've got out here is rear-drive only," one of them said defensively.

"Aw, hell. You're just going to get bogged down on that beach," John said.

"Look, nobody said anything about the beach. All we're supposed to do is take out the road," he said.

John looked into the field full of vehicles. "Looks like you've got enough D-8s to do that job."

The man smiled. "That road is going to be gone by noon, day after tomorrow, believe me. They won't know what the hell hit them."

The other man shot his buddy an annoyed look, and tried to take a closer peek at John's badge. John knew he was about to be in trouble here. He quickly took his cell phone from his belt. "Well, that's good, but hold on," he said. "I've got to find out about those graders." He punched in some random numbers, and then turned his back on the men as if wanting to make a private call, out of their earshot. There was no answer, of course, but he pretended to be speaking to someone. “Bill . . . Yeah, it’s me. I’m out here in Kapalua, and these guys don’t seem to know anything about the 143H . . . Yeah, hold on, it’s in the Jeep.” He trotted over to the Jeep and got in. Starting up the engine, he gave a friendly wave to the men, and drove off, still pretending to talk on the phone. He breathed a sigh of relief when he got to the highway, then found himself laughing out loud. He hadn’t had a feeling like this in years. It was as if he had just pulled off some kind of fun high school prank. It was exhilarating. He didn’t know whether those guys would report the conversation or not. At this point it really didn’t matter. The most important thing was to get out to the valley and warn Joe and the others about what was coming. He headed back to the hotel to change out of his “costume,” still chuckling giddily, a big silly grin on his face.

The two guys in the rented red Trans Am who were waiting for him in the Napili Plaza parking lot wondered what was so damn funny. In any case, they expected to soon wipe the smile off his face, as they followed well behind his Jeep. They knew where he was going, and there was no reason to get any closer.

27

Lani cleared her calendar by 10:00 a.m. and was ready to focus on the question of John's parents. He had been told that his mother was dead. Maybe it was true. But his father might still be alive. She started with a call to the Roman Catholic archdiocesan office in Honolulu. She asked about a priest named either Keoni or John Punahuloa. They had no record of a priest by that name. She said that he might be deceased, or somewhere on the mainland, and the woman who answered the phone said that she only had access to computer records going back around twenty years. If Lani would write a letter, someone could check through the old records manually and would get back to her in two or three weeks. Lani took down the name and address to write to, but she was too impatient to wait for weeks. She wondered if an older priest might remember either Father Tom or Keoni. She had recently gone to a funeral mass for one of her clients at St. Anthony of Padua church in Wailuku, just a few blocks from her office. The service had been conducted by an elderly priest. She didn't know his name, but it was possible that he might know one or both of the men. It seemed well worth a quick trip to the church. It could be a waste of time, but it was better than waiting for three weeks. She drove over to the old stone church on the hillside above town, and located the rectory next door. She wished she knew the name of the priest so she wouldn't have to just ask for "an old priest." But the door was opened by the old man she remembered from the mass. He seemed happy to have a visitor, and invited her into a sitting room. They sank down into easy chairs in a room that was musty and dimly lit, and she guessed that they didn't often receive visitors here. The old priest offered coffee, which she politely declined. He sank back into his chair. His gaze had fixed on a point over her head. He had a vague smile on his face and for a moment he seemed to forget that she was there.

"Father, do you know of a priest named Keoni Punahuloa? He is a Hawaiian man."

It took him a moment to look in her direction. Finally he seemed to focus on her. "Not very many Hawaiian priests," he said. "No, not very many. I don't know that name."

"What about a Father Tom here on Maui? I think he would be about the same age as you. He was a parish priest in Makena."

"Makena? There's no church in Makena."

"It's gone now, but this was thirty years ago."

"There's never been a church in Makena," he said, and his eyes resumed their vacant gaze off to one side. She waited for almost a full minute in the quiet room before she decided that this interview was going to be pointless. Then he suddenly looked at her and said, "Maybe you're thinking of St. Joseph. It's a mission, not a church. But it's in Kaupo, not Makena."

"Was there a Father Tom there?"

"I don't know a Father Tom. You should check with the archdiocese."

He smiled and returned his gaze to some part of the room above her. After a minute or two of silence, she realized this was as much as she was going to get from him. She stood up and said, "That's a good idea. I'll contact them. Thank you so much for your time."

As she was leaving the room, he called out to her, "They're all up there, you know."

"Pardon me?" she said.

He was pointing up, in the direction over the top of the West Maui mountains out the back window of the rectory. "All of them. All the Maui priests. Soon I'll be there too."

She thanked him again and left the room and let herself out. *Well, old man*, she thought, *I hope you join all your friends in heaven some day*. As she walked to her car, she glanced up into the mountains behind the church and saw something she had never noticed before. On the steep hillside there was a cemetery. She walked out behind the church and up a steep path to a small graveyard in a leveled-out area. This was the place the old priest had been pointing to, not heaven. It wouldn't take long to find out if there was a priest named Thomas who died sometime after 1972 or so. Even if there were more than one, she'd be able to get some last names. She walked among the graves, looking at the tombstones. She had been in other Catholic cemeteries, and she remembered elaborate gravesites with towering statuary. The priests themselves seemed to be much more modest with their own burials. On each grave, there was a small stone with name and dates of birth and death, nothing else. There were a couple of Thomases, but the graves were too old to be the man she was looking for.

She realized that the graves were arranged in chronological order, with the oldest ones nearest to the church. She walked out a couple of rows looking for dates within the last 30 years. The newer tombstones, dating back to the 1950s were made of polished marble. They still had the same simple inscriptions of the older stones, but in a small oval on the stone there was a picture of the priest. She walked down the row of graves until she came to one she had hoped not to find. The inscription read, KEONI PUNAHULOA, 01-12-1950–06-23-1972. *Oh my God*, she thought. This young man had died within a very short time after his son left the islands. His life must have been in ruins. There was a picture on this stone, but it was crusted over with red dirt and dust. She took a Kleenex from her pocket and wiped the dust away until she could see the face. When it was revealed, she pulled her hand away in shock. It was the face of John. She started to shiver. It was as if she were looking at Johnny's grave. No wonder Sunny had been so sure who John was. There was no question in her mind now, either.

She went back to her office, shaken. What had happened thirty years ago, after Sunny moved from Makena? Why had John's father died so young? Had his mother died young also? She got out her phone book and looked under Kalakana. There were only a few listings, none for Aileen. She called each of them, asking about a family member named Aileen. No one had heard of the name, or knew of any *'ohana* in Makena thirty years ago. At two of the listings there was no answer, and she made a note of the numbers to call them back in the evening. The whole thing had only taken a couple of hours. John's father was dead and his mother was dead or lost somewhere. Maybe the best Lani could do would be to give John a couple of gravesites to go to. It was beginning to look as she was going to be the bearer of bad news. She hated to have to be the one to bring John to a state of grief, after all these years, over parents he had barely known.

John had driven back to the hotel and had called her office from the payphone there. She hadn't been in, so he left a voice mail message describing what he had found out about the construction equipment, and saying that he was going out to the valley to warn the taro farmers. He quickly changed back into his local-style clothing. He had never before thought of shoes and socks as being a burden, but it seemed that way now. They were hot and tight and uncomfortable, and it felt wonderful to get them off his feet. He grabbed his keys and wallet and went out to his Jeep. He drove to the highway, and headed north. There were a number of cars on the road, and he did not notice the two men in the red Pontiac who followed him. He did notice a second vehicle directly behind him, a big old GMC pickup raised high off the ground on large tires, with three huge, dark, curly headed men crammed shoulder to shoulder in the seat. He shivered involuntarily as he realized that this was at least the third time he had seen the truck in the last day or so. He might not have noticed it at all, except for the neatly lettered sign attached to the front bumper, reading TONGAN BUILT in six-inch-high letters. He had thought it was funny at the time. Now, as he was headed toward narrow roads along the cliffs with little traffic around to witness a possible "accident," it didn't seem funny anymore.

The slow, gawking tourists in the yellow Mustang convertible who had been ahead of him pulled off the road to look at the view. He accelerated suddenly, and for a moment, the truck fell behind. Then as he came around a curve, he checked his rear view mirror, and there it was, closing the distance. He was going as fast as he dared, but they would be more familiar with the road than he was. The last thing he wanted to do was allow himself to be trapped on a narrow road with this vehicle behind him. The men in the truck looked none too friendly, and he wasn't about to stop and ask them what they wanted. Certainly not out here, anyway. He knew he had to act while he still had some distance between himself and them. He rounded a bend and was out of sight of the truck for a few moments. He saw a steep road going down into the trees, with a sign reading PRIVATE. He jerked the steering wheel to the right and bounded down the road, just on the bare edge of control as he tried to slow the Jeep down. As he descended steeply he could see that this was someone's driveway, and it wasn't a very long one. At the end of it was a small white house, which he was now about to demolish. He hit the brakes hard, wishing he had switched into low gear before turning off the road. He realized that he wasn't going to be able to stop in time, and he aimed for a tree just off the drive. He hit the tree with his front bumper and bounced off back onto the drive. He skidded backwards, but was able to stop before he hit the house. The impact stalled the engine, and John sat there in the sudden silence deep in the foliage. As he tried to recover himself, he heard the big pickup roar by on the road above.

About a half-mile behind, the two men in the Pontiac had seen him suddenly turn down the driveway. They thought they were being careful, but evidently he had spotted them. Either that or he wanted to make sure that no one was following him. They were patient men, and they pulled off the road where they could see the driveway entrance. They waited for John to emerge.

John waited fifteen minutes, gradually coming to the conclusion that he had let his paranoia almost kill him. The truck had long gone. If someone had wanted to get him, they would have come back by now, realizing that he had turned off. He felt like an idiot. He got out and checked the Jeep. There was a pretty good dent in the front bumper, but he couldn't see any other damage. Luckily the airbags hadn't gone off. Evidently no one was home in the house, and he was glad he didn't have to make a fool of himself explaining how he had nearly come to destroy their home. He drove back up the driveway, and at the top where it joined the main road, he turned back toward the valley.

The men in the Pontiac saw the Jeep emerge from the woods, and they pulled back onto the road and followed, staying well behind.

John had driven less than 100 yards, when he heard the roar of an engine around the bend in front of him. Before he had a chance to react, the huge GMC pickup with three surprised looking Tongans was filling his windshield, on his side of the road. He swerved to the left, barely avoiding a head-on collision, and then swerved back to his own side of the road. Paranoia, hell! These guys were after him. He hit the accelerator and drove as fast as he dared, roaring around the bend, out of sight of the truck. They would have to slow down before they could turn around. If only he could get to the valley first, he'd have friends there. He would just have to outrun these guys. The men in the Pontiac had been out of sight of the near miss, but they had seen John's car take off like a bat out of hell. The driver of the Pontiac hit the gas.

The Tongans did not turn around right away. They were still rattled by the near collision that had almost killed all of them. Before they had a chance to even slow much, the red Pontiac came racing around the corner straight at them. The truck swerved to the right, as did the Pontiac, but the road was narrow and there was not enough room for the car to maneuver. Its right wheels were forced off the road and up onto the steep slope on the right side. It got sideways up the slope as far as it could before the left wheels bogged down in the ditch and the car lurched to a stop and rolled slowly onto its roof in the middle of the road. By this time the Tongans had rounded the next bend out of sight. They didn't know what had happened to the Pontiac, and they didn't want to know. It was enough for one day. They slowed to a safe speed and headed back toward Lahaina.

John finally arrived at the valley drenched in sweat. He had driven as fast as he could the whole time. He was pretty sure that he had shaken Brewster's guys. The cops were not at the gate, and he realized that they really were no longer needed. After tomorrow, there wasn't going to be any gate or any road. He got out of the Jeep to open and close the gate, then drove up the road into the valley. There was no guard at the spot where the pickup had been before, and he drove right through and up the road to the taro patches. He thought for a moment of just leaning on the horn and drawing a crowd. *The British are coming! The British are coming,* he thought to himself for a crazy moment. No, the thing was to find Joe and let him figure out what to do. Then he found himself thinking about Joe. Could he be trusted? John decided he had to trust him, there was no choice at this point. He walked up the hill to Joe's house. He wasn't there, but John soon found him next to the river, pounding taro into poi.

Joe's face fell when he heard the news that bulldozers were on the way. He got up and washed his hands wearily in the stream. Then the two of them went house to house, taro patch to taro patch, getting everyone together. When they were all gathered down by the stream where they had had the luau the other night, Joe told them what was going on. There were questions for John about what he had heard and seen. He didn't pull any punches. He told them all he knew about Brewster, that he appeared to be manipulating the press, getting people to line up behind him, getting public sentiment in his favor. Mostly it was a quiet and downcast group. After two years of battling Brewster, after the lawsuits, the criminal trespass charges he had brought against them, the battle to convince people not to sell out at the inflated prices they had been offered, they were tired. For two whole days, they thought they had beaten him. And here was John, bearing the news that the situation was even worse than before. John sat quietly and listened while the discussions went back and forth between those who wanted to "do something" and others who were urging caution.

A large and tough-looking Hawaiian man whom John began to think of as "the warrior" spoke up. "I say we go ovah there tonight and we going burn those bulldozers."

Someone else said, "Yeah? And who da hell going feed your kids when you get arrested?"

Another man said, "Eh, cool your jets, brah. Dis no time fo' act like a bunch of hotheads."

John looked around him at the valley and tried to think of himself as a Hawaiian warrior of olden times, defending his land. He recalled an event from Hawaiian history that had fascinated him as a teenager when he was reading about the islands. What was the name of that guy? Finally he remembered, and he spoke up, hoping the others wouldn't mind him putting in his two cents' worth. "I don't know," he said. "Maybe it is time to behave like a bunch of hotheads." This earned him an approving look from the several of the men.

"You mean burn the dozers?" Joe asked.

"No, I think we should act like warriors," John said. "Kalanikūpule's men didn't just give up when they got backed into a valley. They stood and fought."

Someone added, "Yeah, and they wen get pushed ovah da cliff and die, those buggahs."

"We don't have to worry about that here," John said. "But we do have to stand and fight."

"Eh, brah, how da hell we go against bulldozers with spears?"

John smiled. "You remember in China a few years ago, Tiananmen Square . . ."

The warrior's face lit up. "Yeah. Dat guy wen jus' stand in front of da tank."

Joe started to show a little enthusiasm for the concept. "I saw dat. Stopped dat tank cold, brah!"

"They going smash us like one cockaroach," one man said.

John said, "If I know Brewster, there's going to be press there. He needs favorable public opinion. You don't go running people over with bulldozers if that's what you want."

The warrior said, "I go out there and stop da ting myself!"

"That's good," John said, "but what we need are lots of warriors. We need to have people see that this affects all Hawaiians, not just the ones here in this valley."

The warrior said, "I know fifty guys would show up here if they knew what stay going on."

"Can you have them here by tomorrow?" John asked him.

Without hesitation, the man stood up and started sprinting over to his pickup truck. John shouted after him, "We have to keep this quiet. Make sure only the right people know about our plans."

The warrior waved an acknowledgement, got in his truck, and took off down the road.

Joe started to say, "I think maybe some of the canoe clubs—"

"Yeah, war canoes!" another man said.

Joe turned to Oliver. "Oliver, can I use your phone?"

"Help yourself," Oliver said.

They spent the rest of the day spreading the word and preparing for war. Just before dark there was a shout from one of the lookouts they had posted high in a tree. A canoe was arriving. John and the warrior, who had returned with a hundred men, not fifty, went down to the beach in John's Jeep to meet the canoe. John watched as the six men in the bright-orange canoe waited offshore briefly, then paddled vigorously as they caught a wave that allowed them to run the canoe right up onto the beach. He and the warrior greeted the new arrivals warmly and helped pull the canoe above the tide line.

A man in his fifties was the steerer, the last to get out of the canoe. John shook his hand and thanked him for coming. The man introduced himself as Peter Akuna. As usual, John got the funny look he got from locals when they heard the New Jersey coming out of his Hawaiian mouth. Then the warrior came over and told Peter and the other new arrivals that John was the one responsible for all that was happening. The warrior's endorsement changed everything, and John was immediately accepted. He helped unload the canoe of the food, clothing, a video camera, all the things they had brought. John had often paddled canoes in New Jersey, and he found the canoe's structure interesting. He asked Peter about it and got a complete course in canoe construction and paddling. Before long, he found himself an honorary member of Peter's canoe club in Lahaina. It had gotten dark before another canoe arrived, this one bright green and white. And then they started arriving in twos and threes, coming into the bay from both the Lahaina and Wailuku sides, canoes in all colors of the rainbow, plus some made entirely of koa wood. John worked with Peter, helping them land until, once the last of them arrived at midnight, there were around sixty of them pulled up on the beach. Then John collapsed in fatigue on the beach and fell into a sound sleep, surrounded by hundreds of his fellow Hawaiians.

28

By the next morning, at the controls of his own personal Boeing 737, Brewster was on his way to his homecoming. After his triumphant arrival in Hawai'i, a helicopter would transport him to a place on the road where he could join the parade of construction equipment that would be waiting for him. He would then make his entrance into the valley like Patton at the head of the column, riding on the lead tank. The key thing was to keep the momentum going. Operation Clamor had been a huge success. He knew from past experience that once you started construction, there was no turning back. They could try to sue, and he would match them, ten of his attorneys to one of theirs. In the meantime, the bulldozers would be working. During the months and years he could delay legal action, the casino and resort would get built, and there would be nothing anyone could do about it. If they attempted any violence, the press would be there to see it, the police to deal with it. Civil disobedience would be met with handcuffs and pepper spray, carried by the many police officers Bennett was arranging to accompany the equipment. Brewster's day of triumph was at hand. Life was good. He was in command.

Pilot-in-Command. He loved that phrase. It had been a long flight from the mainland. He found that he didn't get nearly as tired on these trips when he flew the plane himself. He knew that his pilots didn't like him to hand-fly the plane. They used the autopilot. *A bunch of airline rejects*, he thought. As soon as he had his final check ride and rating in this aircraft, he was going to can the bunch of them, make himself Chief Pilot, and hire some guys who did things his way. He could out-fly them any day. If only they could keep his wife away from the liquor in back, his arrival in Hawai'i would be perfectly executed. He scanned the horizon through the windshield. *Must have headwinds*, he thought. *Should be seeing the Big Island by now.*

Bob Lunde, the co-pilot in the seat on his right took off his headset and unbelted himself. "I'm going to visit the head, sir. Be right back."

"Okay, I've got the aircraft," Brewster said, thinking, *And I don't need you, dummy.*

The copilot made his way to the back of the cockpit and walked into the main cabin. Frank Edwards, the other pilot, was sitting there looking out the window, concern on his face. He looked up when Lunde entered the cabin.

"Has he figured it out yet?" Edwards asked.

"No," Lunde said.

"When are you going to tell him?"

Lunde looked at his watch. "I think in another half hour or so, it should be obvious to him."

"What if it isn't?"

"We've got plenty of fuel."

"Not enough for Japan."

"Frank, believe me, I'm not going to let this moron put us down in the Pacific."

"Well, he kicked me out of the cockpit, so it's going to be up to you. But my personal limit is one more hour. After that,

I'm going to come up there and hit him over the head with a gold-plated faucet."

"Okay, we're agreed, one more hour. The funny thing is, the son of a bitch isn't a bad pilot."

"Yeah, just can't program a navigation computer for shit."

Brewster's plane touched down nearly two hours late, and his pilots tried to blame it on him. Obviously if they had given him the right information, he wouldn't have missed Hawai'i by 105 nautical miles. And the little shits waited until he had flown well past the islands to tell him there was a problem. They knew an on-time arrival was important, and all they had to say was, "We tried to tell you." Tried, hell. Well now they could take their fired asses back to the mainland on a commercial flight. He delighted himself by making a perfect squeaker of a landing at Kahului.

Bennett had managed to keep the band and most of the dignitaries on hand for the late arrival. Brewster stepped from the plane into the roll-up steps, his arm around his wife as they stood there and waved grandly to the crowd. The high school band, using the instruments Brewster had provided, played "Hail to the Chief," one of Brewster's favorite songs. The press had waited patiently, and they recorded it all as the Brewsters walked down the steps, blowing kisses to the crowd, and stepped onto the red carpet leading away from the plane. They were greeted by politicians Brewster had helped, and their staffs, by labor leaders, by construction workers in hard hats. The teachers at a school Brewster had paid to build turned up with all the kids. Lei after lei was placed on his and his wife's shoulders as he stopped to shake hands with people. *Welcome to the homecoming hero. It was just as he had envisioned it.* They followed the red carpet to where a podium and microphone had been set up on a small raised platform. Brewster stepped up onto the platform and waited for the crowd to quiet down before he spoke.

"Today a great injustice has been corrected. My wife and I are grateful to you, the people of Hawai'i, for recognizing this injustice and for welcoming us home. For yes, this is my new home, Hawai'i *nei*."

He was careful to give this a good Hawaiian pronunciation, "Havai'i nay," this beloved Hawai'i. There was a nice round of applause, and raucous cheering from the union guys. Brewster waited for silence before continuing.

"I am now going to fly by helicopter to the beautiful Kalonahoa Valley. There, we will work together to transform it into what it always should have been, a resort that will draw people from all over the world to Maui, a source of jobs for thousands of Hawaiian citizens, and a major boost to the economy of Hawai'i, while providing a free college tuition to all these young people we see here today."

At a pre-arranged signal from Bennett, and prodded by their teachers, the kids from the school cheered and yelled.

Brewster continued, "And it is thanks to you, the *good* people of Hawai'i, that this is going to happen. I thank you most sincerely for your confidence in me. I will redouble my efforts now to bring to fruition all that I have promised you. *Mahalo* and aloha."

He waved at the crowd majestically as they cheered and applauded, and stood for a moment basking in their admiration, while the band played "Hawai'i Aloha." He noticed Bennett signaling him, and he stepped off the platform and shook a few hands, before striding briskly over to a waiting helicopter, where, taking the controls himself, he lifted off and flew toward the Kalonahoa Valley.

Within fifteen minutes, he was flying over a long column of construction vehicles stopped along the narrow cliffside road on Maui's north shore. At the head of the column was a huge new yellow bulldozer, poised at a bend in the road just before it sloped down the cliff and into the Kalonahoa Valley. The bulldozer had been rigged with flag staffs, and the flags of Hawai'i, the US, and Zodiac International fluttered in the sea breeze. Brewster circled the area, making sure the press was ready with their cameras, before setting the helicopter on the road next to the dozer. He stepped out of the chopper to the yells and cheers of his men in hard hats, sitting astride their noisily idling machines, the air alive with the throbbing power of thousands of diesel horsepower. He waved at them, stepped quickly over to the lead bulldozer, and climbed on board. He was glad he'd had a chance to spend an hour on the mainland learning how to drive one of these. It had to be impressive to people, he figured, when he could smoothly transition from the controls of a helicopter to the operator's seat in a bulldozer. He had an experienced operator standing behind him, just in case.

With a grandiose "forward ho" wave, he put the idling tractor into gear and pressed on the accelerator pedal. The engine speed increased, but the beast didn't move.

The operator said loudly, "Handbrake, handbrake." And Brewster, the camera-ready smile never leaving his face, said to him, "I *know* about the goddam handbrake, you dumb son of a bitch." He released it then and stepped on the gas again, but the dozer didn't move. With some trepidation, the man behind him reached around and gave the gearshift lever another pull, and the machine suddenly lurched forward. The rest of the column followed. Brewster steered it around the bend and into sight of the valley below. *Wait until those mud-stomping peasants see this baby coming*, he thought gleefully.

He had traveled less than fifty yards before a dark-skinned man appeared from out of the bushes by the side of the road a few yards away, and stepped out in front of him. He was bare-chested and barefooted, wearing only a loincloth, and his ankles and head were encircled by grass leis. The man carried a spear.

He didn't even look at the bulldozer directly, as if he disdained to even see this huge yellow machine rapidly closing the distance to where he stood. He just stood there, shoulders hunched forward, spear held in front of him, his demeanor and his posture saying, "No further." Brewster grinned and took dead aim at the man, knowing that the guy would have to move. Suddenly there were ten more men like him on the road, then another twenty. They all assumed the same posture, standing there unflinchingly. Brewster raised the blade of the bulldozer and pressed on the throttle. But about ten feet from the men, he was surprised when the machine suddenly lurched to a halt.

"What the hell?" Brewster said, looking around at the controls to figure out what had happened.

"You can't just run them over," said the operator, who had slipped the bulldozer out of gear.

"Dammit, they're going to move."

The operator looked at the warriors, standing motionless in the road. "I don't think so."

"You're a fucking dumb-ass bulldozer driver. I don't pay you to think."

"You'd just run those people down, wouldn't you?"

"If they don't move, damn right I would. This is my valley now, and you work for me."

"Yeah, well, I just quit, *asshole*."

Before Brewster could stop him, the man reached over and shut down the engine, pulling the key from the ignition switch. He jumped down from the machine and heaved the key as far as he could over the cliff to the rocks 300 feet below. The warriors did not react, but from down in the valley Brewster could faintly hear cheering. He looked down to see that there were now at least 1000 people on the beach—men, women, and children. Looking over the dozer blade, he could see that one of the men on the road was looking up at him. He realized that he knew this man: John

Rossi. It seemed as if everything had started going wrong the day this man showed up on Maui. *Okay, Rossi,* he thought. *It's gloves off now.* Frustrated and angry, Brewster climbed down and stalked back up the road to look for the police he had been promised. By the time he found them he was seething. There were a dozen uniformed cops at the top of the hill, just standing there like spectators. He walked over to the senior man, a Lahaina police sergeant. "I want to see some goddam arrests made," he said. "And I want them now."

Police Sergeant Jay Sakai looked down the road at the warriors, armed with spears, and at the thousand people or so people on the beach below. His watch captain had told him to make sure Brewster's men and equipment could get through to the valley. Sakai was a man who did his duty. But having seen Brewster attempt to run down unarmed civilians, he wasn't so certain about following the order. He was fully aware how well-connected and powerful Brewster was, but now that he had met this man, he did not like him.

"Sir, this is a different situation from what we were expecting."

"So?" Brewster demanded.

"For one thing, we're greatly outnumbered here."

"I don't care. Get reinforcements. Get the National Guard."

"I'm not authorized to do that, sir."

"Well what in hell are you authorized to do?"

"I'm going to call my captain and see what he wants me to do."

Brewster grabbed his arm and got right in Sakai's face. "Listen, you damned idiot, you're going to make some arrests right now, or you're not going to have a captain or a job."

The sergeant had had enough. "Okay, sir. You're under arrest." He motioned to one of his men, who took a set of handcuffs from his belt, and stood ready to clamp them on Brewster's wrists.

Brewster was stunned. "You're arresting me? For what?"

"Assaulting a police officer, for one thing," Sakai said, looking angrily down at Brewster's grip on his arm.

Brewster abruptly let go of him, but the sergeant went on. "Also, it looked to me like you were about to run some people down with that bulldozer."

"They would have moved!"

"You don't know that."

Brewster realized he couldn't win this contest right at the moment. He would have the sergeant fired later. "Well, sergeant, I apologize for interfering with your duties."

The sergeant looked at Brewster for a moment, then motioned to the other cop to put the cuffs away. Bennett came over to talk to Brewster. "I'm having a little trouble with the press," he said. "Maybe if you said a few words to them it would help."

"Get his badge number," Brewster said to Bennett, and stalked off to where the press had set up camp with cameras and microphones. Brewster had managed to change his sour expression into a smile by the time he got there. He held up his hands to silence their shouted questions.

"Well," he chuckled, as if amused by the entire incident. "It looks like a handful of people have obstructed us temporarily." Then he got more serious. "It's a sad situation when so few are able to stop the benefits to so many. I'm confident that we can prevail upon the authorities to take whatever actions are necessary. We must enforce the rights of the vast majority of Hawaiians who want to see this project built and enjoy the jobs, the economic benefits, and the education that will be provided as a result." Brewster now noticed that his 300-foot yacht, *Emperor of the Seas*, was sailing into view. Grateful for the distraction, he pointed it out to the reporters, who promptly aimed their cameras in that direction. "As you can see, my floating headquarters for this operation has arrived. I am going to fly out there now and leave it up to the authorities to resolve this situation in an appropriate manner. Thank you all for coming. We are all certainly disappointed to see the start of construction temporarily delayed. I'm sure it won't be long before we're ready to go." He refused to take any questions. Bennett had signaled to the other helicopter pilot to start his engines, and by the time the impromptu press conference was over, the whirling dust had the reporters holding tightly to everything that might blow away. Brewster and Bennett climbed aboard, and they flew out over the bay to land on the now-anchored ship two miles offshore.

29

Gene McKay, the Maui County District Attorney, and Assistant D.A. Ted Wong, sat in a conference room in the county office building in Wailuku, gloomily going over the color slides and the report from the Honolulu Medical Examiner. It was the third time Jim Putnam's body had been autopsied. McKay had allowed the defense the leeway. He didn't want to have problems at trial in what should have been an open-and-shut case. The problem was that this third and only really thorough examination of the body had revealed evidence of a gunshot wound as the likely cause of death. Even the Maui County M.E.s were now reluctantly conceding the point. Not that this meant that Sunny Waikoloa was innocent of murder, but it made a dramatic difference to the prosecution's case. No longer could they claim that Sunny had been found with the murder weapon in his hand. The club had not been the murder weapon. James Putnam had most likely been killed with a .32 caliber pistol. For the life of him, Gene could not imagine a *kūpuna* like Uncle Sunny Waikoloa packing a handgun. The defense would pounce on the point.

Questions were also being raised by Lani Miller about Brewster's finances. She had sent to McKay's office copies of reports buried in the files of the Department of Business Development. How she had come by them, he didn't know. But a visit to that office had confirmed the authenticity of the documents. He couldn't understand how a man with a private Boeing 737, a permanent wing at the Honoloa Bay Hotel, a 300-foot yacht, and a Honolulu concert hall named after him could be broke. It made no sense to him. But he was not an accountant. He knew that all kinds of shenanigans could be pulled on balance sheets. If Brewster was really in financial trouble, and James Putnam had been about to make public his damaging press release, the delays to the start of his project could lead Zodiac International to take desperate measures. Not that Zodiac could be responsible for a murder, but if he were the defense attorney trying to direct attention from his client, he would certainly take this tack.

And the matter of the car that Lani Miller reported was problematic. The kid who claimed to have seen a yellow Viper had been interviewed by the D.A.'s office. No one could confirm if he had seen the car or not, but according to the interviewers, the kid knew his cars, and from that standpoint he was a credible witness. They had quietly looked for any record of such a car on Maui but had come up empty. That in itself was odd. Maybe the car, if it existed, had nothing to do with the murder. But McKay had often been on the opposite side of a courtroom from Lani Miller, and he had always respected her integrity, if not the kinds of lowlifes she was usually defending. He admired integrity, even if his position sometimes required him to bend a little in the interest of practical politics. In this case, he had to decide whether he was going to have more political problems by attempting to convict Sunny or by looking for a killer with some connection to Charles N. Brewster and Zodiac. At the moment, the political pendulum was still swinging in favor of Brewster, and he sure didn't want Brewster as an enemy. Still, he figured it wouldn't be a bad idea to hedge his bets a little. He said to Ted, "We can't walk into that courtroom and admit that we haven't at least asked Brewster about that car."

Ted said, "I'd be willing to bet you a hundred bucks that it doesn't exist, except in the minds of Lani Miller and a ten-year-old kid."

"Fine, but are you willing to bet your career?"

As Ted mulled this over the phone rang. It was Brewster, calling from his yacht.

"Speak of the devil," Gene said. He pushed the button for the speaker phone so Ted could listen in. Brewster had calmed down considerably from the frustrations of the morning, and he was able to speak in an amiable tone of voice. "Gene, how are you?"

"Welcome back. Or should I say welcome home?"

"The latter, I think. And thank you, it's good to be back," Brewster said.

"What can I do for you this morning?"

"Did you hear what happened out in the valley?"

"No. I've been in meetings all morning."

"They've blocked the road, denied me access to my property."

"Blocked it with what?"

"People, damn it. And the police refuse to do anything about it. I want some arrests made. I want that John Rossi character locked up. He's the instigator."

"I'll prosecute him, if the police arrest him. Why haven't they done so?" McKay asked.

"You tell me. There's a sergeant Sakai out there who should be locked up himself."

"Let me make a couple of phone calls, find out what's going on."

"Thank you, Gene. I knew I could count on you," Brewster said.

"Charles, I wonder if you could do something for me."

"Of course, name it."

"Well, there's a matter that seems to keep coming up, and I'm hoping you can help us out here."

"I'll be glad to help in whatever way I can."

"I appreciate that. Would you happen to know anything about a yellow Dodge Viper?" McKay asked.

There was a perceptible pause before Brewster answered. "I think I might have seen one around. I tend to favor Ferrarris and Porsches, myself."

"That's what I thought," McKay said. He hesitated a moment before adding, "So you've never owned such a car yourself?"

Brewster quickly responded, "No, never have."

"And as far as you know Zodiac doesn't own one either."

"If they did, I guess I would know about it," Brewster said.

Gene had been a criminal lawyer for many years, and he knew an evasive answer when he heard one. But was Brewster being deliberately evasive? And if so, why?

"So you're saying Zodiac International doesn't own a Dodge Viper?"

There was an instant of hesitation, before Brewster said, "Tell me, does this have something to do with John Rossi? I understand he's been poking around in my affairs."

Gene and Ted looked at each other. A question answered with another question. It was a tactic they both recognized.

McKay said, "I honestly don't know, Charles. The issue is being raised by Sunny Waikoloa's defense."

"Well I think he has more connections to this case than you realize. You might want to pick him up and talk to him."

"That's something I'll have to think about. You may be right."

"That it, then? I'm a little pressed for time this morning."

"Charles, does Zodiac own a Dodge Viper?" McKay asked once again. There was no response for a moment, and so he added, "If you're not sure, maybe you can have one of your people provide a list of cars purchased by the corporation."

"No, Gene, Zodiac does not own a Dodge Viper and never has."

"Thanks, Charles. Sorry to have bothered you."

There was a click on the line and Brewster was gone.

"Well, you got your answer," Ted said.

"Yeah, I did," McKay said. But Brewster's initial evasiveness was surprising, and his mind was opening to the possibility that Brewster knew something that he wasn't telling them.

Brewster put the phone down and thought of the Sir Walter Scott line, "Oh, what a tangled web we weave when first we practice to deceive." Brewster was a practiced liar, and he excelled at it, indeed took pride in his ability to do so. But he knew that there were many shades of the truth, and the one thing you didn't want to do was just flat-out lie. When you do that, and the lie is discovered, they've got you. And when you lie to a district attorney, they've got you behind bars. The only way to get out of a flat-out lie was to cover it up with other lies. Eventually you lose track of the lies, and you'll be exposed.

He had tried to avoid a flat-out lie about the car, but they had outmaneuvered him, forced him to deny its existence or they would come investigating. His quick calculation told him they would take his word if he gave it, and that would be the end of it. But now his intuition was telling him he had made a mistake, that Gene McKay had become or was becoming an adversary. Even if the D.A. believed him, John Rossi would never let go of it. What he had to do was get rid of Rossi. It would be no great loss. This one man was in large measure responsible for stopping a project that would employ thousands, and educate thousands more. It was plenty of justification for taking action. He picked up the phone and dialed a cell phone number. He left a one-sentence voicemail message: “I would like you to close out our position on that commodity we have been tracking.”

30

At around 4:00 in the afternoon, John Rossi and Joe Akuna were relieved of their positions on the road, replaced with a fresh group of warriors. Over 100 men had stood there since the initial confrontation, in a standoff with police and construction crews. They would continue their defiance until the police moved in and made arrests, or the bulldozers backed off. So far, the warriors were winning. The cops had made Brewster's crew move their bulldozers to the side to allow traffic to pass. The men on the road made room for cars to go in and out, but no construction equipment was allowed in. Lani had been in court that afternoon, getting a judge to rule that Brewster had no right to destroy the access road, at least for now. Brewster had gotten a different judge to issue an injunction preventing them from blocking the road, so technically the warriors were in violation of the law. If the cops began making arrests, the plan was for the men to fall back to defending the road up into the valley. Well covered by the press, the word of the incident was spreading around the islands like wildfire. It was a Friday, and as people got off work, they began arriving by car and by canoe, to camp out in the valley, at least for the weekend, to lend their support. A lot of them had never ventured to this part of Maui before, and John hoped that once they saw the valley in its pristine state, they would want to help keep it from being "developed."

The men being relieved got a ride down to the beach in the back of someone's pickup truck. They were hot and thirsty, and after drinking two full bottles of water, John waded out into the ocean and threw himself into an oncoming wave. The cool water felt wonderful, and he splashed and floated until he felt restored, then came out onto the beach. He saw Peter, the man he had met the other evening, working on his canoe, and walked over to him.

"Alright, us guys wen give 'em!" Peter said, reaching out and clasping John's hand.

"For now, anyway."

"We can be proud of this. First time in years we wen stop one developer. Not bad work fo' one *malihini*."

Joe had heard them talking and came over to the canoe. "Don't call this guy one *malihini*. This one *Kama'āina*. One *kanaka maoli*, this guy," Joe said, clapping John heartily on the back.

"Thank you, gentlemen. I hope that's a good thing to be," John said in his thick Jersey accent.

Joe and Peter looked at each other and burst out laughing.

"He sure no sound like one *kanaka maoli*," Peter said.

"What does it mean?" John asked them.

Peter put a hand on John's shoulder. "It means you one real Hawaiian kine guy," he said.

"Mahalo," John said quietly, choking down the emotion he felt at their acceptance of him in the land of his birth.

"Hey, you wen see dat stink eye you wen get from Brewster?" Joe asked John. "Dat guy, he no like you."

"I was surprised that he seemed to recognize me," John said.

"Recognize you? I think if he had one gun on him, he shoot you."

"Well, I guess it's a good thing I'm with friends."

"Maybe you should get Lani fo' come ovah here," Joe said.

"Why?"

"Just for da weekend, 'til tings calm down," Joe said. "You know Brewster not one frien' of hers, either."

Joe walked off and left John deep in thought. He had been so busy with all this, he hadn't considered that Lani might be in danger. Suddenly he was feeling very stupid. He told Peter he had to go, and he hitched a ride up into the valley. The only functioning phone was Oliver's, and there were a dozen people waiting to use it. He went to his house and showered and changed quickly, then got into his Jeep and drove out of the valley toward Wailuku. It was a slow, frustrating drive, with dozens of cars coming in. Several times he had to pull over and wait for an incoming line of cars to pass before he could go forward. He finally got to a location where his cell phone would work and called her office. There was no answer, just the voicemail. He tried her house, and there was no answer there either. He punched in the numbers for her cell, and got still another voicemail. He left a message saying that he was on his way. He continued around the island and drove to her office. It was locked up, and her car wasn't there. He got back into the Jeep and headed for Napili. There was a slow tourist car at the head of a line of cars snaking its way across the island. This made it easy for the two men in the brown Buick rental to follow him, from where they had first spotted him at Lani's office, keeping well out of sight. Neither they nor John paid any attention to the fabulous sunset taking place over the ocean to their left.

John drove through Lahaina and past Kā'anapali and finally got to the Napili turnoff. The traffic light was red, but he didn't wait for a left turn arrow. As soon as there was a break in the oncoming traffic, he turned and five minutes later he was pulling up to Lani's house. What he would have given to see her little silver CRV parked there. But the driveway was empty. John pulled in and parked, and walked into the house. His imagination was working overtime. He half expected to see the place ransacked, with signs of a struggle. But everything was normal. He didn't hear the car pull into the driveway. A few moments later, the door opened and she was there.

"Well, you've had a busy couple of days," she said.

He went over to her and hugged her hard and long, not trusting himself to say anything at first. She laughed. "So did you miss me or what?"

He kissed her sweet, precious face, her neck, her shoulders, her lips. The tension of the last few hours began to ebb and he finally found his voice. "Yes, I missed you terribly," he said.

"I missed you too," she said. She took him by the hand and led him toward the bedroom. "Let me show you how much."

And she did. Afterwards, as they lay in the bed, she reached for the TV remote control. "I suppose we'd better watch the news. See what Brewster is up to."

He gently pried the control out of her fingers. "Let's not. I'm tired of him." And then he had an idea. "Let's go over to the Kapalua Bay Hotel, listen to some slack key music, and have dinner."

"What a wonderful idea!"

They showered and dressed and drove to the hotel in her car. As they went in, they noticed the big black Mercedes parked at the lobby entrance. The music was playing as they walked into the lobby, and George Kahumoku was in his usual spot. Again, John was surprised at how empty the place was. There was just one other customer there, a young, smartly dressed woman wearing a scarf over her hair and sunglasses, despite the dim lobby lighting. There was an empty glass in front of her. There was something familiar about her. She made John think of a movie star traveling incognito. The musician smiled and nodded to him and Lani as they took a seat. The music was wonderfully relaxing after the tense events of the day, and John closed his eyes and let the waves of sound wash over him. A few minutes later, he got a poke in his side from Lani. She was looking at the young woman sitting a few chairs over from him. "Do you know who that is?" she asked him.

"No," John said, glancing over at her. "She looks kind of familiar, though. Is she an actress?"

"That's Brewster's wife."

John looked at the woman as surreptitiously as he could and realized that Lani was right. The bartender was bringing her a fresh drink, as George stopped playing and took his break.

"That's her third drink since we got here," Lani said.

"You're pretty observant."

"I'll tell you something else about her. She's a battered wife."

John glanced at the woman, but couldn't see any outward evidence of battery. "How do you know that?"

"Because half my cases are battered women. I know how to spot them."

"You think there's a black eye under those sunglasses?" John asked.

"I don't know," Lani said. "Maybe he doesn't hit her, but she's battered in some way, no question."

"Do you think she would talk to me?" John asked Lani.

"About what?"

"About whether her husband owns a gun. Or a yellow Viper."

Lani chuckled. "No, I don't think she'll talk to you."

"Even if Brewster is beating her up?"

"Even then."

"Can you think of any reason why I shouldn't try?"

"Because you'll probably embarrass yourself?"

John said, "What the hell. Around here, I embarrass myself every time I open my mouth."

Lani smiled at him, and then they saw Brewster's wife finish off her drink and stand up. John got up and followed her toward the lobby entrance. She saw him coming. Her body language said she knew she was about to be hit on, and was used to it. She did not look at John. A large young man John had not noticed before was walking briskly toward them.

John said, "Mrs. Brewster, my name is John Rossi."

She glanced at him then, with perhaps a little recognition.

"Jimmie Putnam was my best friend. I came here to take him home."

Her demeanor changed completely now, and she stopped and took off her sunglasses and looked at him, extending her hand. No black eye, John noticed, just glassy eyed. She was a beautiful woman. The young man had nearly reached them now, but she waved him away.

"Oh, yes, John. I'm so sorry for your loss. I met Jim a few times. He was a nice man." She was looking at him carefully. "But you're Hawaiian, aren't you?"

"I was adopted by a mainland family when I was four. This is the first time I've been back."

"How sad that your first time back has to be for this. I hope my husband has been able to help you," she said.

This was his opening, and John dove in recklessly. "Actually, he's made things very difficult. Do you know if your husband owns a gun?"

She stiffened visibly and put her sunglasses back on. He was losing her. "Mrs. Brewster, a yellow Dodge Viper was seen fleeing the scene of the murder. The D.A. thinks it was driven by the killer. Your husband denies owning such a car. Is that true?"

She stood there looking stunned for a moment. John wasn't being completely honest, of course. The D.A. thought that Sunny was the killer. He was just hoping he could shake something out of her. But Lani was right. Battered or not, his woman was not about to betray her husband. She turned and walked away as quickly as she could on slightly wobbly legs. John followed her to the front of the hotel and as she got into the Mercedes, the door held open by the driver/bodyguard, John said to her, "It's awfully important that we talk about this, Mrs. Brewster."

She did not look at him. The driver closed the car door, and a moment later she was driven off. John went back to where Lani was sitting and sat down.

"I see the old Rossi charm is still working," she said.

"You're right, she wouldn't say anything," John responded glumly.

She smiled at him and held out her hand. "Can we please get something to eat now? I'm starving."

He took her hand and they walked across the lobby to the stairway down to the restaurant.

Later, over dinner at the hotel, John told Lani he was feeling guilty about enjoying such a fancy place while his friends in the valley were probably sitting around a campfire eating who knows what. She surprised him when she laughed out loud at this. "Did you happen to notice a lot of large coolers in those canoes and pickup trucks?"

John remembered unloading quite a few of these the night before. "How did you know that?"

"We're Hawaiians, John. We come prepared to eat. I guarantee you that while you were on that road, a dozen guys were out in the mountains with guns, shooting feral pigs, while another bunch was digging a bunch of *imus* to roast them. They're eating better than we are."

"Okay, you're right. But I think I need to get back out there tonight."

"I understand."

"And I want you to go with me."

"John, I can't do that. I'm needed in Wailuku."

"Well, I'm worried about you."

"What in the world for?"

He didn't want to tell her about being chased along the road by the Tongans. "We've got people mad at us, powerful people."

"Maybe that's a new experience for you, but not for me."

She opened her purse and showed him the compact Colt .380 Mustang pistol she kept in there. "In answer to your next question, I know how to use it too. If anything, it's me who should be worried about you."

She's right, he thought. If he was a target, maybe she'd be safer by not being with him. But he'd seen no sign of the Tongans and was on the alert for them. He knew that once he got into the valley he'd be safe.

An hour later he left her at her house, making her promise to lock up. He drove out to the Napili Market. He wanted to pick up some ice to take out to the valley. But it was after nine, and the market had closed, the parking lot nearly empty. He sat in his car, trying to decide whether to drive down to the Star Market in Honokawai or just get out to the valley. Suddenly the doors of the late-model brown Buick parked a couple of spaces over opened, and two large men emerged and rapidly walked toward his car. He quickly started the engine and was about to drive away, when he heard one of them calling his name.

"Hey, Johnny. Where you goin'?"

It was a voice he recognized, with a thick New Jersey accent. He shut off the motor. This was just too crazy to believe. "Vinnie? What are you doing here?"

Vincent Mancini, his ex-future brother in law walked over to the car, Bruno Ricci at his side. "What am I doin' here? I'm on vacation, what the fuck you think I'm doin' here?"

"But I don't get it, what—"

And then he got it, as Vinnie opened his door and put a big hand on his arm, a deadly serious look on his face.

"They sent you all the way out here to kill me?" John said.

Vinnie snickered, then he and Bruno looked at each other and suddenly convulsed with laughter, holding their sides, unable to talk. John just sat there flabbergasted. They finally managed to compose themselves, and Vinnie grabbed John's arm again, and pulled him out of the Jeep.

"That's a good one. Wait 'til they hear that one back home. No, Johnny, we're not going to whack you. We're taking you home. There's an 11:45 flight to Newark tonight, and you, me, and Bruno are going to be on it." He got more serious. "You made my sister very unhappy. She's unhappy, my dad's unhappy. Now don't go making me unhappy too. Just come along with us. There's going to be a private family wedding ceremony tomorrow afternoon. Then you and Angela can have a nice honeymoon."

"Not in Hawai'i, though," Bruno said very seriously.

Vinnie and Bruno looked at each other and realized this was a pretty good joke, and were once again laughing. John could see nothing funny in the situation. "But we broke up. She's the one who broke it off."

"Hey, you don't break off an engagement with my sister like that."

"But she doesn't want to marry me."

"That's what she's sayin', but she don't really mean it."

"How can you know that?"

Vinnie was getting angry now, and he pulled John toward their car. "The important thing is, my dad don't think so, so you're going back to Jersey and you're marrying my sister, as planned."

They got to the car and Bruno opened the door. John began to struggle, and Bruno grabbed his other arm and bent it until it hurt. Bruno said, "Don't want to have a broken arm on your weddin' night, do you Johnny?" He pushed John into the back seat, while Vinnie went around and opened the trunk and pulled something out, then slammed it shut. He got into the back seat next to John carrying a small leather zippered case.

"Didn't want to have to do this to you Johnny," Vinnie said as he unzipped the case and pulled out a hypodermic needle. He held it up and tapped it expertly to get any air out. "This will help you relax for your journey."

John struggled with all his strength, but with the two of them holding him, he couldn't stop Vinnie from injecting him in the arm with whatever it was. There was no immediate effect, but John acted as if he were getting suddenly drowsy, and he let his body go limp. Vincent smiled at him. "Nice try, Johnny," he said as he closed the rear door of the car and got into the driver's seat. "This stuff takes a few minutes to take effect. Then you won't have to pretend."

John suddenly started kicking and struggling, but Bruno had a good grip on him. He couldn't go back to New Jersey, couldn't marry Angela. How did they expect to get him through a wedding ceremony?

Vinnie started the car, and drove about ten feet before they were hit hard from behind by a bright-blue Mustang.

Vinnie said, "For fuck sakes, can you believe this shit?" He stopped the car and got out.

Bruno called after him, "Forget it, just go."

Vinnie was looking at the back of the car in disgust. "We can't fuckin' go. Fuckin' fender is all bent into the fuckin' tire. Fuck!" He seemed to notice the other car for the first time. Two men were emerging from it, with pistols in their hands. Vinnie looked at them in astonishment. "Now this, I don't fuckin' believe."

One of the men pointed his pistol at Vinnie and said, "Where do you think you're taking him?"

Vinnie glared at him. "To Newark, fuck you care?"

The gunman said, "He's not going anywhere, except with us."

"Who the fuck are these guys?" Bruno was asking.

The gunman said to Bruno, "Okay, now I want you both to get out of that car, real slow. Keep your hands where I can see them."

Bruno and John got out of the car. The gunman asked John, "Who are these guys?" John was starting to feel woozy from the drug. His brain seemed to be slowly disconnecting from his mouth, and his speech was slurred as if he were drunk. "Theeshe are represelatives of a Northern New Jershey crime family," he said.

The two gunmen looked at each other. One of them pointed his pistol at John. "You—get in the car." John was feeling completely disoriented now. He started to get back into the Buick. The gunman yelled at him, "Not that car, this car!" and nodded toward the Mustang. John obediently went to the Mustang and started to get into the driver's seat. "I really don't think I should be driving," he said. The gunman said impatiently to his colleague, "Help him." The other man pulled John out from behind the wheel and put him in the back seat. John just wanted to lie down on the seat and close his eyes for a while, but he was startled by the sudden roar of a high performance engine and a blinding set of high beam headlights coming straight at them from across the parking lot.

The other four men were equally surprised.

"Now who the fuck is *that*?" Vinnie asked.

The four of them ran for cover to avoid being run over by the speeding vehicle headed right toward the two cars. John seemed to have lost any ability to move his arms and legs, but he watched with amusement as all the bad guys dove for cover. He just sat in the seat smiling, and bobbing his head agreeably. The last thing he would remember seeing was the sign on the oncoming GMC pickup reading, TONGAN BUILT. He passed out just before the impact.

31

When Wainani Brewster arrived home, she was distressed to find that one of her husband's cars was parked in front. He was supposed to be on his ship. For a moment, she sat in the car, fearful of going in. Then she thought, *Finally I've got something on you, you son of a bitch.* She got out of the car, knowing that even if he knocked her around, she had a way to get even. Still, out of habit, she found herself trying to open the front door and let herself in as quietly as possible. She was halfway up the stairs when she heard his voice behind her.

"Out for a little sip of something?"

"Yeah? Where have you been, initiating some wide-eyed, big-titted young lady into the mile-high club?"

"My, aren't we feeling courageous tonight? How many glasses of courage did you drink?"

"Fuck you."

"Ah, the quick wit that won the Miss Hawai'i title."

"Go fuck yourself," she said and turned to walk up the stairs.

"Don't you ever, ever turn your back on me when I'm talking to you." The coldness in his voice sent a chill through her.

She could hear him coming up the stairs behind her, but she wouldn't turn around. She felt the goose bumps as he approached.

She would wait until he had raised his hand to punch her before she mentioned the yellow car. She wanted to see the look on his face, and know that she had him. But he didn't punch her this time. He grabbed her long black hair from behind and yanked on it, spinning her around. She lost her balance and fell down the stairs, bouncing down all the way to the bottom. She lay there groaning. He calmly walked down the steps, past her lying there, and went into his den.

She picked herself up and sat on the bottom step. Bruises were already forming on her elbows and knees and forehead. A moment later he emerged from the den, carrying two large briefcases. He glanced at her disdainfully before opening the door and going out. She saw the door close behind him, and a few moments later heard the roar of his Ferrari as he peeled out of the driveway.

He's going to pay for this, she thought. *He's going to pay.* She got herself to her feet, made her painful way upstairs, and drew herself a bath. The household staff was gone for the day, and she had to do everything herself. She sat in the tub for a while, but soon became impatient for action and got out and dried herself. She dressed in jeans and a sweatshirt and packed a few things in an overnight bag. She was feeling more sober. She carried her bag downstairs and walked through the kitchen into the attached garage, where she switched on the lights. The garage was clean and neat and well lighted. Six of the seven parking spaces had cars in them, all but one with car covers to keep the dust off. The uncovered one was "her" car, a silver Porsche Boxster convertible. She drove it once in a while, but she preferred being driven in a limo.

Her husband was changing cars constantly, and she didn't know what any of them were, in fact hadn't been in the garage for weeks. She walked down the line pulling covers off the cars one by one, trying to remember what kind of car it was that that man in the hotel had told her about. All she could remember was that it was yellow, and so far, none of these cars was yellow. The last car at the end had a tightly fitting cover, and when she tried to remove it, it wouldn't come off. She realized that this cover had a padlock on it. She had no idea where the key might be. She yanked at the heavy fabric in frustration breaking a couple of long fingernails before she finally slumped down on the garage floor next to the car weeping in frustration.

After a few moments, it came to her that, as of now, she didn't care about him or any of his things. She was so accustomed to not touching, not moving, and certainly not damaging anything of his. Well, those days were over. There was a workbench full of tools, and in one of the drawers she found a utility knife. She took it out and walked over to the car, and carefully cut a small slit in the cover and pulled it apart. A lustrous yellow finish glowed in the lights. She cut a little more, and then really got into it, and slashed and slashed, laughing, joyfully ripping the cover to shreds. It was a bright-yellow sports car, apparently brand-new. The car door was unlocked and the key was in the ignition. She pushed the button on the garage wall and the door rolled open. She got in the car and started it up. The engine was very noisy. She hadn't driven a stick-shift car for several years, and it took her a few moments and a lot of gear crunching to get the hang of it and get it into reverse. She pressed on the accelerator, intending to back out slowly. The car responded immediately and shot out of the garage backwards. She was able to brake to a stop before it hit the fountain in the forecourt of the house. She put it into first gear and gingerly applied the gas this time, and got it moving out of the driveway.

The night air was cool, and she rolled all the windows down. She felt herself sobering up nicely. She would drive to her sister's house in Kula in upcountry Maui. Kanani and her husband had a farm with a barn, and she would put the car in there. In the morning, when Brewster found it missing, he would be forced to deal with her. The sense of power she felt was reinforced by the power of the car, and although it had at first frightened her, now she found it exhilarating. She came out of a corner and onto a straight section of road, and with a big smile on her face, she punched it.

Brewster's ship-to-shore radiophone rang at 2:00 a.m. as he lay in his stateroom reading. He was dancing close to the edge of disaster, and for the first time he could remember he was unable to sleep. All of his calls automatically forwarded here. He looked at the clock and figured it had to be some idiot on the East Coast who hadn't bothered to figure out what the time would be locally. He picked it up.

"Yes?"

"Is this Mr. Brewster?"

"Yes."

"Mr. Brewster, this is Lieutenant Craft, Maui P.D. I'm sorry to bother you at this hour, but we thought you might appreciate a call. Sir, your wife was involved in an automobile accident."

Brewster sat up in bed. *The bitch. He needed her.* "Is she okay?"

"Uh, well, yes sir, just a few bruises, but I'm afraid we had to arrest her. She was given a breathalyzer test and I'm sorry to say she failed it. We're holding her in jail here in Wailuku. Since it was *your* wife, we thought we should give you a courtesy call. She'll have to appear before the judge in the morning."

"Thank you, Lieutenant. Thank you for calling."

He hung up the phone. *Stupid bitch.* When he had caught her drinking and driving before, he had provided her with a car and a driver. At least he hadn't bought her the Mercedes 600SL he'd thought of initially. If she wanted to wreck a Boxster, fine. He was about to pick up the phone to call his attorney to see if he could get her released, but then thought, *Hell, let her rot in jail for the night.* Now he'd have to be in Wailuku in the morning, playing the concerned husband for the judge. The best he could hope for is that the press wouldn't get wind of it.

32

John awakened to bright sunlight, in a strange bed and a strange room. He had a terrible headache and the most god-awful taste in his mouth. He felt completely disoriented. He tried to force himself to think of the last thing he could remember. Then the light coming through the doorway dimmed and a huge, dark man with a mop of curly hair on his head was standing there looking at him. Now his recollection was stark and clear. Brewster's Tongans had gotten him. He heard the Tongan talk to someone in the other room, "He's awake." A moment later Joe stuck his head in the door. Joe and the Tongans. In that moment he knew that he had not been cautious enough. Lani was right. Joe was in on it, maybe even working for Brewster. But how could that be? Maybe he was hallucinating. Maybe he was dead. Joe came into the room and walked over to the bed. "How you feeling?"

"Where am I?" John asked in a raspy voice.

Two other huge Tongans squeezed through the door and studied him, concerned looks on their faces.

Joe said, "My house. Here in the valley. These guys wen bring you in last night. I going get you someting for drink. You going be safe here." He turned and left the room.

"Safe? Safe from whom?" John rasped after him.

"Hey, brah," one of the Tongans said. "We didn't know what was going on. We just figured no mo' da watching, we bettah grab you before those other guys did."

John was starting to remember. Vinnie was in Hawai'i. He thought it had been a bad dream. He spoke to the Tongans. "Why did Brewster want me brought here?" They put their fuzzy heads together to confer and John heard one of them ask another, "Brewster who?"

"Brewster," John said. "Your boss."

Then one of them said to John, "No, we not working for no Brewster. We working fo' you, brah."

"Is that why you almost ran me off the road?"

The three of them looked at their feet, embarrassed. One of them said, "Yeah, well, we sure sorry about dat. Somebody following you. We trying to protect you."

"Them guys following you, we put them outta business," another man said. They had a good laugh about this. "Got dem again last night, smash dat car good. Dey going have trouble next time try rent one car." They laughed again, ridiculous, high pitched giggles emanating from these huge bodies. John's head was spinning in confusion, and their silly laughter somehow got to him and he had to laugh too, although it made his head hurt worse.

"What's this bullshit about working for me. I don't even know who you are."

"No, it was our little brother, Maka. He say to look after you, so we been doin' it."

John had to think about this for a moment before he remembered their "little" brother from the Maui Business Development Board. He had given John potentially explosive information. Had he figured that he should also provide some protection? It was a nice thing for him to do, if that's what was going on. It would have been a good idea let John in on it.

Charles Brewster called his attorney in the morning, and at 8:30 he flew his helicopter off the deck of *Emperor of the Seas*, headed for Kahului airport. He was met by the attorney, who drove him out to the courthouse and explained that all that was needed would be a brief appearance before the judge. Normally, bail would be set at this time, although the attorney figured that, given Brewster's status in the community, Wainani would be released on her own recognizance. Brewster didn't pay much attention to any of this. He was familiar with the procedures. He would not have come at all, except that if the press had been alerted he would need to play the role of caring husband. He intended to have his wife sent home after the hearing so he could return to his ship and get back to business. It was Saturday, and he was sure that, once the weekend was over, most of the people camped out in the valley would have to go home. Without them blocking the way he would be able to move in with his heavy equipment.

They sat in the empty courtroom waiting for the judge: Brewster, the attorney, and Wainani, who had been brought in by a bailiff. Brewster positioned himself so the attorney was seated between his wife and himself. He didn't want to be anywhere near her. There was no press, and there were no spectators to witness their estrangement. She sat there sullenly and didn't speak to him. The bailiff and judge came in and the bailiff called the case. The attorney stood and handled everything; neither of the Brewsters had to say a word. The door at the rear of the courtroom opened, and Brewster turned and saw Gene McKay, the Maui County D.A., come in. He waved encouragingly to Brewster, who smiled back at him, grateful to have a powerful friend in the courtroom. It was over in a couple of minutes, with Wainani released to go home. After the judge left the chamber, the Brewsters and their attorney stood at the back of the courtroom with the D.A.

Gene said, "I hope you don't mind my dropping in. I heard about your wife, and I wanted to make sure everything went smoothly for you."

"Thank you, Gene. I'm grateful," Brewster told him.

"These things can happen. If there's anything my office can do, please let me know."

They shook hands and were about to walk out when they were approached by the bailiff. He had some forms in his hand. "Excuse me sir, you'll need these to get the car out of police impound," he said. He read off the form, "Yellow Dodge Viper." Looking at the form he added cheerfully, "Looks like it's not too badly damaged, you probably can just drive it right home." He handed Brewster the forms, smiled and said, "Have a nice day."

And Charles Brewster knew right then he wasn't going to have a nice day. He glanced at Wainani. Her sullen look had been replaced with a smirk. He wanted so badly to punch her in the face. He took a few steps toward the courtroom door, but Gene said, "Charles, about that car. I think we need to talk."

"Gene, this is not a good time," Brewster said.

"I understand, but you told me . . ."

Wainani had a smile of triumph on her face. "That's right, honey, tell him about the car. Let's see you explain that away, cocksucker!"

"Dearest, just calm down," Brewster pleaded with her. But she wouldn't calm down. She had lost her leverage with him, but maybe she could still hurt him. "Tell him about the night Jim Putnam was murdered. You were out with that car, for hours. You wanted me to say you were home, but I'm not going to be your alibi."

Now the attorney said to her, "Mrs. Brewster, you shouldn't be speaking of these things."

But she went on. "You spent hours cleaning it. First time I've ever seen you wash your own car," she said triumphantly.

Brewster grabbed Gene's arm and attempted to pull him out of earshot of his wife. He said as quickly and quietly as he could, "You see, I bought that car for her. She wanted a Viper so badly. She's the only one who's ever driven it. When you asked me about it, in connection with the murder, well, I didn't know what to think. Not that I believe for a minute that she could be responsible. Sure, I heard the rumors about her and Jim Putnam, but I . . . ."

They were interrupted by an angry wail from Wainani. "What are you saying to him, you bastard!"

"Don't worry honey, we'll fight this together," Brewster said to her.

Gene turned to Wainani and asked, "Mrs. Brewster, is it true that the car belongs to you?"

The attorney could sense imminent danger to his clients, and he spoke up quickly. "You don't have to answer that, Mrs. Brewster."

She came at Brewster, fists flailing. The attorney and the D.A. had to keep her from hitting her husband. "You filthy, lying son of a bitch!"

She continued cursing and yelling, and the attorney and the bailiff dragged her from the courtroom, leaving Brewster and Gene McKay alone.

Brewster said, "I'm sorry you had to witness that. We've been having some trouble at home. Still, I'm hopeful that we can work it out. She's a wonderful, warm person. She just shouldn't drink."

"Charles, I can't overstate the seriousness of this situation," McKay said.

"Oh come on, you can't be telling me you think she's in any way responsible for murder. I want you to know that if you attempt to charge her, I'll defend her with every dime I have."

"Charles, if I were you, I would follow my attorney's advice and not say anything else. We are going to have to interview both you and your wife."

"I have no problem with that."

"I'm going to give her time to calm down. I need you both to be here tomorrow morning at nine. You'll be interviewed separately. You should both have attorneys present."

Brewster acknowledged with a nod, and left the courtroom.

A few minutes later, Gene was in Ted Wong's office describing what had happened in the courtroom.

"Unbelievable," Ted said, shaking his head.

Gene said, "What I want you to do is grab that car. Make sure the police don't let it out of their sight. In fact, go down to that impound lot yourself. I want the lab guys to go over that car microscopically."

Ted picked up the phone and quickly dialed a number.

Brewster had the attorney take charge of his wife. The lawyer had stuffed the screaming woman into his car and driven off with her. Brewster's Mercedes and driver had come over from West Maui to drive him to the airport. They drove to Kahului, Brewster feverishly deep in thought. How was he going to get out of this? The cops would grab the car for sure, and they would find traces of Putnam's blood. Sunny Waikoloa was going to be set free, and, depending on whom the police believed, either he or Wainani would be arrested for murder. Even if Wainani was the one charged, the scandal would ruin his chances to win over the politicians and the people. He would have to spend millions defending her, or people would think he was a shit. And if he were charged, it was certainly all over for him. Even if he were eventually found innocent, he could end up like O.J., bankrupt and with his reputation ruined.

He was facing the abyss and for the first time in his life he felt frightened. Where do you go to escape prosecution for murder these days? Maybe some small Pacific nation. After all the years of successes he just couldn't believe it had come to this. Now he had to turn his thoughts to escape. One thing he would do was immediately transfer everything of value to the *Emperor of the Seas.* Out there at sea he would be difficult to get to. In less than an hour, he could be in international waters. It would give him time to think, time to let things settle down here. He could quickly put his hands on fifty million, if he had to. It was all someone else's money, but he didn't care about that now. It was time to start making plans to flee, he thought bitterly.

The chauffeur made eye contact with Brewster in the rear-view mirror. "Sir, I'm sorry about last night."

"What?" Brewster said, resenting the intrusion on his thoughts.

"Well, her taking your car and all. I think she was pretty upset by that guy in the hotel."

"What guy?" Brewster asked absently.

"Some guy was hitting on her at the hotel."

"You're supposed to be handling those situations," Brewster said, not really caring about this.

"Sir, I would have, but she waved me off. I think she knew the guy."

"Yeah, okay, fine," Brewster said dismissively.

The driver seemed to want to explain himself. "He looked Hawaiian to me. He came in with another woman, pretty, dark haired, also Hawaiian."

Brewster had a growing suspicion about the man in the hotel, and he was paying attention now. "Did you hear what he said to her?"

"Something about it being important that they talk, something like that."

"That's it?"

"Well, one funny thing, this guy looked Hawaiian but he sure didn't sound like one."

"Meaning what?"

"He had kind of an eastern accent, if you know what I mean."

Brewster knew exactly what he meant and who the man in the hotel was. He hadn't heard from his men yet. He had sent a couple of guys to deal with Rossi last night, and he knew the man would be dead by now. Seething in red-hot anger when he thought of what Rossi had done to him, he wished he could have done the deed himself.

33

John didn't fully recover from the effects of the drug until the afternoon. As his head cleared, his recollection of the previous night's events returned. There had been two mystery guys there, guys with guns. They had to be working for Brewster. If it hadn't been for Vinnie, he'd probably be in a hospital bed right now, or in the morgue, lying next to Jimmie. And if it hadn't been for the Tongans, he'd be in New Jersey, married to Angela. The Mancinis weren't going to give up until he was back in Jersey. Who knew what Vinnie and Bruno were going to try next? He was going to have to stay in the valley until he could figure out some way to get out safely.

He couldn't stop worrying about Lani. He went down to Oliver's place and called her. She was fine, and happy to hear from him. Later that day, by the fifth time he called her, she was beginning to sound a little annoyed with him, and he promised not to call again until she got home that evening. And yes, she would keep her cell phone with her and switched on at all times. Feeling much better, he insisted on taking his place on the road for a few hours. All that day, the warriors willingly moved to allow incoming and outgoing traffic to pass. John was surprised at how many tourists came in to lend their words of support and bring treats like ice cream for the kids. It appeared that not everyone wanted a casino operation here, despite what Brewster might think.

Brewster was holed up on his ship, moored a couple of miles out to sea from the valley. From there, he had complete communications with his operations. By this time all of his thoughts and actions were oriented around escape, so when the call came in from State Senator Alfred Toguchi, he didn't care what the man had to say.

"You know, all this stuff about the people defending their valley, it doesn't play too well for us in the court of public opinion," Toguchi said.

"I understand, Alfred."

Toguchi had been expecting an explosion of temper from Brewster, and could hardly believe the mild reaction. He braced himself for an outburst when he said, "You know, the anti-development crowd is spreading all these stories about you and a bulldozer."

"Yeah, I heard about that," Brewster responded mildly.

"I know I've been saying this for three years now, but I think we maybe have to wait until next year's legislative session. Not much chance of legalized gambling this year, I'm afraid," Toguchi told him. He figured that if this statement didn't cause Brewster to blow, nothing would.

Again, Brewster shocked him by simply saying, "Okay, we'll see what happens then."

"I must say, you're taking this well, being very patient. Maybe we'll finally make a Hawaiian of you yet."

Brewster hung up the phone and thought about that stupid goddam car. Now the police had their hands on it. He had worked hard that night to get the blood out. There had been so much of it. You couldn't bludgeon a human head at close range without getting some on you. The car had been brand-new when he took it to the meeting with Putnam. He'd just gotten it that day, and couldn't wait to drive the damn thing. It wasn't even the kind of car he liked, an American muscle car. He just wanted to try one out, to sample the pure power of the V10 engine. He never kept his cars for long anyway. Afterwards, he'd seen the tour bus coming out of Lahaina, and he'd been forced to drive the other way, to Wailuku. It was dark out there, and there were few houses near the road. He had to hope he hadn't been seen. But someone *had* seen the car. And now, they would find traces of Putnam's blood in it. The car had been safe in the garage. No one knew it was there, and they were hardly about to come to Charles N. Brewster with a search warrant. He could try to pin it on Wainani, maybe even manufacture some witnesses to her "affair" with Putnam, giving her a possible motive. But in the end, it didn't matter. Even if she went to prison instead of him, the scandal would drag on for months, and by that time he would be ruined. It was a question of spending the rest of his ready cash on a legal defense or taking what he had and running. He pulled out the nautical navigational charts of the Pacific. In this yacht he could reach anyplace in the world. He figured that, with the ship and the cash and gems he could take with him, he could find some island kingdom that would welcome him with open arms.

He could scarcely believe it had come down to this. He was going to be like Robert Vesco, a fugitive financier. And all because of one man, John Rossi, an electrician from New Jersey. His phone rang again. He had no desire to talk to anyone, but when he saw the number flash on his caller ID, he quickly picked up the phone.

"I hope it was painful," he said into the phone.

There was a pause on the end of the line. No direct response had been expected or wanted. "Well, sir, um, I hate to have to tell you this, but it did not go well," a man's voice said.

"What the fuck are you telling me?" Brewster said.

"The man has a lot of friends. It was a nightmare, sir. He's out in the valley now, and I don't know of a way to get to him. Maybe we should let things cool down for a few days."

Brewster was overcome by a sudden deadly calm. They had failed. But in failure there was an opportunity for him to deal with Rossi himself. He practically salivated at the prospect. "We will not be letting things cool down," he said icily. "There is a way to get to him. This is what you are now going to do."

After he had dictated the information to the man on the phone, he hung up and punched in a number.

Lani was alone in her office when the phone rang. She was surprised to hear the voice of Charles Brewster. She had never met him before, but she recognized his voice from his numerous appearances on TV. But instead of his usual quiet, imperious tone, he sounded downcast and beaten.

"Mrs. Miller, this is Charles Brewster. I'm hoping you'll be able to help me."

She did not answer immediately, both surprised and suspicious.

Brewster went on. "I know this call is unusual. What you need to know is that I have reason to suspect that your client, Sunny Waikoloa, may be innocent."

She thought, *If he meant to surprise me, he's definitely succeeded.*

"Why aren't you talking to the D.A. about this, Mr. Brewster?"

"I guess you haven't heard about what happened in the courtroom today."

"No, I haven't."

"I suggest that you talk with your Ted Wong about that."

"I'll do that."

"Let me get right to the point, Mrs. Miller. I have some reason to believe that my wife may know something about the murder of James Putnam."

If she had been surprised before, she was rocked now. But she responded automatically as an attorney. "You should retain counsel, Mr. Brewster. And if you're looking for representation, I can't help you."

"I'm not seeking representation. I'm seeking the truth. Are you willing to help me with that? Are you willing to take an extraordinary action that may get your client out of jail?"

"Of course I want to see Sunny Waikoloa go free. But do you expect me to believe that you're calling me to implicate your own wife in the crime?"

"Listen to what I am saying. I don't believe for a minute that Wainani committed murder. That's not my point at all. The fact is, my wife is hysterical. She knows something about the murder, but she won't talk to me, and she won't talk to her lawyer. She says she is willing to trust you. You can find out what really happened. You're an officer of the court, aren't you? Don't you have a duty to find the truth?"

"I also have a duty to behave in an ethical manner. I'm just not sure if—"

Brewster interrupted her. The man was sounding more and more desperate. "I'm asking you for one thing, and one thing only. Just come to my house and talk to her, just the two of you. I'm not going to influence things. In fact, I will not even be there. I've asked the district attorney to be present in the house, but he will not be in the room when you talk to her. Do it for your client, not for me."

Lani's mind was working overtime. It was a chance to free Sunny, if Brewster was being sincere. But was he? This was the man who had slashed John's tires, made threats. What else might he be capable of? "I am going to talk to Ted about this, before I do anything."

"Please do. And as soon as you do, please go to my house. I don't know how much longer she'll be willing to talk."

Brewster gave her the address of his home in Kapalua, and as soon as she hung up, she dialed Ted's number. He was out of the office, but was expected back soon. The whole idea was just too crazy to be true. She sure as hell wasn't going to Brewster's house without some protection. Still, if Brewster was cracking, it could get John off the hook as well as her client. It didn't seem like there would be a lot to lose by driving out there. She made up her mind, and packed her briefcase. Twenty minutes later, about halfway through the central isthmus of the island, she dialed Ted's number again and he answered it himself.

She got right to the point. "Tell me what happened in the courthouse today with Brewster and his wife."

Ted was being evasive, as usual. "I wasn't there."

"Then why did Brewster ask me to call you and get you to tell me what happened?"

"Brewster called you?"

"I just got off the phone with him. He says his wife is hysterical."

"She sure was this morning."

"He didn't sound so good himself."

"I'm not surprised."

"So talk to me."

"You know I'm not going to do that. It's all hearsay anyway."

"Do you think Wainani Brewster killed Jim Putnam?"

Ted did not respond immediately. She knew him well, and his hesitation spoke volumes to her. "I'm not answering a question like that. I'm a prosecutor, for God's sake."

"Where is Gene McKay?" she asked him. "Has he gone out to Brewster's place?"

"I don't know where he is. He's not in the office."

She said, "Thanks, Ted," as sarcastically as she knew how, and hung up on him. So Brewster was telling the truth, at least partially. She called John and left him a voicemail message saying that she was on her way to the Brewster home to talk to Wainani.

At around 5:00 p.m., Brewster sent most of his crew ashore in the launch. There was one man left aboard, deep in the engine room where he oversaw the generators and other equipment that needed to be kept running. The launch was a sturdy thirty-six-foot all-weather vessel with twin inboard diesels. It would be in Lahaina in thirty minutes. The crew had instructions to meet a man named Lester French there and help him load some equipment aboard before taking their shore leave.

When the launch arrived in Lahaina, the crew docked it and shut down the engines. Lester French and another man were waiting there on the dock with a large metal locker, which the crew helped them load on board. The other man then took the boat out to deliver the locker to the ship, promising to be back for the crew later. Lester got in his car and drove to the Kalonahoa Valley. When he arrived about an hour later, he set about to find John. John had just finished his tour of duty on the road and had gone for a swim. The beach was packed with people—men, women, and children. It was like a big family luau, despite the serious reason for their being there. John was helping Peter retie one of the lashings on an outrigger when Lester French came strolling nonchalantly down the beach toward him. John thought he looked familiar, but couldn't place him. After a moment, he suddenly remembered who this guy was: it was one of the gunman who had attempted to hijack him. Lester walked right up to John confidently.

"You son of a bitch. I can't believe you'd just come strolling in here," John said to him.

"Trouble, John?" Peter asked.

Lester said to John, "I need to talk to you. Alone."

"Fine," John told him. "After we talk, we're going to have a conversation with one of those cops up the road."

"You'd better hear what I have to say first."

As Peter watched them curiously, Lester led John toward the water, where the sound of the surf would drown out their words.

"Talk fast," John said. "The police are waiting."

Lester smiled at him. "We have Lani Miller."

John pulled back his fist to hit him, but Lester ably blocked the punch. "Don't go doing that, if you ever want to see her again."

"What do you want from me?"

"Mr. Brewster would just like to talk to you, that's all. But you haven't been so cooperative."

"This is how he sets up a meeting?"

"He has some very private things he needs to say to you. He knew you wouldn't come otherwise."

"You expect me to believe that?"

"No, not really," Lester said indifferently. "Look, the fact is, we have your girlfriend. You want her to live, you're just going to have to go along with this."

"That's bullshit. How do I know you have her anyway?"

"Why don't you try calling her?"

John had a terrible feeling deep in his gut then. If this guy was confident enough to have him do that, it was a bad sign. But if it was a bluff, John was going to call it.

"I will. That's exactly what I'm going to do."

Lester took out his cell phone. The "No Service" message appeared in the window. John said to him, "You don't get cell phone service here. I'm going to drive up the hill and call her. You can wait here."

For the first time, Lester looked a little disconcerted. He didn't like to let John out of his sight. "Don't dawdle," he said. "And don't tell anyone else, or I won't take you to her. She doesn't have much time."

John left him angrily, hurried over to his Jeep, and roared off in a spray of sand and gravel. Peter had been watching the heated confrontation. John had told him about his misadventure the evening before, and he suspected that this man was somehow connected. He walked over to Lester, who was leaning casually against a canoe.

"What was that about?" he asked Lester.

Lester gave him a smirk, and said, "I'd say that was none of your business, old man."

Peter grabbed Lester by the shirt front and said, "Let's try again. What was that about?"

The altercation was beginning to draw a crowd, and Lester was getting spooked. He was not exactly among friends here. A little girl's voice spoke up. "Grampa, what are you doing to that man?"

Peter turned to find himself faced with his wife and children and two grandkids. He let go of Lester and went over to his wife and hugged her. "Aloha Meleana," he said.

"Peter, what's going on here? Who is that?" she asked him.

Peter gazed at his wife, a gentle, kind-eyed woman who looked as if she couldn't imagine hurting another human being, no matter how evil. Peter looked across at Lester, who was chuckling to himself. He went over to him and said, "You know, you're right. It's not my place to ask you any questions." He then called over to a campfire on the beach where a group of men were roasting marshmallows. "Hey, Kelepi, Mateni, Dennis. Can you come ovah here for one minute." Lester was taken aback to see the three huge Tongans who had crashed their truck into his car last night and abducted Rossi. These were people he didn't care to deal with. They came over to Peter and Lester.

"Hey, we know dis guy," Mateni said to Peter.

"Oh yeah, we ran into him last night," Kelepi said.

Mateni snorted and poked Kelepi in the ribs. "Ran into him. Good one."

The three of them laughed, but to Lester it did not sound at all funny. Peter said to them, "Why don't you take him ovah to da rocks there and ask him why John is mad at him?"

Mateni said to French, "You made our frien' mad? We nevah like dat." They went over to Lester and picking him up bodily; they hauled him over to the rocks. About five minutes later they were back, half carrying, half dragging Lester. The front of Lester's pants had a big dark spot where he had wet himself. Peter and several other canoeists came over for a debriefing.

It took John thirty minutes to make his calls and return to the beach. He had tried to reach Lani, dialing each number with an increasing feeling of alarm. Finally he called his voicemail. There was a message from her. The Viper had been located, and Brewster had something important to tell her. She was on her way to Brewster's house, she said.

But where was she now? John knew then that he was going to have to go with this guy. Brewster would try to kill him or have him killed. But if there was any chance to save Lani, he would willingly take it. Life was not worth living without her.

When he got back to the beach, he was surprised to see Peter, the Tongans, and several others talking to Lester French. The women and children had been shooed away, and the men were conferring in quiet, urgent tones. John walked up to them and saw that Lester had a pained, frightened look on his face.

John said, "I have to go with this guy."

"No you don't," Peter said.

"Peter, I do. They have Lani."

"Yeah, and we know where." He pointed out toward Brewster's ship, the lights clearly visible a couple of miles away. "Dat's where he was going take you."

"How?"

"By launch from Lahaina harbor. But we know one better way fo' get there."

John looked at Peter and realized what he was thinking. "He might kill her if he sees a bunch of canoes coming. I think you would put her in great danger."

"What, you think he was going let her go after this? Or you?"

John thought Peter was right, but he was very nervous about this new plan. Peter spoke to the Tongans. "I like you to take Mr. French to Oliver's house and if he no like have both his arms broken, he going call Mr. Brewster on his boat fo' tell him that he has Mr. Rossi and is going Lahaina with him." The Tongans dragged Lester to their truck, threw him in the back like a sack of potatoes, and drove off with him.

Peter said, "That gives us about an hour to approach the boat quietly and get ourselves aboard."

"No, I won't do it that way," John told him.

"Listen, John, we gotta work together."

"Don't you see? If he sees someone besides me, there's no telling what he'll do."

"We going take him by surprise."

"*I'll* take him by surprise, in a one-man canoe. We've got plenty of them here."

Peter snorted. "What, and you going paddle out there yourself?"

"New Jersey is full of lakes. I've been paddling a canoe since I was five years old."

"Not in the open ocean."

"It's a calm sea tonight. The moon isn't up yet. I'll be on that boat before he knows what hit him."

"You don't know how many people he get with him out there."

"My guess is not very many. He wouldn't want any witnesses."

"But you don't know that."

"All I know for sure is that he's got Lani out there, and time is running out."

Peter thought about this for a moment, and then signaled to some of the other men on the beach. They picked up a one-man outrigger canoe and took it down toward the water. John followed them. On the shore, John could hear a bare-chested *kūpuna* begin a chant. He sang a verse, *Hole Waimea i ka ihe a ka makani*, and the verse was echoed by people on the beach and by the men carrying John's canoe. Another verse followed, and then a third. *Hao mai nā`ale a ke Kīpu`upu`u, He lā`au kala`ihi ia na ke anu, I `ō`ō i ka nahele o Mahiki.* By this time dozens of voices were responding.

"What is that?" John asked Peter as he climbed awkwardly into the canoe and was handed a paddle.

"It's a chant of blessing for a warrior about to go into battle."

34

John had sat in the one-man outrigger canoe as they walked it in through the surf, a couple of hundred people standing on the beach watching and chanting. The men had given the boat a shove and John had started paddling. There was a foot-operated rudder they had shown him how to use, and the paddle was gripped a little differently. Other than that, it was a lot like paddling a standard canoe. Now, a half mile from the beach, and with almost two miles to go to the boat, he was having second thoughts. It was lonely and dark out here. The stars overhead formed a vast canopy of white. Earlier, surrounded by friendly people, emboldened by the sound of the chanting, he'd been full of courage. Now he glanced back toward the beach. He was immediately sorry he did. It seemed miles away, and the realization that he was so far from land filled the pit of his gut with dread. He had never felt so isolated. Peter was right. The Pacific Ocean was not Lake Shawnee. He focused on the distant lights of the boat and concentrated on keeping up a steady stroking rhythm.

After forty minutes of non-stop paddling his arms and shoulders were beginning to ache, and Brewster's boat did not seem any closer. He felt a panic rising. The ship appeared to him to be getting farther away. Maybe they had weighed anchor and were sailing off. With Lani! He dug in and paddled as hard as he could. He began to worry that not only might he not be able to catch the ship, but even if he did he would be too exhausted to do anything useful when he finally got there. After about ten minutes, he could see that he was definitely getting closer. His imagination had gotten the best of him—the ship was still at anchor. He let himself slacken the pace a bit to conserve his energy.

Another twenty minutes and he was almost there. The vast, white-painted hull of the *Emperor of the Seas* loomed high above his head, He wondered how he was going to be able to get on board. No one was visible on the ship, and only a few of the cabin windows showed any light. He could only hope he was right about there being few people aboard. The night was intensely quiet, and he could hear the gentle lapping of the water against the ship's hull as he tried to figure out what to do. He could see where the stern was and he paddled in that direction. Now he saw that there was a diving platform and a small open deck at the rear of the ship. He maneuvered over to it and tied his canoe to a cleat. Being careful to keep his balance, he stood up in the canoe and stepped aboard the ship.

There was a ladder, and he climbed it to the main deck. In front of him was a small swimming pool glistening with underwater lights. It was surrounded by a teak deck. There was a door leading into the ship on the far side of the pool. He moved toward it like a cautious deer, his senses sharpened. The doorway led into a lounge. He walked through it and found himself in a bar, with a huge circular counter that looked like it was made from the timber of old Spanish galleons. He went through another door into a dining room with a long polished table and enough chairs to seat twenty or more. The luxuriously thick carpeting felt strange against his bare feet. He exited through a side door, walked along the outside deck, and re-entered the ship through another door farther forward. Here there was a grand spiral staircase that seemed to give access to all of the various decks.

He decided to go up first. Ascending the stairs quickly and quietly to the top deck, he walked warily through a teak double doorway to what he figured must be Brewster's stateroom. There was a large sitting area with sofas and chairs, and walls lined with books. He recognized one of the paintings on the wall as a Renoir. An alcove contained an office with a couple of computers, printers, and fax machines. Back out on deck he made his way to the front of the ship. Through a glass door there he could see the bridge. Various lights and gauges were lit up, but no crew was present. Someone had to be manning this equipment, but where were they? He walked along the outside deck toward the stern, and saw Brewster's helicopter sitting on a small deck there, but not a single soul was around. He was beginning to think he was on a ghost ship.

He went back to the staircase and down four decks to the lowest level. Here he could hear the hum of equipment through the doors that led toward the front and back of the ship. He opened one of the doors slowly. It was some kind of storage room, with a dozen or so large metal lockers stacked up. Brewster had been packing. He realized he wasn't likely to find Brewster down here, so he went up a deck and through a door. He found himself faced with a dimly lit corridor punctuated with nearly a dozen polished teak doors. He crept stealthily down the corridor, slowly opening each door. They were staterooms of varying sizes, all with the beds neatly made and no sign of inhabitants. He began to wonder if this whole thing had been a ruse to get him on board. Maybe the big containers were loaded with explosives. They would blow up, sinking the ship and John with it. And Lani too, if she was really here. But how could they have gotten her aboard? She might have allowed herself to be lured to Brewster's house, but they would have had to carry her aboard by force. How could you force a person onto a launch in busy Lahaina harbor in broad daylight. Then he thought with a start of the containers. They were certainly big enough to carry a person. He turned quickly and raced back down the corridor toward the stairway. Just before he reached it there was a cold voice behind him.

"Welcome aboard. I didn't expect you so soon."

John turned slowly to face Charles Brewster. Brewster was standing down at the far end of the corridor holding a shotgun pointed at John. "You've seen my plane and now you've had an opportunity to see my ship. You're a lucky man, Mr. Rossi."

"Where is she?"

"Why don't we go out on deck? You seem to have worked yourself into a lather."

John gauged his chances of getting the shotgun away from Brewster. Brewster was a good ten feet away. A twelve-gauge fired at that range would kill him, and the distance between them was too great for John to grab the gun away from him. John walked slowly up the stairs to the upper deck, Brewster keeping plenty of distance behind him. They stood on the deck, surrounded by the quiet, dark sea, and Brewster slowly raised the gun.

"I'm used to shooting skeet off this deck. This will be a new experience for me."

"Can you tell me why? Did you murder Jimmie?"

Brewster lowered the gun slightly, but kept it pointed at John's stomach. "This is a murder. That one was an accident. Well, more or less. He was going to issue that press release if I didn't agree to pull out of his precious valley. It would have tied up the project indefinitely. Your friend Jimmie was going to cost me everything."

"But how did you get Sunny out there?"

Brewster laughed crazily. "Sunny was a gift from the gods. He just showed up. Jim asked him to come. I didn't know he'd be there until his truck turned up on the road. Sunny was supposedly going to convince me to pull out of the valley." Brewster laughed, "Your friend was an idiot."

"So you shot him."

"You should have seen the look on his face when I pulled the gun." Brewster was grinning like delightedly. "He was so shocked. The bullet went right into his gaping open mouth."

He was getting into it now, enjoying telling his story for the first time. The raconteur in him had been denied up until now, unable to tell anyone the best story of his life. "So get this, talk about fast thinking, I had this fishhook I'd been wearing around my neck. A Hawaiian good luck thing. And I remembered, can you believe it, about putting a fishhook through the cheek of a traitor. So I hooked him, then bashed his head in. I figured on getting away toward Lahaina, you know, because Sunny was supposed to be coming from the other way. I figure Sunny shows up, reports the crime, and he's going to be a suspect. All I have to do is let the police know that Putnam worked for me. But it gets even better, because Sunny looks at the body, gets blood on him, picks up the club."

Brewster laughed hysterically. "And then, he confesses! He figures it's because of him that Putnam died. The best I was hoping for was that he's found at the scene and becomes a suspect. All I had to do is drive to Wailuku. It's dark out, the road is empty."

"But somebody saw your car."

Brewster's mood sobered. "Yeah, that damn car. If I had known I was going to have to kill him, I would have taken something less distinctive."

He lowered the gun barrel a few inches, and John tensed himself for a lunge for the weapon. Brewster was alert for it, and smiled and raised the barrel again. "Anything else you want to know?"

"Why kill me?"

"Because I goddam well feel like it. A week ago I had it made. Then you show up. I've been on the cover of *Time* magazine, *Fortune*, *Business Week* three times for God's sake! And who the hell are you? Nobody! Now I've got to pack up and leave. You think I'm going to leave you here to gloat? No! You're going to die and I'm going to see it happen myself. You can join your friend Jimmie in hell."

"What about Lani?"

"She's served her purpose."

"Is she aboard? Is she alive?"

Brewster was enjoying John's plaintive questions, his obvious distress. He was grinning now. "Yes to question one, no to question two. Those containers you saw in the cargo room are watertight. She's been in there a good hour or two. I don't imagine she's still with us by now, do you?"

He raised the shotgun to fire. John thought of Lani suffocating to death in one of the containers below. His heart hurt to think of the possibility that he might have been in time to save her, had he known where she was when he first boarded. He looked at Brewster and the dark sea behind him, and thought that this would be the last thing he would see in his life. In an instant, he had the sensation of his life passing before his eyes. It was more like an evaluation. In that brief moment he felt that it had been a good life, especially since he returned to Hawaiʻi. If only he could have saved Lani. He got himself ready to make a final, certainly fatal lunge for the gun. He knew Brewster wouldn't miss him at this range.

From the quiet ocean next to the ship Peter's shouting voice abruptly broke the silence. "Dat one great story, Brewster!"

Startled, both John and Brewster whipped their heads around in the direction of the voice. Brewster, the practiced skeet shooter, had automatically pointed his weapon toward the new target. John saw his one and only chance and he launched himself at Brewster. A split second later, Brewster realized his mistake and tried to bring the gun back around. By this time John was on him. He grabbed the gun by the barrel just as it fired with a thunderous roar into the air. With one swift motion, John yanked the gun out of Brewster's hands and flung it overboard, where it splashed into the water below. Brewster just stood there, stunned. All John could think about was Lani, in an airtight container below. He leaned out over the railing to yell out in the darkness to Peter.

"I've got to go look for Lani."

Suddenly he found himself flailing in the air, pushed overboard by Brewster, who had already hit the stairway to the upper deck by the time John splashed into the water. John came up gasping and choking. But all he could think about was Lani, and he swam quickly for the stern of the ship. He heard some shouts from the water.

"He's going for the helicopter!"

John didn't care about Brewster. He stroked quickly to the diving deck and hauled himself on board. He climbed the ladder two rungs at a time and raced down the deck to the stairway leading down to the cargo hold. Above him, he could make out the whine of the helicopter turbine as it came up to speed.

He slammed open the door to the hold. There were a dozen containers aboard, stacked on top of each other. He pulled the first one off the top of a stack and saw how it was latched, six stainless steel latches arranged around the cover. He quickly flipped open each of the latches and threw back the cover. The container was filled with sealed cardboard boxes. He could see that there was a rubber gasket around the opening, providing an airtight seal. He shoved the heavy container to one side and started on the next one. He worked in a frenzy, pulling down containers, throwing himself on the covers to get at the latches and pulling them open, then going on to the next one. Flooding into his mind was a horrifying vision of opening Jimmie's casket and seeing him lying there so lifelike, but dead.

Then he noticed a container at the bottom of one of the stacks. This one was as tightly latched as the others, but the seal was broken by a piece of leather sticking out. He threw the other containers off and concentrated on this one. It was hard to get the latches open because the leather object had partially jammed the lid. Finally the last latch came loose and John pulled the cover off. Lani was in there, lying on her back like Jimmie in his coffin. John stared in dread at her still form. She didn't look dead, but neither had Jimmie. He bent close to her, listening for breathing or a heartbeat. Sea water from his dunking in the ocean dripped on her face.

"You're all wet," she said.

He pulled back his face and looked at her. She was squinting at the bright lights in the room, trying to open her eyes. His heart swelling with joy, he reached down and pulled her out of the container and embraced her with all his strength.

"I can't breathe," she said.

"Oh, I'm sorry," he said, holding her by the shoulders and looking at her face. "It's a lucky thing that leather thing kept the container from sealing."

"Lucky, hell. I shoved my briefcase strap through there just as they were closing the lid," she said.

He just looked joyfully into her eyes, rejoicing in her spunk and cleverness, thinking of how much he loved her. There was noise and vibration from the deck as the helicopter lifted off. He didn't care. She was alive! After hours in the dark box, it was taking her a while to get used to the bright lights. She finally could get her eyes fully open and her breathing restored to normal.

Suddenly the fears and emotions of the last few hours caught up with her, and she fell into his arms. "Oh, Johnny."

"I thought you were dead," he said.

"And I thought you were. I was trying to conserve oxygen, breathe shallowly. Just before I passed out I heard a gunshot. I thought he had killed you. Then I didn't care if I could breathe or not."

They held each other close, and then they could hear footsteps and shouting from above. "John, John!"

"Down here!"

There was a shuffling of feet coming down the stairs and the door to the hold was flung open. It was Peter. He saw the two of them holding each other, and he smiled. John went over to him and embraced him in a bear hug. "Thank you. Thank you for my life. I'd like you to meet Lani. Lani, this is Peter."

She went to Peter and gave him a hug. "Mahalo for everything."

"I should have known you weren't going to let me go out here alone," John said to Peter.

Peter said to Lani, "This guy like do it all by himself, take all the credit."

"Yeah, he's a pretty independent guy. I guess he's got a lot of friends now, though," Lani said.

"He sure does," Peter said. He looked around at the mess John had made with the containers and their scattered contents. "Let's get the hell out of here."

They went out of the hold and climbed the stairs. When the three of them emerged on deck, a loud, resounding cheer went up from the water all around them. The whole ocean seemed to be alight as a huge number of torches flickered and reflected off the water. The ship was surrounded by dozens of canoes, each one carrying six paddlers. Over 100 men's voices cheered and shouted.

"He get plenny friends, alright," Peter said to Lani.

A man came up to Peter and said, "Brewster got away in the helicopter. Our cell phones aren't working. We've got somebody trying to figure out the radio."

"You heard what he said to me?" John asked Peter.

"Everybody did. And that includes one municipal court judge and one high school principal. Brewster's finished. But we get one long night ahead of us."

"What do you mean?" John asked.

"You've got about a thousand people waiting on the beach fo' put one lei on you. Then we going have one hell of a luau. I hear you're quite an ukulele player."

35

Brewster radioed ahead from the helicopter to the airport to let them know he was coming. The plane was normally kept ready to go at a moment's notice, and this was not an unusual request. He congratulated himself on having the foresight to have an alternate means of escape and he reached over to the left seat of the chopper to reassure himself the briefcase containing the cash and diamonds was with him. He approached Kahului airport from the northwest, which gave him a direct approach to the general aviation area. He set the chopper down just a few yards from his plane. He could see lights in the cabin windows, which meant the plane was powered up with the APU running. The wheel chocks had been removed and it was ready for engine start. The plane's own self-contained cabin steps were extended, and Brewster climbed quickly aboard. He asked the man from the flight office who was in the cockpit to go and check catering supplies in the hangar.

"Your crew hasn't arrived yet, sir."

"Fine, I'll wait for them in the cockpit," Brewster told him.

He watched the man descend the stairs and walk across the apron into the hangar. As soon as he was out of sight, Brewster raised the cabin steps and turned the handle to lock the door. He walked quickly back into the cockpit, pulled out the pre-takeoff checklist, and began the engine start procedures.

In the terminal across the runways, Frank Edwards, now a passenger, was waiting for his American Airlines flight to Los Angeles to board when he happened to glance across at the general aviation terminal. He saw the 737, of which he had recently been captain, rolling toward the end of the runway. The plane had no taxi or navigation lights displayed. He poked his friend Bob Lunde, his former co-pilot on the same airplane. Lunde looked up from his novel.

"Look at that," he said to Lunde

Lunde looked out, and then stood and went to the window.

"What the hell is he doing?"

In the Kahului airport control tower, the ground controller and tower controller, who sat side by side at their consoles overlooking the runway, couldn't believe what they were seeing.

The ground controller spoke into his headset. "Boeing 737 on east taxiway, Kahului ground, say your intentions."

There was no response, and the plane kept on rolling toward the departure end of the runway.

"Boeing 737, hold right where you are, sir. You have landing traffic."

In the sky about two miles from the end of the runway were the bright landing lights of an approaching jetliner.

"Boeing 737, I say again, stop your aircraft now. You have traffic on final approach."

The plane kept on rolling, and made the turn toward the runway. The tower controller needed no further time to make his decision. He spoke briskly and calmly into his headset.

"United six-five heavy, abort your landing and go around. Traffic on runway."

After a moment there was a response from United Flight 65. "Roger, we can see him now, we're going around, United six-five."

The tower controller said to his colleague, "That's the Zodiac plane, isn't it?"

"Yeah, I'm pretty sure it is." He spoke into his microphone, "Zodiac 737, you have not been cleared for taxi or takeoff, if that is your intention. Hold short of the runway, sir."

There was no response from the plane. It rolled into position for takeoff on the end of the runway.

In the terminal, the two astonished pilots watched as the United 777 from Los Angeles thundered overhead at 500 feet of altitude, engines at full power for the aborted landing. Oblivious to all this, the Zodiac 737 went to full throttle and accelerated down the runway, picking up speed. About halfway down the runway, the lightly loaded plane lifted off and climbed into the night sky.

36

John and Lani were paddled to the beach in Peter's canoe. Before leaving the ship, someone had gotten the radio working. It had been hard to convince the police to take their story seriously, but once they heard from the judge, they agreed to check on the three Maui airports and other places that might report a helicopter landing in the night. Peter beached his canoe with dozens of helping hands from the people on the beach. The first canoes to arrive had been the speedsters, the competition canoe clubs. They raced each other to the shore to let everyone know what had happened, and to pass the good news that Brewster had fled and the police were looking for him. By the time Peter's canoe slid onto the beach, there was pandemonium and joy, and wild cheering for the conquering heroes. They stepped out of the canoe, and Peter spotted his wife coming toward him.

"Come on, I like you come meet my *'ohana*," Peter told John and Lani.

John started to walk with Peter, but Joe spotted him and raced over to grab him in a big bear hug. After what they had just been through, John hated to be separated from Lani for even a couple of minutes, but within seconds, he found himself surrounded by a crowd of happy people, and every one of them wanted to clap him on the back, shake his hand or pile yet another lei on his shoulders.

Peter just stepped back and smiled at the spectacle. He was joined by his wife, and he introduced her to Lani. “Lani, this is my wife, Meleana.”

Meleana Akuna smiled at her husband, and at Lani, and hugged them both.

“You gotta meet John,” Peter said.

He pointed out John, who was unable to extricate himself from the crowd and just smiled at them and shrugged before getting pulled down for an elderly woman to put a lei on him.

Meleana looked over at John and turned white as a ghost. She stumbled in the sand and nearly fainted. Peter and Lani caught her before she fell, and they helped her sit up in the sand.

“Mele, what happened, are you okay?” her worried husband asked.

She was coming around now. “Oh, I’m so sorry, it just came over me. It’s just that that young man looks so much like someone I used to know.”

“Really? Who?” Peter asked.

“It doesn’t matter. It was a long time ago.”

Lani was thinking of John’s resemblance to his father. This woman was about the right age. She sat next to Mele and looked into her eyes. “Auntie, what is your full name?”

Meleana looked at her strangely. “Meleana. Meleana Akuna.”

“Is that your married name?”

“Of course, yes.”

“Is your maiden name Kalakana?”

Meleana smiled at her. “How did you know that? Have I met you before?”

“No. I’m Sunny Waikoloa’s attorney.”

“Uncle is the reason why I’m here. I knew him many years ago.”

Lani was almost holding her breath. "I believe he told me about you. Have you ever used any other first name?" she asked Meleana.

"No. Well, I had a Christian name, but I haven't used it in years. Aileen."

Lani's mind was racing. If what Sunny had told her was accurate, this woman could be John's mother. But there was one more question she had to ask. It involved having a child out of wedlock, and it might be embarrassing to this obviously happily married woman with children and grandchildren. She leaned in close to Meleana's face and spoke softly so Peter couldn't hear what she was saying.

"When you were very young, did you have a child named Keoni who you had to send away when he was around four?"

Meleana was startled. "Sunny told you this?"

"Yes."

Meleana had a small knapsack slung over her shoulder. She pulled the bag onto her lap, and took a wallet out of her purse. She flipped through a clear plastic folder of photos until she found the one she wanted. She held it out for Lani to see. It was an old snapshot of a little boy. Meleana gazed at it longingly. "I tried to get him back. Six months after they took him, Father Tom was dead and Keoni's father had committed suicide. All the records were sealed. I was very young. They had made me sign a lot of forms I didn't understand. I didn't know he was going to be adopted. I tried for years to get him back. They wouldn't tell me anything."

Meleana's eyes had filled with tears, and Peter asked, "Sweetie, what's wrong?"

"I'm sorry if I've caused you any embarrassment," Lani said.

"No, it's okay, Peter knows, the whole family knows."

"That little boy has gotten to be kind of a legend in our family," Peter said, pointing at the picture.

"I've never forgotten him, not for one day," Meleana said.

She kissed the picture lightly and carefully closed the wallet and put it back in her purse. And now Lani was certain that she had found John's mother. Down the beach, John emerged from a crowd of people and walked toward them. As he got closer, and she could see his face more clearly, Meleana rose to her feet. Lani could see that Meleana was squeezing her husband's hand tightly, tears streaming down her face. Lani knew then that Meleana had recognized her son. John walked up to them and took Lani's hand, and she said, "Johnny, there's someone I want you to meet."

37

Vinnie Mancini and Bruno Ricci were ensconced in their suite overlooking the ocean in the Westin Kāʻanapali at 2:00 p.m. on a perfect, sun-drenched Hawaiian day. The drapes were drawn to darken the room. They were engrossed in a game on TV between the New York Knicks and the Philadelphia 76ers when there was a knock on their door. Opening it, Bruno was surprised to see John Rossi standing there.

"You guys are still here?" John said.

There was no response from either of them, just an astonished look.

"Mind if I come in?" John said.

Bruno moved away from the door and John walked into the room. The two of them watched him as he settled comfortably into an easy chair.

"You guys enjoying Hawaiʻi ?" John asked them.

Vinnie said, "I never been so fucking bored in my life. Fuck you doing here, anyway?"

"You guys want to catch the next flight back to Newark?" John asked.

"Fuckin' A. As long as you're going to be with us," Vinnie said.

"I have another idea," John said. "Let's call your father."

"What for?"

"I have a proposition for him."

"Johnny, I can tell you right now, Mr. M. ain't interested in no proposition," Bruno said.

"Let's just call him. Okay?"

Vinnie and Bruno looked at each other, then Vinnie shrugged and picked up the phone and dialed. "Your funeral," he muttered as he punched in the number. The phone was answered on the other end and Vinnie said, "Pops, it's me . . . No, I'm still here. But we have Johnny with us. . . . No, he came to us. He wants to talk to you . . . Okay, hold on." He handed the phone to John.

"Hello, Mr. Mancini," John said into the phone.

Angelo Mancini sighed deeply. "Hello, John. Have you finally come to your senses?"

"Yes sir, I have. I really have."

"Good, glad to hear it."

"What I'd like, sir, is to work for you."

There was a pause on the end of the line, and Vinnie and Bruno looked at each other as if John had lost his mind.

"What do you mean, work for me?"

"Sir, how do you and your colleagues feel about the prospect of gambling coming to Hawai'i ?"

"If you're thinking about me starting up a casino in Hawai'i, you've got the wrong guy."

"No sir, what I'm proposing is that I work here as your representative to help insure that there is no casino in Hawai'i. I have, in fact, been working to your benefit here. And I think I can say that thanks to my efforts, there will be no casino here, at least for the foreseeable future. This means that any interests that you or your colleagues might have in the gaming industry in, say, Atlantic City or Nevada, will not be impacted."

There was a pause from the other end. "Okay, yeah, I guess. What's your point?"

"Sir, Angela does not want to marry me."

"She may be saying that now, but only because you took off on her."

"Do you want your daughter to be married to someone who took off on her?"

"Okay, let me ask you a question. How do you think it feels to me, when I've told dozens of friends and family members about my daughter getting married, to tell them her groom has dumped her and run off to some damn island? Do you know how embarrassing that is to me? It's not something I can allow, John. Not in my position."

"I understand, sir. And maybe you can find some way to force us to get married, even though your daughter doesn't want to. But what if I didn't run off to Hawai'i. Suppose you sent me here, as your representative, to disrupt any prospects of competition for gambling, and it's worked out so well that you're asking me to stay permanently. But Angela doesn't want to relocate here, so the engagement has been called off. Isn't that better than getting your daughter to marry someone she doesn't want?"

There was silence at the other end. Finally, Angelo said, "Put Vinnie on."

John handed the phone to Vinnie, who looked at John while he listened to his father. Then his dubious expression turned to elation. He hung up the phone and let out a whoop.

"We're outta here," he said joyfully to Bruno. He stuck out his hand to John and shook it vigorously. "Johnny, have a nice life. I never liked you anyway." He chucked John playfully in the back of the neck, then turned toward the closet. "Where the fuck's my suitcase?"

John said goodbye to them, and went to the door. Bruno was standing near the sliding glass doors onto the balcony, looking down at the sparkling water and the sun-splashed beach below, a disgusted expression on his face. He said to John, "You really prefer this to Newark?"

"Yeah," John Rossi said. "Yeah, I do."

As John was opening the door to leave, Vinnie said to him, "I give ya credit. You're a brave man, come walkin' in here alone. Brave or stupid."

Neither, thought John, as he stepped out into the hotel hallway and motioned to the three large Tongans waiting there to walk with him to the elevator.

EPILOGUE

The Zodiac International Boeing Business Jet had been fueled sufficiently to fly a direct route over the Pacific to many different countries in Asia, the South Pacific, or the Americas. It did not show up at any of these places. By approximately 7:00 a.m. on the morning after its unauthorized takeoff from Kahului International Airport, it would have run out of fuel. The plane would never be seen again.

On Tuesday, January 24, exactly two weeks after his incarceration, Uncle Sunny Waikoloa, accompanied by John Rossi and Lani Miller, walked into the bright sunlight outside of Wailuku police headquarters, a free man.

Sunny Waikoloa officiated at the June wedding of Keoni Punahuloa Jr. and Ka'ohelelani Miller surrounded by a few hundred close friends and family in the Kalonahoa Valley.

Hawai'i remains one of two states that do not allow any form of legalized gambling. However, for the past several years, gambling interests have been by far the largest single contributor to political campaigns.

ABOUT THE AUTHOR

An author of several popular books about Hawai'i, island-based Paul Konwiser is a founding father of the Hawaiian Slack Key Guitar Concert Series, now in its twenty-second year on Maui. He is the recipient of four Grammy Awards for Best Hawaiian Album. His long involvement with Hawaiian cultural activities has led him to write *Island of Shadow and Light*, a novel set on Maui.